MW01256768

A
Lady's
MISHAP

THE LOCKWOOD FAMILY

LAURA BEERS

Text copyright © 2025 by Laura Beers
Cover art copyright © 2025 by Laura Beers
Cover art by Blue Water Books

All rights reserved. No part of this publication may be reproduced, stored, copied or transmitted without the prior written permission of the copyright owner. This is a work of fiction. Names, characters, places and incidents either are the product of the author's imagination or are used fictitiously. Any resemblance to actual persons, living or dead, business establishments, events or locales is entirely coincidental.

1

London, 1813

Lady Elodie Lockwood stared at her reflection, wondering how many ostriches had been harmed in the making of her headpiece. She counted seven large, white feathers that extended from the diamond-encrusted bandeau atop her head. The feathers swayed slightly, mocking her with every tiny movement she made. It was absurd, outlandish, and—worst of all—balanced precariously on her head as if daring her to make a wrong move.

She turned her attention towards her Court dress. It was white satin, opulent and stiff, with an exaggerated hooped skirt that made her look like a walking bell. The long, narrow train behind her was impractical, and yet, somehow, it seemed the least ridiculous element of her entire costume. *The dress is too much. The headpiece is too much.* But she had no say in the matter. Court dress was rigid and dictated by the queen.

And today was her presentation to Court.

She was supposed to make a good first impression, so her mother repeatedly reminded her. But no matter how hard she tried, there was a gnawing fear in the pit of her stomach that she would fall short.

Her lady's maid, Molly, was busy tidying her bedchamber when a knock came at the door. It was opened, revealing her mother, Lady Dallington, her eyes wide with approval as she took in Elodie's appearance.

"Elodie, darling," her mother breathed, eyes sparkling with pride. "You look magnificent."

Elodie pressed her palms against the rigid fabric of her hooped skirt. "I look awful in this dress."

"Nonsense," her mother replied, stepping forward. "It is perfect. I am sure you will make quite the impression on the queen today."

There was no point in arguing. Any attempt to resist would be met with the same determined resolve. *Do what is expected, smile, and do not trip over the train.* That was what had been going through her head all morning. She hoped she would not find a way to mess it all up.

With resignation, Elodie turned towards her dressing table, spotting a piece of buttered bread on a silver tray. She reached for it, only for her mother's sharp voice to cut through the air.

"No bread for you!" her mother exclaimed.

Elodie froze, fingers brushing the golden crust. "Whyever not?"

Her mother hurried over to her and picked up the bread. "I will not risk butter stains on that gown after all the effort we have put into your appearance."

Elodie frowned. "I am not a child anymore, Mother. I am eighteen years old."

"That may be true," her mother replied, inspecting the bread as if it were a dangerous object. "But too much is riding on today to be careless. Molly, take this away, please."

With a wistful glance at the perfect piece of buttered bread, Elodie watched Molly carry off her would-be breakfast. What was she going to eat now? Apparently, her mother wanted her to die from starvation.

"May I at least have a glass of water?" Elodie asked.

Her mother conceded. "You may."

Elodie reached for her glass and took a long, satisfying sip.

"Good gracious, Child," her mother admonished. "Not so much. We must leave soon, and there won't be time for unnecessary stops on the way to Court."

Placing the glass down, Elodie said, "I am hoping the water will keep me from dying of hunger."

Her mother didn't appear the least bit sympathetic to her plight. "You had all morning to eat."

"That is not the least bit true," Elodie replied, waving her hand at her elaborate dress. "I have spent the entire morning being stuffed into this contraption. I have not had a moment to think of food, let alone eat it."

Her mother merely smiled. "It is the curse of being a lady, my dear."

"I would rather be judged on my wit or intellect. Why must my appearance be all that matters?" Elodie asked. "I feel like a performing monkey, paraded around for the eligible bachelors and their overbearing mothers."

"I wish you would stop referring to yourself as a 'performing monkey.'"

Elodie's lips twitched. "I could be a performing hippopotamus. However, that does not have the same ring to it, especially since they are rather vicious animals. Monkeys are at least adorable."

Before her mother could respond, the clock on the mantel chimed, marking the passage of time and bringing Elodie one step closer to the moment she dreaded most.

Her mother had no such reservations. "Shall we depart for Court?" she asked, her voice taking on a far too cheery tone.

"I suppose so," Elodie said.

Ignoring her lackluster response, her mother approached the door and opened it. "You have been preparing for this your entire life. You will make us all proud."

Elodie didn't respond, though doubt gnawed at her. She wanted to make her family proud, but the truth was that she had no idea how she would manage it. Her heart ached for her twin sister, Melody, who had married Lord Emberly and was now traveling on her wedding tour. They had always planned to face Society together, but now Elodie was alone in the dreaded marriage mart.

Elodie's steps faltered slightly as they passed by Melody's bedchamber door. She was happy for Melody, but her sister was her best friend. They had always been a team for as long as she could remember.

Her mother's eyes held compassion. "I know you miss Melody, but you can do this on your own. I know you can."

"We were supposed to do this together," Elodie responded with a sad smile. "Melody would have been the diamond of the first water, and I would be the bluestocking, picking up stray bits of rubbish."

Her mother's brows knitted in confusion. "Good heavens, why would you pick up rubbish?"

Elodie shrugged. "I would not want anyone to trip on it."

"Do not pick up rubbish."

"Fine," Elodie huffed. "I won't. Not even at the palace."

"Especially at the palace."

Elodie held up her hands in mock surrender. "You have made your point. I won't pick up rubbish for any reason, ever, ever again. In fact, I will kick the rubbish on the ground to prove a point."

As they descended the stairs, Elodie saw her dark-haired brothers, Bennett and Winston, waiting at the bottom of the entry hall. Both stared up at her, their eyes widening as they took in the entire spectacle of her attire.

"Not a word from either of you," Elodie stated firmly.

Bennett smiled. "You look lovely."

Elodie placed a hand over her stomach, feeling the absurd layers of fabric beneath her fingers. "I do not need false flattery, Brother. I have ostrich feathers on my head and I am not afraid of using them."

"You will do no such thing," her mother asserted. "Ostrich feathers are not weapons, especially ones dipped in gold."

Winston stepped forward, his expression softening as he met her gaze. "You will certainly make quite a statement at Court."

"I would rather be judged for my intellectual prowess than my appearance," Elodie shared. "Perhaps I could engage the queen in conversation about the struggles of the people—"

"You will do no such thing," her mother interrupted swiftly. "You do not speak unless spoken to. Even then, you will answer only what is asked. No more, no less."

Elodie sighed deeply. "I know, Mother. You have reminded me at least a hundred times this morning. I am not a simpleton."

Her mother placed a hand on Elodie's shoulder. "I am sorry. I want everything to go perfectly for you. This is your moment to shine."

"I daresay that it is *your* moment to shine. I do not care about being presented to Court," Elodie responded.

From the corridor, her father's voice carried towards them. "It is your duty. Every young woman worth her salt is presented to the queen."

Duty.

How that word grated on Elodie's nerves. It seemed every time she voiced her wishes, her father would remind her of her obligations—to marry well and produce heirs. The very thought of it made her stomach twist. Yet despite her resistance, she had seen the possibility of happiness through her siblings' marriages. They had all found love. And now, she couldn't imagine settling for anything less.

As he came to stand before her, her father's eyes held a tenderness she rarely saw when he looked at her. "You look lovely, my dear."

Elodie should have taken the compliment and moved on, but she had to voice her thoughts. She did this quite often, much to the chagrin of her parents. "I think this is a silly tradition. Hundreds of debutantes are lined up to be presented to the queen, and she barely glances at us."

Her father slipped his arm around his wife's waist. "It is a long-standing tradition that I have no intention of breaking. It signals the start of the Season and your entrance into Society."

Bennett moved to stand next to Elodie. "I do hope you have left your bent nail behind."

"I did, only because this gown has no pockets to hide it in," Elodie confirmed.

"Good. You will have no need for it at the palace," Bennett said. "Besides, Winston and I will be there to protect you should anything go awry."

Elodie smiled, but her heart was sad. The bent nail reminded her of Melody and how she had learned the truth about her sister's covert activities. How she missed her sister, especially at a time like this.

"Did I say something wrong?" Bennett asked, growing concerned.

Elodie shook her head. "No, I was just thinking about Melody. We were supposed to debut together."

Bennett placed a reassuring hand on her shoulder. "I know, but you are strong enough to do this on your own."

"Am I?" Elodie asked, voicing her fears.

Bennett grew solemn, but the familiar warmth in his eyes remained. "You will never know how strong you are until being strong is your only choice. And I think, dear sister, you are one of the strongest people I know."

Elodie offered him a grateful smile. "Thank you, Brother."

But Bennett wasn't done. He leaned closer and said, "And you are most proficient at buttering your bread. Do not discount that skill."

She laughed softly, the tension easing from her shoulders. "It all comes down to the perfect ratio between bread and butter."

Their mother clasped her hands together. "Come now, let us not dawdle. We must adjourn to the coaches. We cannot afford to be late."

Elodie glanced back at the grand staircase. "What of Delphine and Mattie?"

"They had an appointment with the modiste and will meet us at the palace," Winston informed her.

Bennett offered his arm. "Allow me the honor of escorting you to the coach."

"Thank you," Elodie said, slipping her hand on his arm.

As they reached the door, their lanky butler, White, stepped forward and pulled it open with a bow. He smiled—something rare for him—and said, "I wish you the best of luck, my lady."

Elodie tipped her head in acknowledgment as Bennett led her out the door and into one of the awaiting coaches. Maneuvering into the coach was no small feat. Her voluminous gown took up half the space, but eventually, she managed to settle in. Her brothers followed, sitting across from her as the coach jolted forward, merging into the busy London streets.

She saw Winston eyeing her headpiece and felt the need to defend herself. "I know it is audacious, but Mother insists I wear it. Ostrich feathers have been worn at Court for hundreds of years."

"You look beautiful, Sister," Winston said.

Elodie huffed. "Do not lie to me."

Winston shifted in his seat. "Today is an important step towards your future. Do try to enjoy it."

Elodie forced a smile, knowing full well that enjoyment was the last thing she felt. How she despised being on display. She would much rather slip into the background and observe from the shadows, but she knew her family would never allow that. So she braced herself for the charade to come.

For a fleeting moment, as the coach rattled down the road, she entertained the wild idea of jumping out and running away from it all. But she wouldn't make it very far. Not in the slippers she was wearing.

Anthony Sackville, Viscount Belview, sat at his polished mahogany desk in the study of his townhouse. His irritation was steadily growing as he studied the accounts. His younger brother, Stephen, had once again exceeded his generous allowance by a shocking margin. Lavish spending on gambling, fine clothes, and other frivolous pursuits seemed to have become Stephen's trademark. How had Father allowed this to go on for so long?

Leaning back in his chair, Anthony closed his eyes for a moment. His father, the Earl of Kinwick, was gravely ill and was confined to their country estate on strict orders from his doctors. Despite his weakened state, the earl had insisted Anthony attend the Season. He had resisted the idea, preferring to remain by his father's side. But his father's stubbornness had won out, as it always did. Now, here he was, in London, wrestling with his brother's irresponsibility and feeling the weight of familial duty pressing heavily on his shoulders.

Frustration coursing through him, he opened his eyes and stared at the ceiling. Something must be done about Stephen.

His reckless spending could not continue. If only Father had curbed this years ago.

His brooding was interrupted by a knock at the door. Anthony sat up straight as Percy, his narrow-shouldered butler, entered the room with a solemn expression.

"My lord," Percy began, "a Mrs. Talbot has requested a moment of your time."

Anthony's brow furrowed. The name did not sound familiar. "Mrs. Talbot?" he asked, leaning forward. "Am I acquainted with her?"

Percy's face remained impassive. "I do not believe so."

He sighed, placing the ledger aside. Perhaps it was another tenant, but he couldn't be sure. "Very well. Send her in."

Moments later, a petite woman stepped into the room. She was older, her silver hair neatly pinned beneath a simple bonnet. Though clean and well-maintained, her modest blue gown marked her as a woman of humble means. Her chin was raised in a manner that suggested quiet defiance, and there was an unmistakable resolve in how she carried herself.

"Thank you for agreeing to see me, my lord," Mrs. Talbot said. "I shall only require a moment of your time."

There was something about the woman that set Anthony on edge. He gestured towards the chair opposite his desk. "Please, have a seat. How may I help you, Mrs. Talbot?"

She glanced at the chair but remained standing, her posture rigid. "I am here because my correspondence to your brother, Mr. Stephen Sackville, has gone unanswered. I had little choice but to seek you out."

Anthony's stomach twisted. *What did Stephen do now?* "If this is about money—"

Mrs. Talbot cut him off, raising her hand. "This is not solely about money. It concerns his daughter—Miss Emma Sackville."

Anthony blinked, momentarily stunned. "I assure you that my brother does not have a daughter."

"You would be mistaken," Mrs. Talbot said. "My niece, Jane, married your brother five years ago. They had a daughter, Emma. Since then, your brother has not lived up to his responsibilities, leaving Jane and the child practically destitute."

Anthony's pulse quickened. *Married? A child?* His disbelief was palpable. "My brother is not married," he asserted, though his voice lacked the certainty he wanted it to have.

Mrs. Talbot reached into her reticule and pulled out a worn piece of paper, holding it out to him. "This is proof," she said. "They eloped to Scotland and were married by an anvil priest. I believe you will find it all in order."

Anthony took the paper and unfolded it carefully. His eyes reviewed the document, and his heart sank. It was a marriage license, just as Mrs. Talbot claimed. This document changed everything. "I had no idea," he admitted, looking up from the paper.

"I thought as much," Mrs. Talbot said, her voice softening. "Jane has passed away and I can no longer care for Emma. I have come to deliver the child to her father."

Before Anthony could respond, Mrs. Talbot turned to the door and waved her hand. A small girl appeared in the doorway. She had soft brown braids and wide, nervous eyes that darted around the room. She clutched a cloth doll tightly to her chest, her worn frock neat but clearly old.

Anthony stared at the girl. The resemblance was undeniable. The girl's features were a mirror of Stephen's at that age. The same dark eyes and the same untamable curls framed her face. Any protest died on his lips as reality crashed down upon him.

"This is Miss Emma Sackville," Mrs. Talbot announced, placing a hand on the child's shoulders. "She is four years old."

Anthony couldn't take his eyes off the little girl, feeling entirely out of sorts. He prided himself on being a man who was always in control, yet he had no idea how to handle this sudden revelation. "I need time to sort this out," he managed. "Perhaps I could pay you to continue caring for her, at least until I—"

"No," Mrs. Talbot interrupted firmly. "I am moving in with my sister and we have no room for a child. Besides, is it not time Emma knew her father and lived the life she deserves?"

"I know nothing about children," Anthony admitted, his voice strained.

Mrs. Talbot gave him a pointed look. "Then it is time that you learned, my lord. She is your niece, after all. Her father may be irresponsible, but you can do right by her."

She pointed to the marriage license still in Anthony's hand. "Keep that safe for Emma's sake. She will need it when she grows older."

Anthony placed the paper down on his desk. "I do not doubt Emma's parentage," he said slowly, his mind racing. "But I am... taken aback. My brother said nothing of a marriage or a child."

Mrs. Talbot scoffed. "Your brother is a scoundrel. He promised Jane the world and abandoned her when it suited him. He should be ashamed."

"If what you are saying is true, I would wholeheartedly agree," Anthony said. "However, this home is not prepared for a child. Could you not take Emma for a few more days—"

"Absolutely not!" Mrs. Talbot declared. "You have plenty of servants who could tend to a child. It is time you took responsibility for your family. I made a promise to Jane on her deathbed that I would bring Emma here."

Anthony had so many questions, but he didn't quite know where to start. But before he could ask anything more, Mrs. Talbot knelt beside Emma, offering her a tight embrace. "This is Lord Belview. He is your uncle, and he will take good care of you. Be sure to mind your manners here."

Emma nodded, her eyes still wide with uncertainty.

Mrs. Talbot smiled warmly at the child. "Your mother loved you very much and she wanted this life for you. You will do well here, far better than what I could have given you."

Rising, Mrs. Talbot brushed invisible dust from her skirts. "Emma will need new clothes at once. Her minimal belongings are with your butler."

Anthony remained rooted to his spot, utterly unsure of how to proceed. He wasn't prepared for this—none of it.

"I shall leave you to it, my lord," Mrs. Talbot said.

"Wait," Anthony called out, scrambling for some sense of control. "How can I contact you?"

Mrs. Talbot reached into her reticule and pulled out a slip of paper. "Here is my address in Cornwall. You may send letters there."

Anthony accepted the paper and glanced down at the address. "Can you not delay your trip? I will pay you handsomely to stay and care for the girl."

A frown came to Mrs. Talbot's lips. "This *girl* is your niece. I expect you to do the honorable thing by her, considering she is the granddaughter of an earl."

Anthony was at a loss for words. He simply nodded, knowing there was little he could do. He would ensure Emma was cared for, but he still needed answers—answers only his brother could provide. With a final glance at the little girl, Mrs. Talbot left the room, leaving Anthony alone with the four-year-old.

For a moment, the silence stretched between them. Anthony was uncertain how to interact with a child, so he crouched down to her level. "Good morning, Emma," he greeted. "Are you hungry?"

The girl just stared at him.

Anthony decided to try again, hoping the child was not mute. Surely, Mrs. Talbot would have said something if she had been. "Do you like chocolate?"

Emma shrugged, clutching her doll tighter. "I have never had chocolate," she murmured.

He felt immense relief at hearing her speak. "Well, we will need to rectify that at once," he said, rising. "Percy!"

The butler appeared promptly in the doorway. "Yes, my lord?"

"Please ensure Miss Emma is given breakfast, including some chocolate," Anthony instructed, touching Emma's small shoulder gently. The thinness of her frame alarmed him. How could Stephen have allowed this?

Percy tipped his head. "Yes, my lord. And Mrs. Clarke?"

"Yes," Anthony replied. "I will need to speak with the housekeeper at once to arrange for new clothing and care for Miss Emma."

Turning back to the child, Anthony smiled faintly. "Go with Percy. He will make sure you have something nice to eat."

Emma obediently followed Percy from the room. Anthony watched her go, feeling a mixture of helplessness and determination. What in the blazes was he supposed to do with a child? But there was no time to dwell on that thought. He needed answers. And those answers could only come from one person.

Anthony strode out of his study and made his way up to the second level, heading straight for Stephen's bedchamber. He didn't bother knocking, simply pushed the door open with force. "Stephen!" he shouted.

His brother, sprawled across the bed in disarray, groaned and pulled the covers over his head. "Must you shout, Brother? I had a late night."

Standing beside the bed, Anthony glared at his brother. "I had a most enlightening conversation with a Mrs. Talbot," he began.

Stephen peeked out from under the covers, squinting up at him. "Who is that?" he asked, clearly disinterested.

"She is the aunt of your *wife*," Anthony responded.

Stephen slowly sat up, rubbing his temples. "What nonsense are you spouting? I have no wife."

"According to your marriage license, you do."

"I have no time for your games."

"This is no game," Anthony shot back. "Did you or did you not elope to Gretna Green with a woman named Jane?"

A flicker of a smile crossed Stephen's lips. "Ah, Jane Gardner," he mused. "Yes, I remember her. She was quite the comely lass. But we weren't truly wed. I paid the anvil priest to pretend to marry us."

Anthony's jaw tightened. "Pretend or not, your signature is on the marriage license."

Stephen waved his hand. "It was all part of the ruse. A fake signature."

"Do you remember anything about that day?" Anthony asked, his patience wearing thin.

Stephen lowered his hand to his lap. "I remember Jane wouldn't... entertain me until we were married. She was quite the prude, so I staged the whole thing."

"You fooled yourself, Brother," Anthony declared. "That marriage was valid, and you had a wife."

"*Had*?" Stephen asked, a look of confusion passing over his face.

"Yes, Jane has passed away," Anthony shared, wondering what kind of reaction he would get from his brother. Would Stephen show any remorse for his actions?

Stephen sighed deeply, but there was no sign of sorrow. "Is that what this is about?" he asked, rubbing his face. "I haven't seen Jane since we spent those two weeks in Scotland."

"No, this is about your *daughter*, whom you had with Jane."

His brother's mouth dropped. "What in the blazes are you talking about? I have no daughter."

"You do, and she is currently eating breakfast."

Stephen threw off the blankets, his feet hitting the floor with a thud. "That is impossible! I would have known if I had a child."

"From what I understand, Jane tried to tell you, as did Mrs. Talbot," Anthony said, folding his arms.

Stephen walked over to the table and poured himself a generous glass of brandy. He downed it in one gulp. "That child is not mine. Send it away."

"You can't deny her, considering she looks just like you did at her age."

Shaking his head, Stephen refilled his glass. "We were careful... I was careful. This is ridiculous. Send her to a workhouse for all I care."

Anthony pressed his fingers to the bridge of his nose, struggling to control his anger. "I do not know what delusions you have been entertaining, but you left Scotland with a wife. And now, you have a legitimate daughter. You cannot toss her aside."

Stephen sank into a chair, looking defeated but defiant. "Jane is lying. She probably concocted this whole story to trap me."

"There is nothing to fight, Brother!" Anthony exclaimed, tossing his hands in the air. "You were legally married, and Emma is your daughter. You have a responsibility to her."

"I don't want it."

"She has a name. Emma. And she is four years old." Anthony stepped forward and snatched the brandy glass from Stephen's hand. "You are coming to meet her."

"I won't do it," Stephen declared. "I want nothing to do with this child."

"You will, or I will cut your allowance," Anthony said.

Stephen narrowed his eyes. "You wouldn't dare."

Anthony stood his ground. "I would. I control the family funds now, and I won't support you unless you take responsibility."

Standing abruptly, Stephen's nostrils flared. "What would Father say about you lording over me?"

"Father isn't here," Anthony replied, "and frankly, I do not care what he would think. You have made your choices, and now it is time to face the consequences."

Stephen stared daggers at him. "We will see about that. I will write to him. I have no doubt he will side with me."

"Write him if you wish," Anthony said, walking to the door. "But it won't change anything. You have a daughter, Stephen, and it is time for you to do the honorable thing."

Anthony left the room without waiting for a response, his footsteps echoing in the corridor. He couldn't help but feel like he was dealing with not one but two children. One was four-years-old and the other was a grown man incapable of taking responsibility for his actions.

2

Elodie stood at the back of the drawing room at St. James's Palace, her heart pounding in her chest. The air was thick with the hum of murmured conversation as everyone watched the debutantes being presented to Queen Charlotte. The grand opulence of the palace—gold-leafed moldings, crystal chandeliers, and walls lined with rich tapestries—was lost on her. It should have been exciting, but the only thing Elodie could think of was the impending moment when all those eyes would be on *her*.

She was prepared for this. After all, she had taken endless lessons on how to approach the queen with grace, how to execute the perfect deep curtsy, and how to walk backwards out of the room without falling flat on her face. Yet no amount of practice had prepared her for the reality of being here, surrounded by so many watchful strangers.

Bennett leaned in and whispered, "Just breathe, Sister."

"Thank you for that reminder," Elodie responded dryly. "If you hadn't, I surely would have stopped breathing altogether and died."

Her brother chuckled. "Your nerves are showing. You will be fine."

Elodie bit her lower lip. "What if I fall in front of all these people?" she asked, her voice laced with genuine fear.

"You won't," Bennett assured her. "And if you do, rest assured, I will be the first one to laugh."

"Thanks, Brother," she responded as her eyes roamed over the room. "But there are so many people here. What if—"

Bennett interrupted her gently. "None of these people matter. The only one who does is the queen. Focus on her, and if she asks you anything, just say the opposite of what you presume to be right."

Elodie's fingers fidgeted with the edge of her long, white gloves. "What if she asks something unexpected, something I don't know how to answer?"

Bennett grinned. "I promise you, the queen isn't trying to stump you. Just be yourself and do exactly what you have practiced."

"Moo..." Elodie muttered under her breath. "I feel like a cow being herded about."

He gave her an amused look. "It is not as bad as you are making it out to be."

Before Elodie could respond, their mother appeared at her side, placing a hand on her arm. "The Lord Chamberlain is about to announce your name."

Elodie took a deep breath and squared her shoulders, despite her stomach being twisted with nerves. She was determined to appear more confident than she felt. As her name echoed through the room, Elodie began the walk towards the queen, her eyes fixed on the red carpet ahead of her, trying not to focus on all the eligible bachelors and their families.

When they reached the front, they stopped before the throne, and Elodie dipped into the deep curtsy she had practiced endlessly. She rose and smiled at Queen Charlotte, who regarded her with a critical, but not unkind, gaze. The queen's powdered hair was swept back into a loose chignon, her aged features still sharp, though the wrinkles around her eyes betrayed her years. She appeared older than Elodie had imagined, but her eyes gleamed with a sharpness that suggested nothing escaped her attention.

The queen turned her attention towards Lady Dallington. "I was informed you had twin daughters. Where is the other?"

Lady Dallington met the queen's gaze. "Yes, Your Majesty. My other daughter, Lady Melody, recently married Lord Emberly. They are currently on their wedding tour."

"Lord Emberly," the queen repeated, a note of approval in her voice. "That is quite the advantageous match for a young woman."

"It was a love match," Lady Dallington said.

The queen raised an eyebrow and turned her attention to Elodie, her penetrating gaze sharp enough to make Elodie's pulse quicken again. "And what of you, Lady Elodie?" she prodded. "Do you also wish for a love match?"

Elodie hesitated for only a moment, then lifted her chin, determined to speak truthfully. "I do, Your Majesty."

Queen Charlotte studied her, the silence stretching just long enough to make Elodie wonder if she had said something wrong. Finally, the queen spoke, her tone almost thoughtful. "You are a pretty enough thing, but you must be mindful to choose wisely."

"I will," Elodie replied.

The queen's eyes perused the length of her with faint amusement before settling back on her face. "You are much shorter than your brothers."

Elodie's lips twitched, unable to stop herself. "You might say that I *look up* to them."

The queen let out a laugh. "Dear heavens, that was awful,"

she said with a slight smile. "But you are a delight, Lady Elodie."

With a graceful wave of her hand, the queen signaled that their audience was over. Elodie felt a rush of relief as she dipped into one final deep curtsy. Rising carefully, she took slow, measured steps backward, mindful not to trip over the long train of her gown.

As Elodie reached the threshold of the drawing room, she let out a long, shaky breath. Relief flooded her body, and her shoulders finally started to relax. *It is over.* She hadn't tripped over her gown, she hadn't misspoken, and—almost unbelievably—she had made Queen Charlotte laugh. That had certainly not been part of the plan.

She stepped into the cool air of the corridor and placed a hand on her stomach. She had an overwhelming desire to return home and shed the layers of her Court dress. The feathers and the heavy satin felt like a cage she longed to escape. But as she turned to her mother, she saw the frown creasing Lady Dallington's brow.

"Why did you insist on making a joke in front of the queen?" her mother asked, her voice tight with disapproval.

"I thought it was prudent, given the circumstances."

Her mother's brow arched. "Prudent? It was risky and foolish. A lady's presentation to Court is not the place for humor."

"It worked, though," Elodie countered. "The queen laughed."

Her mother pressed her lips into a thin line. "This time, yes. But next time, if there even is a next time, you might not be so lucky."

Bennett's cheerful voice echoed from down the corridor, his figure emerging from the crowd. "Why the gloomy faces?" he asked, his grin wide. "I would say that was a rousing success."

Their mother gave a small nod, though her tension

remained. "It was," she agreed. "I suppose I can finally breathe."

Elodie turned, her eyes widening slightly in surprise. "You were nervous?"

"Of course I was. I have been nervous for years. I never know what will come out of that mouth of yours," her mother shared.

Bennett arrived at Elodie's side, his hand coming to rest on her shoulder. "You were brilliant," he declared. "I do not think I have ever heard the queen laugh before. But your joke was truly awful."

Elodie couldn't help but laugh. "I know, but I thought I should at least try."

Bennett shook his head in mock dismay. "In the future, leave the jokes to me, would you? Everyone knows I am the funny one in the family."

"You? Funny?" Elodie teased. "I have never noticed."

"Perhaps not, but I have been told by multiple people that I am quite witty," Bennett said, puffing out his chest.

Elodie glanced around the corridor dramatically, then back to him. "By chance, are these 'people' with us now?"

Bennett chuckled. "We will have to continue this conversation later. The rest of the family is waiting for us by the coaches."

Their mother offered Elodie a warm smile. "I am very proud of you, Elodie. You did what was expected of you, and you did it quite well."

Elodie's heart swelled with a mixture of relief and gratitude. "Thank you, Mother."

"Now, let's go home and get you out of that gown," their mother said. "It is not the least bit flattering on you."

Placing a hand over her heart, Elodie feigned outrage. "That hurts, considering this is my new favorite gown. I think I will wear it all the time."

Their mother just laughed as she started walking down the hall. Elodie lifted her skirts slightly, the heavy fabric rustling as she followed. Bennett walked beside her, casting a sideways glance.

"Delphine didn't enjoy wearing her Court dress to be presented to the queen, either," he informed her.

"I am not surprised," Elodie said. "This gown could hurt children, given the chance."

"You have now officially entered Society. What do you intend to do first?"

Elodie already knew that answer, and it should come as no surprise to her brother. "I think I shall go home and take a nap."

Bennett shot her a sidelong look. "You always take naps."

"That is because naps are the best," Elodie replied. "In my dreams, I can be anyone I want to be."

"And who exactly do you want to be?"

Elodie's smile faltered for a moment as she considered the question. "I am not sure yet. I just know that I want to do more with my life than what is expected of me."

Her brother's expression grew more serious. "You don't wish to marry?"

"I do," Elodie said quickly, "but in due time. There are so many things that I want to do first, things I want to see and experience."

Bennett leaned in closer, his voice dropping to a playful whisper. "Do not let Mother or Father hear you say that. The word 'spinster' is practically a curse word to them."

Elodie rolled her eyes. "I am only eighteen. I am hardly on the path to spinsterhood yet. It is not that I don't want to marry, but I want my life to have meaning beyond the usual expectations. I want more than just balls and suitors."

"You will find your way, Elodie. I am sure of that."

Hearing her brother's encouraging response, Elodie felt a

spark of hope. She was now a part of Society, but she was determined to chart her own course through it, even if it meant defying expectations.

As they stepped out of the grand entrance of St. James's Palace, Elodie spotted her sisters-in-law, Delphine and Mattie, waiting by one of the coaches. The two of them beamed when they caught sight of her.

"Elodie!" Delphine exclaimed, her eyes sparkling as she hurried over. "You were absolutely brilliant."

Mattie nodded enthusiastically. "I agree. I was so nervous when I spoke to the queen that my voice barely came out as a whisper. She had to ask me to speak up. Twice."

"I was nervous, too," Elodie admitted. "But I suppose the joke helped... at least a little."

Her father, who was standing nearby, cleared his throat. "The joke may not have been entirely appropriate, but the queen did not seem offended. You were fortunate she took it in good humor," he said, gesturing towards the waiting coaches. "We can discuss this further once we are home."

Mattie quickly looped her arm through Elodie's. "Come ride home with us," she said, already pulling her towards one of the coaches.

Winston held his hand out and assisted them both into the coach. It took some effort for Elodie to be situated, but after a brief struggle, she finally settled on perching at the edge of the bench. Mattie and Winston followed, taking the seats across from her.

Once the coach jerked forward, Elodie reached up and removed her elaborate headpiece. She held it out in front of her, wrinkling her nose in distaste. "At least I will never have to wear this monstrosity again. It is hideous."

Winston grinned. "Hideous or not, you wore it well, Sister. A vision of elegance," he teased with a wink.

"Well, at least it is over," Elodie said.

Her brother's smile widened. "Oh, on the contrary, Elodie. It has only just begun. Now the true fun begins."

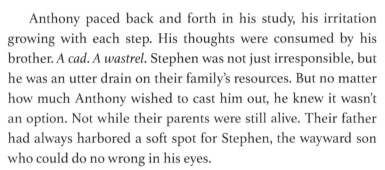

Anthony paced back and forth in his study, his irritation growing with each step. His thoughts were consumed by his brother. *A cad. A wastrel.* Stephen was not just irresponsible, but he was an utter drain on their family's resources. But no matter how much Anthony wished to cast him out, he knew it wasn't an option. Not while their parents were still alive. Their father had always harbored a soft spot for Stephen, the wayward son who could do no wrong in his eyes.

A sharp knock on the door broke Anthony out of his musings, and Mrs. Clarke, the portly, silver-haired house-keeper, entered with her usual gentle grace. She had been with the family for as long as Anthony could remember, her presence a constant source of order amidst the chaos.

She smiled kindly, her eyes crinkling at the corners. "I understand we have a new resident, my lord."

Anthony nodded and gestured to the chair opposite him. "Yes, we do. And I need your help."

Mrs. Clarke seated herself while Anthony returned to his desk, sinking into his chair with a heavy sigh. He pinched the bridge of his nose for a moment before continuing. "We will need to hire a nursemaid for Miss Emma."

"I have already made a few inquiries, but until then, a maid will see to her needs," Mrs. Clarke said. "She will need a new wardrobe—something fitting for her new station."

Leaning back in his chair, he replied, "Yes, see to that as well. Dresses, shoes, whatever is required." He paused, the next question hesitating on his lips. "Do four-year-olds need toys?"

"Yes, my lord, children that age tend to play with toys."

Anthony ran a hand through his hair, feeling entirely out of his depth. "Has my brother even bothered to meet his daughter?" The bitterness in his voice was hard to mask.

"Not that I am aware of, but I am sure Master Stephen is simply overwhelmed," Mrs. Clarke attempted.

"It is his daughter."

Mrs. Clarke's eyes held compassion. "I am sure that Master Stephen will do right by her."

Anthony wasn't quite convinced. He knew his brother all too well. Stephen had always cared only for himself, leaving others to clean up his messes. Mrs. Clarke, however, always saw the best in people, a trait Anthony admired but could never fully adopt.

Mrs. Clarke rose from her seat, smoothing down her apron. "If that will be all, my lord?"

Anthony stood as well. "Please ensure that Miss Emma feels at home. No expense is too great for her comfort."

"It warms my heart to see you taking care of her, my lord. You are doing more than your duty," Mrs. Clarke praised.

"She is my niece, after all. It is the least I can do."

Mrs. Clarke gave him a knowing look. "It is more than that."

With that, the housekeeper took her leave, and the room fell into an uneasy silence. Anthony turned towards the window, staring out into the gardens. The weight of his father's illness hung over him like a shadow, along with the growing responsibility of running the estate, and now he was caring for a niece he had not even known existed. It was almost too much to bear. How much more could he take?

He needed air. Without another thought, he strode out of the study, passing by servants who quickly stepped out of his way, and exited through the back door into the gardens. The cool breeze offered a brief moment of clarity, but his sense was fleeting. Movement from the corners of his eyes drew his attention, and there, by an upper window of the townhouse, sat

Stephen with a drink in his hand, lounging as if nothing in the world could trouble him.

Before Anthony could stop himself, his frustration boiled over. "Stephen!" he shouted, his voice cutting through the quiet.

Stephen glanced down at him, a smirk playing at his lips, before pulling the drapes closed, dismissing him entirely.

"*Stephen!*" Anthony called again, louder this time. "Get down here!"

A sudden loud voice came from the adjacent townhouse, interrupting his fury. "Good gracious, Anthony, will you stop all that yelling? Some of us are trying to take a nap!"

Anthony's head snapped to the side, and there, leaning out of her window with a frown and slightly disheveled hair, was none other than Lady Elodie. Despite her tousled appearance, she was as breathtaking as ever. Her golden hair fell in loose waves around her face, and a light sprinkling of freckles danced across her nose. It was a sight that stirred something deep within him, though she seemed utterly unaware of her effect on him. To Elodie, he had always been nothing more than a nuisance.

"My apologies, Elodie," he said, his tone harsher than intended. "Please, return to your nap."

Elodie's brow creased in concern. "You woke me from it. The least you could do is explain why you are shouting at Stephen like a madman."

"It is none of your concern," he replied stiffly, trying to regain some semblance of control over his spiraling emotions.

In response, Elodie leaned a little further out of the window, her blue eyes sharp with annoyance. "You made it my concern when you decided to yell loud enough for half the block to hear. Naps, in case you didn't know, are sacred in my household."

Despite his anger, a small smile tugged at Anthony's lips.

Elodie, with her biting wit and sharp tongue, had always been able to cut through his frustration. But he quickly stifled the smile, refusing to let her see how much her presence affected him. Not now. Not when everything was falling apart.

"I will be sure to keep my voice down in the future," he replied.

Elodie gave him a long, scrutinizing look as though she could see through the carefully built walls he had put up. "Why do you look so bothered?"

"Leave it alone," he said tersely, turning to leave.

"I would have," she called after him, "but sleep now eludes me, thanks to your shouting. And now I find I am much more curious about you."

The last thing Anthony needed right now was Elodie's meddling. He wasn't in the mood for her questions, not when his thoughts were still tangled with the mess of his brother. "Good day, Elodie," he said as he headed towards the back door of his townhouse.

"Wait!" Elodie shouted. "I will be down in a moment."

"That is wholly unnecessary—" Anthony began, but his protest died on his lips as Elodie disappeared back into her bedchamber, leaving the window wide open.

He groaned inwardly. Normally, he would have leaped at the opportunity to speak to Elodie, even if it was just a playful exchange. But today? Today, he didn't have the energy to pretend all was well. He would have preferred yelling at Stephen for all the trouble he had caused. Still, being rude to Elodie was out of the question.

Resigned, Anthony sat down on a weathered stone bench in the gardens. Time crawled. Though it was likely only moments, it felt like hours before he saw Elodie's head pop up over the hedge that separated their properties. Her hair was now neatly pulled back into a chignon, and her expression held the familiar annoyance she reserved for him.

"What did Stephen do now?" she asked.

Anthony stood up and walked to the small wooden gate between their gardens, pulling it open. "Why did you not use the gate? Our parents installed it for a reason."

"This way is much more clandestine, don't you think?" Elodie replied, her lips curving into a slight smile.

"I would prefer to see you when I am speaking to you."

"Very well, if you insist," Elodie said, hopping down gracefully from the bench she had perched on. She dusted off her skirts and walked over to him. "Now, what has you so upset? I haven't seen you this bothered since Stephen put manure in your bed."

"If I recall, you helped him," Anthony said.

Elodie waved her hand dismissively. "That was only because you left me up in that tree for hours. I had to get back at you somehow."

"You could have climbed down from that tree at any point. It wasn't that high," he pointed out.

"Yes, but I thought I had found the perfect hiding spot. You were just terrible at seeking."

Anthony chuckled, feeling some of the tension drain out of him. "You always hid in the same spot and giggled every time I came near."

"Well, I was a child, and you were ten years older," Elodie defended. "I would hope that you were better at hide and seek than me. What else do they teach you at Eton?"

"I suppose it would be only fair if I told you now that I never did try to 'seek you.' I was far too busy to be playing games with you."

"Pity," Elodie teased.

He found himself smiling. "Thank you. I needed a reason to smile, especially with Stephen being... well, Stephen."

Elodie's eyes twinkled with interest. "Oh, let me guess what he has done this time," she said. "Did he gamble away the family fortune?"

"No, but not for a lack of trying."

She tapped her chin thoughtfully. "Did he race his horse through the busy streets of London again?"

Anthony gave her a curious look. "How did you know he did that?"

"Stephen's antics are constantly in the newssheets. It is practically morning entertainment," Elodie replied. "Though, I daresay I wouldn't find it so amusing if he were my brother."

"My brother is a princcock!"

Elodie gasped dramatically, bringing a hand up to her chest. "Language, Anthony! I am a lady, after all."

"My apologies—" he began, only to be cut off by her laughter.

"I am merely teasing you," Elodie said, her laughter fading into a smile. "You seem to forget that Bennett and Winston are my brothers. I have heard far worse."

"I did not forget, but I do not wish to burden you with my problems."

Her smile dimmed. "I am not a child anymore."

That fact was becoming increasingly difficult for Anthony to ignore. Gone was the little girl who used to hide in trees and giggle behind hedges. Elodie had grown into a striking young woman—far too comely for his peace of mind. "I am well aware, but this is a family matter."

Elodie's eyes narrowed slightly as she considered him for a long moment. She moved to brush past him, her skirt rustling as she moved towards her townhouse. "I gave up a perfectly good nap for this," she muttered over her shoulder. "Good day, Anthony."

He reached out, gently grasping her arm before she could leave. "Are you upset with me?"

"Yes," Elodie said plainly.

"Elodie—" he began.

She pulled her arm back. "I don't know why I bother. Go tell the woodland creatures your problems, for all I care. Perhaps they will have a solution for how to deal with your brother."

"I did not mean to offend you."

Some of her anger seemed to dissipate at his words. "I know," Elodie admitted, crossing her arms over her chest. "But I am tired of being treated like I am still a child. I can do more than eat biscuits and play the pianoforte, you know."

Anthony's lips twitched into a faint smile. "But you eat biscuits so well," he teased.

"That I do," she agreed, though her frown remained.

He looked at her for a long moment, realizing he had a decision to make. He could keep her at arm's length, as he had always done, protecting her from the mess his brother had created. Or he could trust her with the truth. After all, it would not be long before the *ton* caught wind of Stephen's latest misdeeds. Better for Elodie to hear it from him.

Gesturing towards a bench, Anthony asked, "Would you care to sit with me for a moment?"

Elodie offered him a slight nod before walking over to the bench. She sat down and smoothed down her skirts. Anthony joined her but left more room than what was considered proper.

For the first time that day, Anthony felt the possibility of sharing the weight of his burdens with someone. And perhaps, just perhaps, that someone was Elodie.

3

E lodie had done her good deed for the day. Here she was, sitting next to the man who vexed her with almost every word that came out of his mouth, and she was being somewhat cordial. Yet, she couldn't ignore her curiosity. Anthony was not a man who typically let his emotions get the better of him, and his earlier shouting at Stephen had been so out of character for him. What had caused him to react in such a fashion?

Stealing a glance at him, she had to admit, even begrudgingly, that he was not an unhandsome man. His strong jaw and dark hair gave him a certain charming appeal. But then again, she had no desire to be attracted to the man. He had loved nothing more than tormenting her in their youth, and it hadn't gotten much better over the years.

Anthony sat with his arms crossed tightly over his chest, a sure sign he was upset. Not that she noticed such things about him. He sighed deeply. "I am truly sorry I woke you up from your nap with my shouting."

"It is all right," Elodie said. "There is always tomorrow."

He gave her an amused look. "Do you take a nap every day?"

Elodie found that question to be most absurd. "Of course I do. Don't you?"

Anthony shook his head. "No. I do not have time for such things."

She feigned shock, putting a hand to her chest. "That is truly a shame, and I suggest you take a hard look at your life choices."

He smiled, just as she had intended. "I am relieved that you are here. Truly. I was worried when you were abducted a few weeks ago."

"It was nothing that I could not handle," Elodie said.

Anthony raised an eyebrow. "I am surprised your abductors didn't release you when they realized what a minx you are."

Rolling her eyes, Elodie leaned back slightly, letting the cool garden breeze brush her face. "It doesn't quite work that way, but Lord Emberly handled the matter swiftly. I consider it an adventure."

"An *adventure*?" Anthony repeated, incredulity clear in his voice. "Only you would look at an abduction as an adventure."

"Perhaps, but it is over and done with," she said, intentionally keeping her responses vague. She didn't want to share that she discovered her sister was an agent of the Crown. That was not her secret to tell.

Anthony uncrossed his arms, seemingly more at ease now. "Dare I ask how your presentation to the queen went today? I had planned on attending, but things went awry rather quickly this morning."

Elodie smiled proudly. "It went well. I even made the queen laugh."

Anthony's brows shot up in surprise. "That is no small feat. What did you say?"

"She commented on my height compared to my brothers

and I told her that 'I looked up to them,'" Elodie said. "You just had to be there to get the humor."

Anthony grinned. "I suppose so."

With a glance at her townhouse, Elodie said, "My parents were not entirely pleased with my joke, but it all worked out in the end. I didn't trip and Bennett even said it was a 'rousing success.'"

"That is high praise."

"Indeed," Elodie said, giving him a pointed look. "But I know what you are doing. You are trying to distract me from the fact that you were shouting at Stephen like a wild banshee earlier."

Anthony winced slightly. "Guilty as charged," he admitted. "Though, I must say, I have been enjoying our conversation. I did not think we could ever speak so cordially."

"That is because you have a habit of saying the most absurd things," Elodie countered. "You always have."

"And yet," Anthony shot back, his tone playful, "I think you secretly like me."

Elodie huffed. "I do not like you. I merely tolerate your existence. There is a vast difference."

"No, I think there is more to it."

"You would be wrong," Elodie said. "You are friends with my brothers, and our townhouses are situated right next to each other. If not for those things, we wouldn't exchange a single word."

Anthony clucked his tongue. "Ah, but I treasure each and every moment with you, Elodie."

She knew he was teasing, as he always did, but something about his tone made her defensive. It was just this way with him. One moment he was making her laugh, and the next, he had her on edge. "Just tell me why you were shouting at Stephen."

He grew solemn. "Apparently, my brother eloped to Scotland five years ago with a young woman. They were married by an anvil priest."

Elodie's eyes widened. "Who was this woman?"

"I don't know much about her," Anthony shared. "She passed away and now Stephen has a daughter."

Elodie gasped. "Stephen has a daughter?"

"He does," Anthony confirmed. "Emma is four years old, and I haven't the faintest idea what to do with her."

"She isn't a pet, Anthony. You don't have to play fetch with her," Elodie said dryly. "Has Stephen hired a nursemaid for her?"

Anthony pursed his lips. "My brother hasn't even met with her yet. If he had his way, he would send her to a workhouse and wash his hands of her entirely."

Elodie's heart sank at the thought. "That is awful."

"It is the truth."

Shifting on the bench towards Anthony, Elodie said, "I don't know much about children, but I can only imagine this poor girl is terrified. Her mother is gone, and her father is... well, Stephen." Anthony's jaw clenched. "Emma shouldn't be my responsibility, but Stephen is useless. I want to do right by her, but I am at a complete loss."

Elodie tilted her head slightly, studying him. "You are the most infuriating man that I know," she began, her tone lighter now, "but you are honorable. I am sure you will figure it out."

Anthony's lips quirked into a smile. "Why, Elodie, are you flirting with me?"

Elodie's mouth dropped open. "Good heavens, no! I would never flirt with you."

"I don't know. It sounded a lot like flirting," Anthony said. "I am flattered, but I think it is best if we remain friends."

Elodie shot to her feet and placed her hands on her hips, glaring down at Anthony with all the frustration she could muster. "You are *bacon-brained*! A *peagoose* of the highest order."

Anthony tsked. "More flirting, Elodie. Please, you are only embarrassing yourself now."

"Why do I even bother trying to have a civil conversation with you?"

Before Anthony could respond, Bennett's voice came from behind her. "I see that I came at the right time," he said, strolling towards them.

Elodie spun on her heel to face her brother. "Bennett, I think we should sell our townhouse and move far, far away."

"For what purpose?" Bennett asked.

"I cannot abide living next to *him*," Elodie replied, waving her hand in Anthony's direction.

Anthony placed a hand over his heart with mock sincerity. "That hurts, Elodie. Truly. What would I do if I didn't see your smiling face every day?"

"You would survive," Elodie muttered.

Rising from the bench, Anthony flashed her that vexing smile of his. "I suppose our time together has come to an end. Shall we reconvene at the same time tomorrow?"

Elodie ignored his question, knowing full well it was meant to get a rise out of her. She turned to Bennett instead. "We should go inside."

"Before we go," Bennett began, "Mother wanted me to extend an invitation to Anthony for dinner this evening."

Elodie's stomach dropped. She could practically feel Anthony's triumphant smirk without even looking at him.

With a polite nod, Anthony replied, "I would be honored."

Elodie resisted the urge to groan. The last thing she wanted was to spend even more time in Anthony's company. But she knew what her mother was up to. She was attempting to play matchmaker. It was an endeavor her mother could never resist, no matter how obvious her schemes became.

Anthony bowed. "Until this evening, then."

She watched as Anthony disappeared into the hedge of his

gardens, his leisurely stride somehow managing to irritate her
further. "Why did you have to invite him to dinner?"

Bennett seemed unbothered by her irritation. "Mother was
rather insistent on the idea."

"You could have told her no."

With a knowing look, Bennett replied, "You know Mother
does not like being told no. Besides, I have no issues dining
with Anthony, and neither should you. He has been a family
friend for years."

Elodie pressed her lips together, her annoyance barely
concealed. "I think you have terrible taste in friends. There are
hundreds of gentlemen in London you could befriend instead
of Anthony. Just say the word, and I will find you a better one."

"I have never quite understood your aversion to him."

"He was awful to me when we were children," Elodie said.
"Do you remember when he pretended he was dead?"

Bennett let out a bark of laughter. "Oh, I remember that
well! Anthony smeared beet juice all over his shirt and waited
for what felt like hours until you came outside."

"It wasn't funny."

"It was a little funny," Bennett said, his smile widening. "I
can still see your face when Anthony jumped up and pretended
he was a zombie. It was quite a brilliant performance!
Although his mother wasn't amused that he had ruined a
perfectly good shirt."

Without another word, Elodie brushed past her brother
and headed straight for the townhouse. There was no point in
continuing this conversation. Bennett saw nothing wrong with
Anthony's teasing, but he hadn't been on the receiving end.

Bennett quickly caught up to her, falling into step beside
her as they approached the door. "I must admit, I was surprised
to see you outside, conversing with Anthony. Is it not your nap
time?"

"Anthony was shouting at Stephen and woke me up," she

revealed as a footman opened the rear door. "I came to see what the hubbub was all about."

"I always find it interesting how different Anthony and Stephen are," Bennett said.

Elodie cast a sidelong glance at her brother as they stepped inside. "That they are," she agreed. "Stephen may be irresponsible, but he has never been unkind to me."

Bennett placed a hand on her sleeve and gently turned her to face him. "That may be true, but I would prefer if you did not associate with Stephen anymore. He has a reputation of being a rake."

"I am well aware, but that doesn't mean he will do anything to jeopardize mine."

"It is a chance that I am not willing to take, considering reputations can be ruined by even the tiniest of infractions."

Elodie gave her brother a reassuring look, hoping to ease his worries. "I have been preparing for my entrance into Society my entire life. I know exactly what is expected of me—by our family and by the *ton*. I am not going to let Stephen ruin that."

Her brother didn't look convinced, and his brow creased with worry. "Why don't we skip this Season?" he asked. "We could travel back to our country estate and get you far away from all of Society's pressures and expectations. You could even ride your horse wearing trousers again, like you used to."

"I can do this, Brother," Elodie assured him.

Bennett looked at her for a long moment before placing both hands on her shoulders. "I know, but I am just worried for you. It is the job of any good brother."

"You are a good brother..."

"Why do I sense a 'but' coming?" Bennett asked.

Elodie laughed. "*But* you don't need to protect me all the time. I am not a child anymore."

Bennett dropped his hands to his sides. "Well, I am sorry, but that isn't likely to happen. As the self-appointed protector of this family, it is my responsibility—*nay*, my duty—to look after every last one of you."

A teasing smile tugged at her lips. "Very well, then. But, just so you know, I am still not giving you any of my buttered toast. You will have to make it on your own."

Bennett let out an exaggerated groan. "Drats, foiled again."

Elodie giggled as they continued down the corridor, and she looped her arm through his, feeling a deep sense of gratitude for her brother. No matter how protective or overbearing he could be, she knew his heart was always in the right place. And more than anything, she knew Bennett—and their whole family—would always be there for her, no matter what challenges Society or the future threw her way.

Anthony hesitated outside the nursery door, his hand resting lightly on the handle. He had seen the fear in Emma's eyes when she looked upon him, and it struck him like a blow. He needed her to know that she was safe here. With him. The thought of failing her tightened his chest, but he resolved to try. No matter how long it took, he would prove to her that this was her home now. A place where she would never have to fear anything ever again.

He exhaled softly, steadying himself, before turning the handle and stepping quietly inside. The nursery was modest yet cozy, with lavender-papered walls and shelves lined with toys. Emma sat on the edge of her bed, clutching a doll tightly. Her eyes widened when they landed on him, her posture stiffening.

"Emma," he greeted gently. "I came to say goodnight."

Her gaze dropped to the floor, and she murmured, "Goodnight."

He lingered near the doorway, feeling like an interloper in his own home. He shifted awkwardly before taking a tentative step closer. "Do you require anything? If you do, you need only to tell me."

She shook her head.

"Emma..." he began, his tone carrying a warmth he hoped she could feel, "I am glad that you are here. Truly, I am."

Her eyes flickered up briefly, a spark of uncertainty in their depths. "Thank you," she said quietly, her voice almost a whisper.

Anthony knew he needed to be patient with Emma. This adjustment was not easy for either of them, but he was determined to make it work. Emma deserved stability, kindness, and the chance to feel safe again. If that required every ounce of his patience and effort, so be it.

"May I read you a book?" he asked.

Emma looked up at him hesitantly before giving a small nod.

Anthony walked over to the bookshelf, scanning the neatly arranged spines. "Now, let's see," he mused aloud. "Which book shall we read tonight? *A Token for Children*? Or perhaps *The History of Little Goody Two-Shoes*?"

In a soft voice, Emma replied, "*Little Red Riding Hood*."

"An excellent choice." Anthony retrieved the book and sat down next to Emma, keeping a careful distance to avoid overwhelming her. "Have you read this book before?" he asked as he opened the book.

Emma's small fingers fidgeted with her doll. "My mother used to read this book to me. It was the only book we had."

Anthony's heart clenched at the quiet sorrow in her words. Gently, he placed a reassuring hand on her thin shoulder. "Now that you are here, you can have as many books as your heart desires."

Emma didn't respond, but the corners of her lips curved

ever so slightly, a faint and fleeting smile that filled Anthony with hope. It was a beginning, and for now, that was enough. He withdrew his hand and turned to the first page, settling into a steady rhythm as he began to read. He was pleased when Emma inched closer to him with every turn of the page.

As he finished the chapter, Anthony glanced at Emma and noticed her eyelids drooping heavily. Her head tilted slightly, fighting against sleep. He closed the book with a soft thud, marking the page with his thumb. "We will read more tomorrow night," he promised. "For now, it is time for you to get some rest."

Emma slipped under the covers, her head resting on the pillow. Anthony tucked the blanket snugly around her and rose to his feet. "Goodnight, Emma," he said, blowing out the flickering candle on the bedside table.

Not wanting to be late for dinner, Anthony stepped out of the nursery and headed out the main door, walking the short distance to Lord Dallington's townhouse. The chill of the evening air bit at his skin, but he barely noticed, his thoughts still lingering on the brief but significant exchange with Emma.

Upon reaching the door, he knocked, and it was promptly answered by the butler, who stepped aside to let him into the entry hall.

As Anthony entered, he caught sight of Elodie descending the staircase in a pale blue gown. The color accentuated the brightness of her eyes, though, as usual, those eyes flashed with her familiar look of annoyance. At least she was consistent.

He bowed, hoping to disarm her with his charm. "My lady, you look particularly lovely this evening."

Elodie reached the bottom of the stairs and stopped just in front of him. "Thank you, my lord. You look... tolerable."

"Only tolerable?" he asked. "Perhaps I am handsome enough to tempt you. We could make a go of it, you and I. Just say the word, and we could elope to Gretna Green."

Elodie's lips pressed into a tight line as she took a deliberate step back. "I would never marry you. Not even if you were the last man on earth."

Undeterred, Anthony took a step closer. "'The lady doth protest too much, methinks,'" he said, quoting Shakespeare.

She held her ground but arched an eyebrow. "And I think you need to look elsewhere for a wife. Maybe you could purchase one at the market? I am sure you could get a good deal."

Anthony puffed out his chest with exaggerated pride. "I am a viscount. You could not even imagine how many women flock to me on a daily basis."

Elodie rolled her eyes. "Oh, poor lord. What it must be like to be you," she mocked.

"It is a terrible burden to be considered such an eligible bachelor and being this devilishly handsome."

"Dear heavens, you cannot truly be this cocky!"

He smirked. "But you agree, don't you?"

"To what?"

"That I am devilishly handsome," he said with a wink.

Elodie shook her head, exasperation clear in her every move. "I can see why you are not married. People must think you are mad."

"I am not married by choice," Anthony contended. "I am waiting for you to reconsider. Quite frankly, you could do a lot worse than me. I have a title, a fortune, and I would not mind seeing you in trousers every day."

"You would be so lucky," Elodie replied sharply. "But I would never wear trousers around you, my lord."

He leaned in, his tone dropping to a whisper. "It is a shame that I have seen it, then. You seem to forget that I visit your brothers often at your country estate."

Her eyes widened slightly, and a hint of color rose to her cheeks. "A true gentleman wouldn't comment on such things."

"A true lady wouldn't wear something so revealing," Anthony shot back.

Elodie tilted her chin. "There is nothing wrong with wearing trousers when riding a horse. They are much more practical than wearing a riding habit."

"I won't argue with you there," Anthony agreed. "If I were your husband, I would buy you as many pairs of trousers as you would like."

"As tempting as that sounds, I will have to pass," she remarked dryly.

Anthony held her gaze. "If you change your mind, you know where to find me. But be warned—I won't wait forever."

She took a step closer to him. "I am not sure why it is so hard for you to grasp but let me be perfectly clear. I will never, *ever* marry you."

"I will put you down for a *maybe,* then," Anthony quipped.

Elodie let out a long, frustrated groan before turning on her heel and marching towards the drawing room. Anthony watched her go, unable to resist the smile that tugged at his lips. Teasing Elodie had always been his favorite pastime. He rather enjoyed watching the way her eyes flashed with fire or how she never hesitated to spar with him. She was utterly fascinating, making her the most interesting person he knew.

The truth of the matter was that he teased Elodie to keep her at arm's length. If she ever discovered that there was some truth behind his words, he would scare her away, and he did not want to live in a world without Elodie in it.

He was pulled from his thoughts by a familiar voice. "Anthony!" Bennett called from the corridor, striding towards him. "I hadn't realized you arrived."

Anthony turned to greet him, noticing Delphine by Bennett's side. He tipped his head towards her, noticing the warm smile. "My lady, marriage certainly agrees with you."

"Thank you, Lord Belview," she responded. "I would have to agree with you on that."

"Please, you must call me Anthony. All my friends do."

Delphine's smile only seemed to grow. "Very well, but it is only fair if you call me by my given name."

Bennett cast a curious look towards the door to the drawing room. "I thought I heard Elodie's voice."

"You did, but she got rather frustrated with me," Anthony admitted.

"What did you say this time?" Bennett asked.

Anthony couldn't help but laugh. "I may have suggested that a marriage between us would be mutually beneficial."

Bennett huffed, though his eyes gleamed with amusement. "Why would you even suggest such a thing? You two would kill one another within a week."

"That we would," Anthony agreed, "but I do so love to goad your sister. It is almost too easy."

Turning towards Delphine, Bennett explained, "Anthony and Elodie have been at odds with one another since our youth. It is the one constant that I can count on."

"Interesting," Delphine murmured, her gaze flickering between Anthony and her husband.

"Come, let us adjourn to the drawing room while we wait for the others," Bennett suggested before leading his wife to a room off the entry hall.

Once inside the drawing room, Anthony saw Elodie sitting on the settee, engaged in her needlework.

Bennett leaned closer to Anthony, his voice dropping to a whisper. "Be very still. You don't see this often. Elodie despises needlework."

Without looking up, Elodie replied, "I can hear you, Brother."

"At least your hearing is sharp," Bennett joked. "What are you making, or should I ask, what are you attempting to make?"

Elodie lowered the handkerchief to her lap. "It is a handkerchief for Melody. I thought I could give it to her when she returns from her wedding tour."

Bennett nodded approvingly. "That is rather thoughtful of you."

"It is," Elodie agreed. "But I forgot how much I despise needlework. I know it is a skill I'm supposed to have, but it is terribly tedious. I would much rather be doing anything else."

"It is a good thing you were born a lady," Bennett said.

Elodie held up the handkerchief. "I also wanted to embroider a flower above her name, but it looks like a drunk hippopotamus."

Delphine came to sit down next to Elodie. "And how, pray tell, do you know what a drunk hippopotamus looks like?"

"I don't, but it is a common enough phrase," Elodie said.

"Is it?" Delphine asked.

Bennett sat down in a chair across from them. "Allow me to translate. It is a 'common enough phrase' for Elodie. No one else says such things."

Elodie shrugged. "It will catch on. Mother even called me a drunk hippopotamus once while describing my dancing."

Anthony chimed in. "Was that meant to be a compliment?"

"No, but I took it as one," Elodie replied.

Bennett grinned. "Only you would, my dear sister."

A comfortable silence fell upon the group until Winston and Mattie stepped into the room. Delphine patted the seat next to her, beckoning Mattie over. "Come sit with us."

Mattie hurried over and sat down. "What were you discussing before we arrived?"

Elodie extended the handkerchief to Mattie. "This is my fifth attempt at a handkerchief for Melody."

Mattie took it, running her fingers over the uneven stitches. "I see Melody's name, but what is above it?"

"It is supposed to be a flower," Elodie admitted.

"Oh, dear," Mattie murmured, placing the handkerchief on the table. "It is... well, it is nice."

Elodie leaned back against the settee. "Why do these 'womanly pursuits' always elude me?"

"You are proficient at the pianoforte," Mattie offered. "And if eating biscuits were a skill, you would be a champion."

Elodie's eyes brightened at that thought. "You are right. I would be the greatest biscuit eater. There would be sonnets written about my biscuit-eating abilities."

Winston leaned closer to Mattie. "Why did you have to encourage her?"

Mattie simply shushed him. "Let her have this one."

As she uttered her words, Lady Dallington swept into the room on her husband's arm. Her eyes immediately sought out Anthony's and a bright smile lit her face. "Anthony, I am so pleased that you joined us this evening."

Anthony stepped forward and bowed. "I am honored by the invitation, my lady."

"You are always welcome in our home," Lady Dallington responded.

Lord Dallington tipped his head. "Belview. How is your father?"

At the mention of his father, all humor drained from Anthony's expression. "His health is most dire, I'm afraid. But he was adamant that I come to Town for the Season. You know how much he values duty."

"I do," Lord Dallington said.

Lady Dallington clasped her hands together. "Shall we adjourn to the dining room?" she asked, her tone light, attempting to lift the mood.

Anthony stood back and everyone started filing out of the room. Elodie came to stand next to him. "I am truly sorry about your father. Lord Kinwick is a good man."

"The best of men," Anthony responded, offering his arm. "May I have the honor of escorting you to dinner?"

For a moment, Elodie hesitated, but then she placed her hand lightly on his arm. "Thank you," she said. "How is Emma faring?"

"She seems to be doing well," Anthony replied. "I read her a book at bedtime. I even got the faintest of smiles out of her."

"That is encouraging, is it not?"

Anthony nodded. "I thought so."

They started walking towards the dining room and a silence descended over them. Finally, he spoke. "I have not forgotten about the carriage ride I promised to take you on to Hyde Park."

"Oh, wonderful," Elodie muttered.

Anthony found her lackluster response to be rather amusing. "Shall we go tomorrow during the fashionable hour?"

Elodie's gaze shifted to her mother ahead of them and a flicker of something unreadable crossed her face. "I suppose that would be all right."

Leaning in, he asked, "Are you only agreeing to the ride because you are worried your mother would get upset if you refused?"

A small smile came to her lips. "Is it that obvious?"

"Painfully," Anthony said with a chuckle. "But I will take it as a victory, nonetheless. I can think of nothing better than spending an hour with you, confined to a snug open-drawn carriage."

"You make it sound so inviting."

"Going to Hyde Park during the fashionable hour is not for the faint of heart. Everyone will be watching, gossiping."

"That sounds awful."

Anthony straightened up. "Good, then I have properly warned you. But I do have one firm rule for our outing."

She furrowed her brows. "And what might that be?"

"Under no circumstances are you allowed to kiss me in Hyde Park," Anthony said in a mock-serious tone.

Elodie blinked. "I beg your pardon?"

"I don't care how handsome I look, or what witty things I say. You must refrain from kissing me. Can you promise that?"

Elodie let out an exasperated sigh, slipping her hand from his arm. "There is something *seriously* wrong with you, my lord," she said before stepping into the dining room.

Anthony watched her go, chuckling under his breath.

4

E lodie sat down at the long, rectangular table and tried to mask her displeasure when Anthony chose the chair right next to hers. How was it that he always managed to turn the simplest interactions into battles of wit and will? Getting along with him seemed utterly impossible. Still, a part of her felt a twinge of sympathy for him. He was grappling with his father's dire health and his brother's reckless behavior. Neither of which was an easy burden to bear.

Her mother, seated at the head of the table, tapped her fork delicately against her glass, signaling for everyone's attention. Her face lit up with pride as she beamed at the family. "I am so pleased that we are all here—minus Melody, of course, who is on her wedding tour—and that Anthony could join us on this special occasion."

Anthony nodded politely, but Elodie bristled at the formality of her mother's tone. She knew what was coming next.

"Most of all," her mother continued, her gaze shifting to Elodie, "I want to commend Elodie for her presentation at Court today. She did a marvelous job."

Bennett raised his glass in mock solemnity. "Bravo, Sister. You are now officially a part of the cattle mart. What would you say? Ah, yes... mooo."

Delphine swatted at her husband's arm. "Do not tease Elodie. She will have such fun this Season."

"I don't deny that," Bennett said, setting his glass down. "But let us not pretend. The sole obligation of a debutante is to find herself a husband. Fortunately for you, Delphine, I rescued you from the marriage mart. You are welcome."

Delphine laughed, giving him an indulgent look. "I am indeed fortunate, but I believe Elodie will have her own adventure. And her own love story."

Mattie, who was seated across from Elodie, chimed in. "Perhaps we could go to Vauxhall Gardens. I have yet to see the fireworks."

Winston reached for Mattie's hand, his gaze softening as he looked at his wife. "I will take you wherever you so desire. All you need to do is ask."

Elodie watched the exchange with a mixture of pleasure and a bit of jealousy. Her brothers were undeniably happy, each having found love that was genuine and true. But would she be so lucky? Or would she be forced to settle for a match devoid of affection, made purely for duty's sake? No. She would not settle. She would marry for love, or not at all.

As the footmen began to place bowls of soup in front of them, Lady Dallington took control of the conversation, her voice light and cheerful. "I thought we could go around the table and share one thing we have recently learned. It is always enlightening."

Bennett groaned, though his eyes twinkled with mischief. "Must we do this every time we dine as a family? Elodie always shares some obscure animal fact—fascinating, but completely useless—and Winston, well, I suspect Winston just makes something up."

Winston raised an eyebrow. "I do not make things up!"

"I am simply stating that my facts are far more interesting than anyone else's," Bennett said with a dramatic sigh. "But I suppose it is the burden of being so gifted."

Winston huffed. "Gifted? In what way are you 'gifted,' Brother?"

"It is common knowledge that the eldest son is usually the smartest and the most responsible," Bennett said. "And our family is no exception."

Elodie tried to hide her smile as she reached for her glass. Bennett was clearly trying to provoke Winston into a debate, and it was working.

Winston picked up his spoon. "In the case of our family, I would argue that Melody is the smartest."

"Melody?" Bennett asked, feigning shock. "She is clever, I will grant you that, but she doesn't possess my intellectual prowess. Even my wife agrees with me."

"She has to agree with you," Winston retorted.

Delphine nodded. "It is true. No matter what idiotic thing my husband says, I will always side with him."

Bennett gasped dramatically, clutching his chest. "Idiotic? That hurts, my dear. Aren't you supposed to be my greatest supporter?"

"I am, always," Delphine said, her eyes sparkling with affection as she placed a hand on his sleeve. "And you will always be my favorite person."

Elodie decided it was as good a time as any to interject. She raised her hand, catching everyone's attention.

Her mother sighed. "Yes, Elodie?"

"I have an interesting fact," Elodie began, with a pointed glance at Bennett, "and it does not involve an animal. Two years ago, a woman named Sarah Guppy became the first woman to obtain a patent for an innovative method of bridge piling."

"A woman securing a patent?" her father asked. "What nonsense is that?"

Elodie bristled. "It isn't nonsense, Father. Sarah Guppy is a respected inventor, though her contributions are often overlooked because she is a woman."

Lord Dallington gave Elodie a dismissive look. "Women have no business in such matters. She should be at home managing her household, not wasting time on fanciful inventions."

"Why can she not do both?" Elodie asked, her voice firm. "Why must a woman's role be limited to managing a household when she has so much more to offer?"

Winston placed his spoon down and spoke up. "I have to agree with Elodie on this. If a woman has talents and interests outside the home, she should be allowed to pursue them. It is no different than us following our own interests." He glanced at Mattie, who gave him an approving smile.

Elodie gave Winston a grateful nod. "Thank you, Brother."

"I also side with Elodie," Bennett said. "Delphine runs her own business, and I could not be more proud of her."

Their mother interjected, "Does anyone else have something of interest to share? Perhaps a topic that won't lead us into a debate?"

A small silence ensued before Anthony cleared his throat. His voice, usually steady and teasing, carried a more somber tone. "I could take a go at it, but I should warn you that it is not entertaining in nature. That said, it is as good a time as any," he began, pausing for a brief moment as if bracing himself. "My brother, Stephen, eloped to Gretna Green five years ago and now has a child. His wife recently passed away and the child is now living with us." His gaze swept the table. "I thought you should know before the *ton* catches wind of it."

Lady Dallington was the first to break the stunned silence. "Well, I appreciate your candor. That was both interesting and rather scandalous," she murmured. "How was Stephen able to keep that quiet for so long?"

Anthony frowned, his jaw clenched briefly. "Stephen is an idiot," he said bluntly, his tone edged with frustration. "He didn't even realize the marriage was valid. He was quite drunk at the time, no doubt."

Bennett wiped the sides of his mouth with his napkin. As he placed the napkin back onto his lap, he said, "I wish I could say that I am surprised, but nothing truly surprises me when it comes to Stephen."

"Are you certain this child is Stephen's?" Winston asked.

Anthony bobbed his head. "There is no doubt in my mind. She has his features and there is too much of a resemblance to question it."

"Thank you for sharing that with us, Anthony," Lady Dallington said. "I can only imagine what your family is going through during such a difficult time."

Elodie stole a glance at Anthony. His usually relaxed and confident demeanor had shifted. His jaw was tight, and his eyes were clouded with something deeper. But what that was, she could not say. She felt the strangest urge to reach out and offer some sort of comfort, but she held back. It wasn't her place to do so. And besides, where had such a thought even come from?

She couldn't quite explain it, but for the briefest of moments, she saw Anthony not as the infuriating man she had always known, but as someone carrying a burden heavier than most. Her heart softened, though she quickly reminded herself of the walls she kept firmly in place when it came to him.

As the footmen began to collect the bowls of soup, her mother broke the tension with a graceful smile. "It might be best if we forgo any further interesting facts this evening."

"I think that is wise," her father agreed.

Her mother then turned her attention to Elodie, her tone

taking on a more purposeful note. "We have Lady Montrose's ball tomorrow evening."

Elodie tried to suppress the groan building inside her, managing only to mutter, "Wonderful." Balls were her least favorite part of the Season, and the prospect of dancing filled her with dread. She had never been particularly graceful on the dance floor, and her coordination always left much to be desired. Still, she would be expected to go to the ball unless she could find a reason to skip it.

Her mind raced with possible excuses before she forced a half-hearted cough. "I am starting to feel a bit ill. If I go to Lady Montrose's ball, I might grow even sicker and die."

Her mother was not the least bit convinced. "It is a risk that I am willing to take."

Anthony leaned in with an amused glint in his eyes. "I will dance the first set with you, whether you are sick or not."

"What joyous news," Elodie said dryly. "Now I have something to look forward to."

Not easily deterred, Anthony continued. "It will be like old times. And I promise you that I will not let you fall."

As much as Elodie wanted to retort with something biting, she couldn't ignore the truth behind his words. Anthony might be infuriating, but he was also in earnest. She knew, deep down, that he would never let her falter. It was both comforting and irritating—just like Anthony himself.

The footmen placed plates of food in front of them and Elodie reached for her fork and knife. For a few moments, the sounds of clinking silverware filled the room as everyone began to eat.

Then, as if unable to leave the matter of the ball alone, her mother spoke again. "I hear that Lady Montrose's son is quite handsome and considered one of the great catches of the Season."

"He is also a known rake," Bennett said. "I think it would be wise if Elodie avoided him at all costs."

"Lady Montrose has assured me that the rumors about her son are grossly exaggerated," their mother remarked.

Bennett exchanged a knowing look with Winston before responding. "A mother would do just about anything for her child, even turn a blind eye to the truth staring her in the face."

"Very well, I believe you," their mother said. "Elodie will stay away from Lord Montrose and any other rake. We must protect her reputation."

Elodie placed her fork and knife down with a little more force than intended. "Do I have a say in all of this?"

"No," everyone at the table said in unison.

Elodie rolled her eyes. Exasperation echoed in her voice as she said, "I can take care of myself. I do not need to be coddled at every turn."

Anthony leaned in again and whispered just loud enough for her to hear. "I am no rake, but if you are looking for trouble at the ball, you know where to find me."

She shot him a sideways glance. "I will be sure to stay as far away from you as possible."

He grinned. "Pity. We could have quite the fun adventures together."

Elodie didn't know why, but Anthony's words seemed to ring true to her, leaving her with a sense of anticipation she could not quite shake.

With the morning sun streaming in through the windows of his bedchamber, Anthony carefully adjusted his cravat as he stared at his reflection in the mirror. Behind him, his dutiful valet, Rollins, stood at attention.

"Will there be anything else, my lord?" Rollins inquired.

Satisfied with his appearance, Anthony dropped his hands and turned to face the valet. "Do you know if my brother has met with his daughter yet?"

Rollins's eyes flickered with sympathy. "According to the maids, your brother only left his room last night after you departed for dinner. He has not returned home since."

Anthony clenched his jaw, muttering under his breath, "Botheration."

"I'm truly sorry, my lord. I wish I could have delivered better news."

Anthony moved towards the door but paused, his hand resting on the polished brass handle. "I suppose I had half-hoped that Stephen would step up for the sake of his daughter. But once again, I was wrong. My brother will never change."

"Perhaps he just needs more time," Rollins suggested.

Anthony let out a huff of frustration. "Time? That is all I seem to give him, and he never fails to disappoint me. Time and time again."

Without saying another word, Anthony turned the handle and stepped out into the corridor, the familiar knot of frustration tightening his chest. He had no idea why he continued to expect anything from Stephen. His brother had made a life out of proving him wrong, consistently failing to live up to even the smallest expectations.

Anthony headed towards the dining room on the main level and was relieved to find it empty. He preferred solitude in the morning, a chance to gather his thoughts without interruption. Settling into his seat at the long table, he reached for the newssheets, scanning the Society page first. To his surprise—and relief—there was no mention of Stephen or the newly revealed daughter. At least that particular disaster hadn't reached the *ton* yet.

He had just begun reading an article on the war when the

sound of unsteady footsteps caught his attention. Stephen stumbled into the dining room, his appearance as disheveled as ever. His cravat hung loosely around his neck, his shirt was untucked, and his hair stuck out at odd angles, as though he had just crawled out of bed.

"You look dreadful," Anthony remarked, folding the newssheets and setting them aside.

Stephen raised a finger to his lips, swaying slightly. "Shh. You are entirely too loud for this ungodly hour."

"I am speaking no louder than I normally do," Anthony said.

Grumbling, Stephen collapsed into a chair. "Why is it so bright in here?"

Anthony glanced at the long windows lining the room. "It is morning. I can't control the sun."

Stephen waved his hand lazily. "Close the drapes. The light is unbearable."

A footman rushed to obey, pulling the heavy curtains shut and plunging the room into a dim, shadowy state. Stephen sighed with exaggerated relief, sinking further into his chair. "Much better. Now, food. Quickly," he snapped, rubbing his temples as if warding off the remnants of a long night.

Anthony watched him with thinly veiled irritation. "I take it you have just come home."

Stephen gave a mocking grin. "Brilliant deduction, Brother. Clearly, you have missed your calling as an investigator. Now, kindly leave me alone."

"You seem to be in a delightful mood this morning," Anthony said dryly, folding his arms. "I imagine this charming behavior is related to the fact you have just learned you have a daughter?"

Stephen groaned, leaning back in his chair. "Do we have to talk about this?"

Rising from his seat, Anthony crossed the room and threw

the drapes open again, allowing the sunlight to flood back in. "Have you at least met her yet?"

Stephen shielded his eyes, scowling. "No, and why would I?"

"Because it is the right thing to do."

"Do not lecture me on what is 'right.' You always think you are so much better than me," Stephen grumbled.

Anthony returned to his seat. "I don't know why I bother with you."

A footman placed a plate of food down in front of Anthony and he reached for his fork and knife. As he started eating, he tried to ignore Stephen's loud, incessant chewing. But he finally had enough. "Do you mind?"

Stephen paused, looking blankly at his brother. "What did I do wrong now?"

"You are chewing entirely too loudly," Anthony replied.

With a devilish grin, Stephen deliberately took another bite, this time chewing with exaggerated slowness, his mouth wide open. "Better?" he mumbled through his half-chewed food, clearly enjoying himself.

Anthony glanced heavenward. "You are impossible."

"Yet you keep trying to change me," Stephen said, still speaking through his mouthful of food.

"I suppose I am hoping you realize that you are wasting away your life."

Stephen shrugged. "I think I am doing just fine."

Before Anthony could argue that point, Percy entered the dining hall with a silver tray in his hand. "The messenger has returned with a letter from your mother."

Anthony rose and retrieved the letter from the tray. He unfolded it and read the brief note.

"What did Mother say?" Stephen asked.

Anthony crumpled the letter in his hand as he turned to Stephen. "Mother and Father are overjoyed at the news of

their granddaughter and they are traveling to Town immediately."

For the first time that morning, Stephen had the decency to
look ashamed. "Father is coming?"

Anthony's lips pressed into a thin line as he tried to keep his
emotions in check. "Yes, he is. And we both know he should be
resting, not making the journey into Town. His health—" He
hesitated. "He should be in bed, conserving his strength, not
traveling."

Stephen shifted in his seat, appearing uncomfortable, but
he offered no further comment. Anthony could barely stand to
look at him any longer. The sense of betrayal, of disappointment, twisted in his chest.

Without another word, Anthony turned on his heel and
strode out of the dining room. He needed air. He exited the
main door and stepped onto the pavement, inhaling deeply as
the cool air hit his face. Perhaps notifying their parents about
Emma had been a mistake. He wanted them to know the
truth, but he hadn't anticipated they would come rushing to
meet their grandchild, regardless of his father's declining
health.

As his thoughts churned, something unexpectedly struck
him on the back of the head. Startled, Anthony glanced down
to see a green grape rolling away on the cobblestones. His brow
furrowed. What in the blazes? Was someone throwing grapes
at him?

He turned his head and found Elodie leaning out of an
upper-level window, a grape poised in her hand. A mischievous
grin lit up her face. "What is wrong?" she called out.

"Why do you suppose something is wrong?"

Elodie arched an eyebrow. "Must we truly go through this
song and dance? I have been throwing grapes at you for several
minutes and you only just noticed."

"That is because you hit me on the back of the head."

Elodie's smile grew, her eyes sparkling with triumph. "You have to admit that it was an impressive throw."

"I admit nothing," he retorted with mock seriousness, though he couldn't suppress his amusement.

Just then, Lady Dallington appeared beside Elodie, her expression far less jovial. She whispered something to Elodie before turning her attention to Anthony. "Lord Belview, would you care to come inside for a cup of tea?"

Anthony inclined his head graciously. "Brilliant idea, my lady."

With a nod of approval, Lady Dallington closed the window, disappearing from sight.

Anthony made his way to the front door, knocking lightly. A moment later, the door swung open, and he stepped into the grand entry hall just as Elodie descended the staircase, followed closely by her mother.

As Elodie approached him, she lowered her voice. "My mother is not pleased that I was throwing grapes at you."

"I would imagine not," Anthony said.

Spinning on her heel, Elodie faced her mother. "Anthony said he enjoyed having grapes thrown at him. In fact, he found it quite invigorating."

Lady Dallington's expression remained solemn. "A lady does not throw fruit at a gentleman," she chided. "Furthermore, a lady most certainly does not converse with a gentleman out of a window."

Elodie didn't look the least bit repentant. "But what if the gentleman was starving and in desperate need of sustenance? What if tossing him a grape at that precise moment would save his life? I could be a heroine!"

"That scenario is utterly ridiculous," Lady Dallington said.

"Is it?" Elodie countered, tilting her head as if seriously considering the possibility.

Lady Dallington sighed deeply. "You are going to be the

death of me, Child," she muttered. "Just promise me that you won't throw fruit at gentlemen."

Elodie bit her lower lip, clearly fighting back a laugh. "I can't promise that, Mother. I am a saver of lives!"

Turning towards Anthony, Lady Dallington's expression was one of exasperation. "Will you kindly talk some sense into my daughter?"

Anthony bowed. "It would be my pleasure, my lady," he said, though he was quite certain convincing Elodie of anything was an impossible task. Still, there was no denying that it would be entertaining to try.

"If you will excuse me, I would like to return to my breakfast," Lady Dallington said. "Why don't you two continue this conversation in the gardens? And afterward, we can have that cup of tea."

"I would like that very much," Anthony responded with a smile.

As Lady Dallington walked away, Elodie crossed her arms, raising a playful brow at Anthony. "Well, let's hear it, then. Persuade me with your so-called wisdom."

Anthony chuckled. "I don't have any, considering nothing I say will change your mind. But, if I may ask, why exactly were you throwing grapes at me?"

Elodie grinned, completely unabashed. "To get your attention, of course. You looked troubled."

"And you thought throwing grapes at me was the best way to get my attention?"

"It worked, did it not?"

Anthony couldn't help but shake his head. "I must agree with your mother. You are impossible."

"Thank you," Elodie said.

"That wasn't a compliment."

Elodie laughed. "It certainly sounded like one."

Despite himself, Anthony felt a warmth spread through

him. Elodie had a way of always brightening his mood. She was utterly unpredictable, always saying and doing the most unexpected things, and yet, that was what he found so refreshing about her.

Elodie's smile faded. "Now, what has you so upset?"

He extended his arm towards her. "Perhaps we should continue this conversation in the gardens as your mother suggested."

While he led Elodie towards the rear of the townhouse, Anthony found great comfort with her by his side. But he knew that she did not feel the same about him.

5

As Anthony led Elodie towards the gardens, she found herself half-wishing she had taken a few grapes for the conversation. She was, after all, hungry. She had been on her way to breakfast when she had spotted Anthony standing out on the pavement. He looked troubled, his expression distant, and for some inexplicable reason, she could not just walk away. And so, when she saw the bowl of grapes, an impulsive plan had formed in her mind. It wasn't her finest idea, but it had worked. She had gotten his attention.

Anthony cleared his throat, breaking the silence between them. "How are you faring this morning?"

Elodie glanced up at him, the corners of her mouth quirking. "I am hungry," she admitted.

"Shall I leave so you can have your meal?"

"No, it is all right. I would prefer if you would just tell me what is wrong so I can help you fix it."

"Why do you suppose it is something that can be easily fixed?" he asked, sounding skeptical.

Elodie shrugged. "Sometimes problems seem bigger in our minds than they truly are. I can help with that."

Anthony didn't look entirely convinced. "Yet you were the one who decided to throw grapes at me on the pavement."

"It wasn't my finest plan," Elodie admitted with a grin. "But truthfully, I have wanted to hit you with something for ages, and the grapes were the closest thing at hand."

A smile came to Anthony's lips. "You are a minx."

Elodie laughed. "You can call me names all morning, but it won't distract me from the fact that you are troubled. So, what is it? Is it your brother again?"

His smile faded. "It is. He still has not met his daughter."

"Perhaps it is too overwhelming for him."

Anthony stopped walking, turning to face her with a furrowed brow. "You are taking his side now?"

"I am not taking anyone's side. I am simply pointing out that Stephen has never been particularly adept at handling unexpected news."

"That is true," Anthony conceded, though frustration lingered in his voice, "but it is *his* daughter."

Elodie gestured towards a nearby bench. "Shall we sit?"

"If you don't mind."

As she settled onto the bench, she looked at him thoughtfully. "What is it you want from Stephen, truly? What is it you expect him to do?"

Anthony sank onto the bench beside her, his posture tense. "I want him to be responsible."

"Like you?"

He shook his head. "No, not like me. I want him to be held accountable for his actions. Up until now, he has lived without consequences, always skirting around responsibility."

Elodie shifted slightly, turning more towards him. "You can't change Stephen. You can only change how you react to him."

"You are terrible at giving advice," he muttered.

"On the contrary, I think I am rather brilliant at it," Elodie said, holding back a grin.

He gave her a look, half-skeptical, half-amused. "Oh? Do enlighten me."

Elodie leaned back slightly. "I once thought that if I acted more like Melody, life would be easier. She followed the rules, and for a time, I thought if I did the same, I would have no troubles at all. But I was wrong. I was just pretending, fooling myself into thinking that her life was perfect because she did everything right."

"You? Pretend to be Melody? I would have liked to have seen that."

Elodie waved a hand dismissively. "It was very short-lived. I still had to act like a performing monkey and bite my tongue at every turn. And let me tell you, that is not something I am particularly skilled at."

Anthony chuckled, the tension in his shoulders easing just a bit. "Biting your tongue? That hardly seems like you."

"Precisely," Elodie replied. "You can't force yourself—or anyone else, for that matter—to be someone they are not. Stephen has to make his own mistakes. It is *his* life, and he can live it however he sees fit."

He stared at her, his eyes holding uncertainty. "So I am supposed to give up on him?"

Elodie met his gaze steadily. "No, not give up. Trust him."

"Trust?" Anthony scoffed. "Stephen has given me no reason to trust him. He is a rake who squanders money. My money!"

She hesitated, trying to find the right words. "I just think—"

But before she could finish, Anthony abruptly rose to his feet, cutting her off. "No, you do not get to voice your opinion on this. You know nothing about what I have had to endure because of my brother."

Elodie rose. "Anthony—"

He interrupted again. "Why should I take advice from you? Your life is perfect. You don't understand."

"Perfect?" Elodie asked, rearing back. "My life is far from perfect."

Anthony ran a hand through his hair. "Oh, yes, your biggest concerns are what gown to wear each day and what color ribbons to put in your hair."

Elodie frowned. "You are angry."

"Of course, I am angry!" Anthony shouted. "My brother is a blackguard and now my father is traveling to see his grand-daughter. The trip might kill him. But does Stephen care? No. He is too busy being reckless and irresponsible."

"I'm sorry," Elodie said, feeling helpless as she watched him struggle with the weight of his emotions. She wanted to comfort him, to say the right thing, but nothing she could think of seemed adequate.

Anthony turned his back to her, but not before she caught a glimpse of his eyes brimming with unshed tears. His voice, when he spoke again, was softer, filled with grief. "My father is dying, Elodie. And there is nothing I can do to stop it."

Her heart ached for Anthony. The raw pain in his voice, the vulnerability he rarely showed, stirred something deep within her. Without thinking, Elodie stepped forward and gently placed her hand on his back. It was a small gesture, but it was all she had to offer. She wanted to let him know he was not alone in his sorrows.

After a long moment, Elodie broke the silence, her voice light as she attempted to bring some levity back to the moment. "Would you like me to fetch some grapes for you? I find they are excellent for when one is brooding," she said while offering a soft smile.

Anthony turned towards her, a hint of a smile on his lips. "No, thank you."

"What can I say to make you feel better?"

His gaze softened. "Just you being here is enough."

"I can't stay long, though," Elodie said. "I need adequate

sustenance if I am expected to save you from all of life's troubles."

As she uttered her words, the sound of a child's voice drifted up from beyond the gardens' hedges.

Anthony must have heard it too because he asked, "Would you like to meet my niece, Emma?"

"Not yet," Elodie said as she went to stand up on the bench to peer over the hedges. Her eyes roamed over Anthony's gardens until they landed on a small, dark-haired girl walking along a path. "She is much smaller than I imagined."

Anthony joined her, standing beside her on the bench, his gaze following Elodie's. "She is only four."

"She looks like a miniature version of Stephen," Elodie remarked. "I am not quite sure if that is a blessing or a curse."

"Let us hope she grows out of that," Anthony joked.

Elodie hopped down from the bench. "I am ready to meet her now. Although, I must confess, I have not spent much time around children. I hope I do not say the wrong thing."

Anthony smirked. "I have no doubt you will."

"Thank you for the vote of confidence," she retorted.

Extending his arm, Anthony said, "Allow me to escort you to my gardens."

Elodie gave his arm a dismissive glance. "I am more than perfectly capable of walking a hundred feet on my own."

"I am only trying to be a gentleman."

"Well, you can stop," Elodie teased, brushing past him as he lowered his arm with an exaggerated sigh.

"Very well. Come along, then," he said before he opened the gate that separated their townhouses.

Elodie stepped through and headed towards Emma, who stood quietly, clutching a small doll, her wide, apprehensive eyes fixed on her. The sight tugged at Elodie's heart. She had no idea what to say or how to put the child at ease.

Anthony came to stand next to her and provided the introductions. "Lady Elodie, may I have the honor of introducing you to my niece, Emma?"

Elodie crouched down to meet Emma at eye level. "It is a pleasure to meet you, Miss Emma."

The little girl hesitated for a moment, then awkwardly dropped into a small, wobbly curtsy, her tiny legs trembling as she stood back up.

"How old are you?" Elodie asked.

Emma held up four fingers without a word.

"Four," Elodie said. "That is a wonderful age. You know, I believe four is old enough to take care of a pet. Don't you agree?"

Emma's eyes lit up. "Yes, I do."

"If you could choose," Elodie began, leaning in, "would you rather have a cat or a dog?"

"Dog," the girl promptly replied.

Anthony interrupted, "Lady Elodie, I do not think—"

Elodie turned to look up at Anthony. "Do you not think every little girl should have a dog?"

He glanced at Emma and let out a resigned sigh. "I suppose a dog would not be the worst thing in the world."

A bright smile came to Emma's face, the happiness spilling over into her eyes. "I have always wanted a dog."

Anthony moved to crouch down beside Elodie. "Then you shall have one. It may take a few days, but I promise I will find you the perfect dog."

Emma's excitement was so genuine, so infectious, that it brought a smile to Elodie's lips. "Thank you, my lord," she whispered.

A maid quietly stepped forward, gently placing a hand on Emma's shoulder. "If I may, it is time for Miss Emma's breakfast."

Anthony tipped his head in acknowledgment, though his eyes lingered on his niece.

Elodie nudged his arm playfully with her elbow. "You did a good thing, you know."

Turning to face her, he asked, "A dog? Truly?"

"Just think about how happy it will make your niece," Elodie said. "Besides, I will help take care of it. I will even take it for walks in the park."

"I shall hold you to that." He glanced upwards, squinting slightly as the sun broke through the clouds. "I should go review the accounts before we depart for our carriage ride through Hyde Park."

"And I need to eat," Elodie declared, patting her stomach. "Next time, instead of throwing grapes at you, I shall eat them."

"I am sure that your mother would prefer that."

Just as she began to turn and walk away, Anthony's voice stopped her. "Thank you. For everything."

Elodie turned back to face him. "You can repay me by finding Emma a cute puppy. There is nothing worse than an ugly dog. It is awkward when one has to pretend they aren't repulsed by an unfortunate-looking dog."

Anthony bowed. "You have my word."

———————

Anthony sat at his desk, staring at the ledgers, though his mind was elsewhere. The numbers blurred together, and he was tired from grappling with his emotions. He glanced at the long clock in the corner and noted that it was nearly time for his carriage ride with Elodie. Despite the tiresome day, he found himself looking forward to the outing. There was something about being in Elodie's company that made the world seem a little brighter.

Just as he rose from his chair, Percy stepped into the room. "The carriage has been brought around front, my lord."

Anthony nodded his thanks and paused. "I have decided to get Miss Emma a puppy. Do you know where I might find one?"

"Do you have a specific breed in mind?" Percy asked.

"No, but the only requirement is that it not be... ugly," Anthony replied with a faint smile.

Percy gave him a bemused look. "Is there such a thing as an ugly puppy?"

"Apparently so," Anthony said. "Lady Elodie was quite insistent on that point."

His butler's lips twitched. "I shall endeavor to find a suitably non-ugly puppy for Miss Emma."

"I think a puppy might bring some joy to Emma. She could use a bit of happiness right now."

"I have no doubt it will," Percy agreed. "Children do have a particular fondness for animals."

With that settled, Percy exited the study, and Anthony crossed to the mirror on the wall, adjusting his cravat one last time. He couldn't help but feel a sense of anticipation for his ride with Elodie.

As he made his way out of the study and into the entry hall, he was met by his brother. Stephen descended the stairs, looking surprisingly put together for this time of day.

"Where are you off to in such a hurry?" Stephen asked, eyeing him curiously.

"I am taking Elodie on a carriage ride through Hyde Park," Anthony replied, adjusting his gloves.

Stephen's eyebrows shot up. "During the fashionable hour? Tell me, are you courting the lovely Elodie?"

Anthony would love nothing more than to court Elodie properly, but she seemed immune to his advances. "We are simply family friends, enjoying a ride."

Stephen came to a stop in front of him, his grin widening. "If you are not interested in pursuing Elodie, may I have a go at her? Elodie is quite... charming."

Anthony's blood boiled at the mere suggestion, his hands balling into fists. "Absolutely not!" he snapped, stepping closer to his brother. "You will stay far away from Elodie."

"Why so protective? Surely there is more to it than her reputation."

"There is nothing more to it than protecting her from *your* reputation," Anthony replied tightly. "You are a rake, and I will not allow you to ruin her name."

Stephen held his hands up in surrender. "You made your point, but I can't help but wonder if there is more to it than that."

Anthony had no desire to discuss his conflicting emotions with his brother. "Good day." He strode past his brother, stepping outside, and made the short walk to Elodie's townhouse.

He lifted his hand to knock, but before he could, the door swung open and Elodie slipped out, nearly bumping into him.

"We should go, and quickly," she said as she hurried down the steps.

Anthony followed her. "Whatever for?"

"Trust me."

Just as he offered his hand to assist her into the coach, the door opened and Bennett and Winston stepped out with solemn expressions on their faces.

"Drat," Elodie muttered under her breath.

Bennett and Winston came to a stop in front of Anthony. Bennett spoke first, his voice firm. "If you are anything less than honorable with our sister, we will hunt you down and kill you."

Winston shook his head. "We will challenge you to a duel first, of course. Then kill you."

Bennett nodded, as if this were a perfectly reasonable course of action. "Indeed. A duel first, then death."

Anthony smiled. "You have nothing to worry about. We are simply going for a carriage ride."

Bennett gave him a long, assessing look before turning his gaze to Elodie. "Hand it over," he demanded.

Elodie gave him an innocent look. "Hand what over?"

"The nail," Bennett replied, holding his hand out expectantly. "You know, the one you threaten people with."

She reached into her reticule and pulled out a rusty, bent nail. She placed it in Bennett's palm. "Do not lose this."

Bennett held the nail up. "I wouldn't dream of it."

Anthony held his hand out to Elodie. "Shall we?"

Once Elodie was situated in the carriage, Anthony took his seat across from her. The coach jerked forward, but his eyes lingered on Bennett and Winston, who stood rooted in place, watching them with narrowed eyes.

"Dare I ask about the nail?" Anthony asked, breaking the silence.

Elodie waved her hand in front of her. "It is nothing."

"It doesn't seem like nothing."

Elodie studied him for a moment, then let out a small sigh. "When Melody and I were abducted, I found the nail and thought I could use it to protect myself."

"A nail?" Anthony raised an eyebrow. "You were going to defend yourself with a rusty nail?"

A smirk came to her lips. "Do not underestimate a nail. It can be quite effective. One good scratch, and someone could bleed."

Anthony feigned horror. "The terror. A bleeding scratch."

Elodie adjusted the straw hat that sat slightly askew on her head. "We women have very few ways of protecting ourselves. Besides, the nail reminds me of my sister."

His teasing faded as he caught the shift in her tone. "You must miss her terribly."

Elodie's gaze dropped to her hands. "I do. Melody has always been more than just my sister. She is my best friend. We have never truly been apart until now."

Anthony leaned forward, his voice softening. "I have always admired the bond you two share. I have been envious, to be honest. Stephen and I... well, you have seen us. Our relationship has always been strained at best."

Elodie's eyes returned to meet his. "It is different when you are a twin. We may look alike, but our personalities could not be more different. It is those differences that have kept us close."

"At least Lord Emberly lives only a county away from your family's country estate," Anthony attempted.

"It is not the same."

Anthony could hear the sadness in her voice and decided it was time to change the subject, hoping to lighten the mood. "I am working on getting a non-ugly puppy for Emma."

That was the right thing to say because Elodie's eyes lit up. "That is wonderful news! I have no doubt that Miss Emma would appreciate the gesture. I have always wanted a pet, but my father refused."

"Did he give you a reason?"

Elodie pressed her lips together. "He told me that if I wanted to cuddle with something, I should get myself a husband."

Anthony chuckled. "Well, I cannot entirely fault your father's logic."

"It is idiotic!" Elodie declared, crossing her arms in defiance. "Why can't I have a dog or a cat, for that matter? Although, if I could choose, my ideal pet would be a unicorn."

"Unicorns aren't real."

Elodie gave him a thoughtful look. "Aren't they?" she asked. "Fine. My second ideal pet would be a miniature horse."

"What would you do with a miniature horse?" Anthony asked.

Elodie looked at him like he was a simpleton. "The same thing I would do with a dog or a cat. I would love it."

Anthony settled back in his seat. "A miniature horse is a waste."

"I disagree. The Prince Regent has many miniature horses."

"Yes, but he is also known for his wasteful spending," Anthony argued.

Elodie fidgeted with the reticule around her wrist. "Regardless, I would name the miniature horse Henry."

"Henry?" Anthony echoed, stifling a laugh. "Why Henry?"

"Because I have always wanted to name a horse Henry."

"And if it is a girl?"

"Henrietta, obviously."

Anthony grinned. "Those are absurd names for horses."

"So says you," Elodie shot back. "I think they are perfectly fine names for a miniature horse."

"Remind me not to let you help select our non-ugly dog's name," Anthony teased.

Elodie narrowed her eyes playfully. "Those are perfectly acceptable names."

"So says you," Anthony said, using her words against her. "But I prefer stronger names for my horses."

"But a miniature horse is different," Elodie defended. "They are little, cantankerous things. Much like me."

As the carriage entered Hyde Park and joined the elegant parade of carriages along Rotten Row, the fashionable hour was in full swing. The air buzzed with the sound of horses' hooves and the low murmur of conversations from other carriages.

"Have you been to Rotten Row before?" Anthony asked.

"I have walked it, but not during the fashionable hour," Elodie shared, her eyes wide as she took in the spectacle. "There are so many carriages ahead of us."

"It is the place to be seen," Anthony said.

Elodie's eyes remained straight ahead, her posture stiffening. "I do not wish to be seen. I am perfectly content with being a wallflower."

Anthony gave her a knowing look. "I daresay that is impossible. You are far too beautiful to be a mere wallflower."

But rather than accepting the compliment, Elodie's expression shifted, annoyance flashing in her eyes. "I don't want to be known as only a pretty face."

"I never said you were."

Elodie's back went rigid. "One of the teachers at my boarding school used to tell me that being beautiful was the greatest asset for a genteel woman. That nothing else mattered."

"I disagree with your teacher."

"As do I, but I don't think she was entirely wrong," Elodie said. "Most gentlemen only care about a woman's appearance. They seem to dismiss her mind entirely."

Anthony gave her a reassuring smile. "Only the foolish ones do that. Any man worth his salt values more than just beauty."

"It is a shame you do not believe in unicorns," she said lightly.

"I would not tell people that you believe unicorns are real."

Elodie sat straighter in her seat and adopted a mock-serious tone. "People once thought that the world was flat, but Christopher Columbus proved them wrong when his ship didn't fall off the edge of the earth. The same argument could be used for the existence of unicorns."

Anthony looked heavenward, though he couldn't stop the smile that tugged at the corners of his mouth. "What other mystical creatures do you believe in?"

"None. Just unicorns," Elodie said, her eyes twinkling with mirth.

As he went to reply, he caught sight of something in the distance. "Do not look now, but your brothers are trailing us on horseback."

"I am not the least bit surprised."

"I think it is admirable, actually," Anthony remarked. "That they are so protective of you."

A smile came to Elodie's lips. "It is true. They are the best of brothers, at least when they aren't stealing my buttered bread."

"They steal your bread?"

Elodie bobbed her head. "Oh, yes. They may be protective, but when it comes to buttered bread, all bets are off."

"I will make sure to keep that in mind," Anthony said as their carriage continued its steady pace along Rotten Row, surrounded by the watchful eyes of the *ton*. For the first time, he didn't care who saw them—he was just happy to be in Elodie's company.

6

Elodie smoothed down the skirts of her jonquil gown and let out a sigh. Today was her first social event as a debutante. She could do this. All she had to do was smile, make polite conversation, and dance a few sets. Her heart sank at that word.

Dance.

She was dreadful at it, the worst by far. If she could manage to make it through the evening without stepping on someone's foot, she would count it as a win. The thought of falling, of making a fool of herself in front of all those eyes, haunted her. She would be ruined and be an utter disappointment to her parents. And to herself.

Molly finished fastening the last button on the back of Elodie's dress. "Are you all right, my lady?" she asked. "You seem rather tense."

Elodie bit her lip, voicing the fear that had been gnawing at her all morning. "What if I fail?"

"Tonight, or in general?" Molly asked, no doubt in an attempt to lighten the mood.

Elodie turned to face her, her expression serious. "What if I do something intolerably stupid and I am forever ruined?"

Molly's eyes filled with compassion. "Whatever happens, your family will still love and support you. You are not alone in this."

"I hope so," Elodie murmured.

The door swung open and Lady Dallington swept into the room, her eyes immediately locking onto Elodie with a gleam of approval. "You look absolutely lovely, my dear," she said. "And I have the most wonderful news."

Elodie forced a smile, trying to muster some enthusiasm. "What is that?"

Her mother's smile grew even brighter. "The queen has named you the diamond of the first water."

"Me?" Elodie asked in disbelief.

Her mother nodded eagerly. "Isn't it splendid? Do you know what this means? You will have your pick of suitors! Every eligible gentleman will want to dance with you tonight."

Elodie slowly sank onto the edge of her bed. "I don't want to be the diamond."

Her mother's smile faltered slightly, but her tone remained cheery. "You have little choice in the matter. Most young women would be thrilled to receive such an honor."

But Elodie did not feel thrilled. She felt only dread. All eyes would be on her tonight, every step she took scrutinized, every word she spoke dissected. The very thought of it made her feel like she could not breathe.

Her mother moved to sit beside Elodie on the bed. "I know this is not what you wanted, but it is what you deserve. I may be biased, but you are far too beautiful and clever to be a mere wallflower."

"I am scared, Mother," Elodie confessed.

"You, scared?" her mother asked, her voice light. "I didn't think that was possible."

Elodie met her mother's gaze. "What if I say or do the wrong thing? What if I make a fool of myself?"

Her mother squeezed her hand gently. "You won't. And even if you do stumble, you are not alone. We are family. We will stand by you, no matter what."

"Can I at least bring my nail?" Elodie asked. "Just in case I need to defend myself from any unwanted attention."

Her mother laughed. "Very well, you may bring it. But I insist that you do not threaten anyone with it."

Elodie's lips twitched into a small smile. "I can't promise that. Sometimes the nail has a mind of its own."

Her mother rose from the bed. "Come now, it is time. We must leave for the ball. We wouldn't want to be late."

Elodie stood and tucked the bent nail into her reticule. Somehow, having it with her made her feel better, as if Melody were with her in spirit, watching over her. Together, Elodie and her mother left her bedchamber and started down the corridor.

"You may recall," her mother began, "I was named the diamond when I was younger."

"I am well aware, considering you tell me that story often," Elodie teased.

Her mother grinned. "I just want to remind you that I had a life before I became your mother."

As they descended the grand staircase, Elodie spotted her brothers, Bennett and Winston, standing in the entry hall with their wives. The moment they saw her, they burst into applause, grinning from ear to ear.

"Bravo, Diamond!" Bennett called out, his voice full of playful mockery.

Elodie rolled her eyes. "What are you fools doing?"

Winston approached her and kissed her on the cheek. "Well done, Sister. You did not embarrass this family, as Bennett claimed you might."

Bennett stopped clapping, feigning innocence. "I never said

such a thing! I may have thought it, once or twice, but I would never say it out loud."

Delphine stepped forward. "Ignore my husband," she said. "We are all so proud of you."

Mattie bobbed her head in agreement. "You have already achieved more than most debutantes dream of."

Elodie tried to return their smiles, but inside, the dread still lingered. She did not want this. "Thank you," she murmured.

Mattie placed a gentle hand on her sleeve. "It will be all right. You can do this."

White stepped forward and announced, "The coaches are out front."

"Thank you, White," her mother acknowledged before turning back to her family. "Your father has sent word that he will meet us at the ball. Shall we?"

Elodie followed her family outside to the waiting coaches, her mind racing with thoughts of all the ways she could embarrass herself tonight. And the list was plentiful. As she sat across from her mother in the lead coach, her eyes drifted to the window.

Her mother's voice broke through the silence. "Do not fret. You were born to do this."

"That is easy for you to say," Elodie muttered. "But as you so kindly pointed out before, I have flaws. Loads of them."

"Everyone has flaws," her mother began. "It doesn't mean that you are broken or imperfect. You can either live with them, or you can change them. It is your choice. But your strengths— and weaknesses—have made you into an incredible young woman."

"You have to say that since you are my mother," Elodie muttered.

Her mother leaned in, her voice firm but kind. "You have always been my most challenging child. I never know what to expect from you. But I know this—you are capable of far more than you realize. You will take this Season by storm."

"I wish I had your confidence."

The coach came to a rolling stop and the sound of the gathered crowd filled the air. A footman opened the door, and Elodie stepped out, her heart pounding. Her mother's final words echoed in her mind as they lined up with the other guests waiting to enter the ball.

The eyes of every debutante and matron turned towards her, whispers and stares following her every move. It had begun.

They entered the grand townhouse and her steps faltered at the sight of the ballroom. It was a sea of people, the crowd thick with eager faces surrounding the chalked dance floor. It was a *crush*. But it wasn't unexpected. After all, this was the first social event of the Season.

From behind her, Bennett's voice broke through her thoughts, soft with concern. "Elodie? Are you all right?"

"I am," she replied before taking a deep breath. She squared her shoulders and followed her mother through the hordes of elegantly dressed people. They found a spot near the back of the room, and Elodie couldn't help but feel the curious glances cast her way. She was the diamond of the Season now, and everyone was watching.

As her eyes scanned the room, they caught sight of a familiar figure. Anthony. He stood across the ballroom, his dark eyes meeting hers. He tipped his head in acknowledgment and smiled. It was a smile that sent a strange, unexpected flutter through her chest.

She must be going mad. Anthony was the last person she should be thinking about. He was infuriating, and she desperately wanted to dislike him. It must be the nerves she was experiencing this evening.

Her thoughts were interrupted as Mattie looped her arm

through hers, pulling her close. "You are the diamond of the first water. You will have your pick of suitors. Now, who shall it be? An earl? Or perhaps a duke? However, I believe all eligible dukes are over fifty. Is that a problem?"

Elodie suppressed a shudder. "I am not marrying a duke."

"A prince, then?" Mattie teased.

Elodie grimaced. "Good heavens, no. I would make a terrible princess."

From behind them, Winston's voice joined them. "That you would," he agreed. "You would demand a unicorn as a wedding present."

"What else would I ask for?" Elodie joked.

The orchestra started warming up in the corner and Winston raised his voice to be heard over the music. "Who shall you dance with first?"

"I promised it to Anthony," Elodie said. "Although, he didn't so much ask as he informed me that he was dancing the first set with me."

Winston's eyes held approval. "Anthony is a good choice. He will look after you and help ease you into the night."

"Elodie's dancing has improved greatly," Mattie chimed in.

"She had nowhere to go but up," Winston retorted.

Elodie placed a hand on her stomach to calm her nerves. Just as she was debating whether to bolt from the ballroom or not, Anthony appeared before her. The way he looked at her, so steady and reassuring, made her let out a breath she had not realized she was holding.

Anthony bowed. "Lady Elodie," he greeted.

She dropped into a curtsy, knowing what was expected of her. "Lord Belview."

He offered his arm, a teasing glint in his eyes. "I have come to claim the dance you promised me."

Taking his arm, Elodie swallowed her nerves. "Please do not let me make a fool of myself."

"I won't," Anthony assured her. "I have you."

And with those words, she felt herself begin to relax. Anthony might vex her endlessly, but in that moment, she felt safe with him. She wouldn't fall. She wouldn't fail. Not with him guiding her.

They walked together to the dance floor, joining the other couples as the orchestra began the opening strains of a quadrille. It was a dance she knew well, and as they moved through the steps, she kept her head down, focusing intently on each movement. Yet, as the music continued, something unexpected happened—she began to enjoy herself. Her earlier dread melted away, replaced by a surprising sense of lightness. The dance, one she had feared so much, seemed to fly by.

The music came to an end and Elodie dropped into a curtsy. Anthony approached her with his arm out. "You dance splendidly."

Elodie huffed, half in disbelief. "There is no need for faradiddles, my lord."

"I am not lying," Anthony replied with a smile. "I am merely stating the truth."

He led her back towards her family, but as they neared the group, Elodie hesitated. She was not quite ready to let go of this moment with him, something she found odd—and a little confusing. Without really thinking, she blurted out, "Would you mind escorting me to the veranda for a moment?"

"Not at all," Anthony said, guiding her towards the French doors that led outside.

Once they stepped into the cool night air, Elodie slipped her hand from his arm and walked over to the iron railing, taking a deep breath. The fresh air was a welcome reprieve from the stuffy ballroom. She gripped the railing, staring out at the moonlit gardens.

"It is a beautiful night," Anthony said, joining her at the railing.

Just as Elodie was about to reply, a faint sound caught her attention. It was distant, muffled, but it was most definitely a woman's voice. "Shh," she whispered, holding up her hand. "Do you hear that?"

Anthony looked at her, bemused. "Hear what?"

Elodie was quite certain that she hadn't imagined it. She stepped away from the veranda, following the sound down a tree-lined path.

"Elodie," Anthony called after her, his voice tinged with concern. "This is not wise."

Ignoring his protests, Elodie rounded a corner and froze. Ahead, a blonde-haired young woman stood with her back against a tree, visibly frightened, while a man loomed over her.

Anthony caught up to her, his expression darkening as he took in the scene. "What is going on here?" he demanded.

The tall, dark-haired man turned around with a scowl. "Nothing that concerns you, Belview."

"I doubt that, Montrose," Anthony responded, stepping forward. "Let the young lady return to the ball."

Montrose advanced towards Anthony, coming to a stop in front of him. "This young woman wants to be here."

Elodie, feeling a surge of anger, spoke up. "I truly doubt that."

"Elodie…" Anthony's voice held a warning, but she was not about to back down. Montrose's eyes flashed with anger as he turned his attention towards her. "If you wait your turn, perhaps I will get to you next."

Without thinking through the repercussions of her actions, Elodie swung her arm back and punched Montrose squarely in the nose. He staggered, clutching his face, his expression turning thunderous.

"You little chit!" Montrose growled. "You may have gotten one good shot in, but now it is my turn to teach you a lesson."

In an instant, Anthony stepped in front of Elodie, his fist

connecting with Montrose's jaw in a swift, powerful strike. Montrose crumbled to the ground, unconscious.

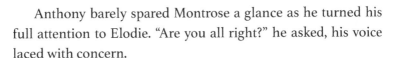

Anthony barely spared Montrose a glance as he turned his full attention to Elodie. "Are you all right?" he asked, his voice laced with concern.

Elodie nodded. "I am. But what about you?"

"I am perfectly well," Anthony assured her, his eyes scanning her face for any sign of distress. Then he turned to the young woman Montrose had cornered. "Did Lord Montrose hurt you?"

The young woman shook her head, her voice trembling. "No, but he would have if you had not arrived when you did."

Anthony was relieved they had intervened in time. He had seen too many situations like this end tragically, and the thought of Elodie or anyone else being harmed stirred a protectiveness inside of him.

Elodie's gaze shifted downward, focusing on Montrose's unconscious form. "He's not dead, is he?" she asked, her voice quiet.

"No," Anthony replied. "He is just unconscious. He will no doubt wake up with a nasty headache, but I do not want either of you near him when that happens. You should return to the ball and not speak of what transpired here."

Elodie hesitated for a moment before she conceded. "Very well," she said, turning to the young woman. "Shall we go back together?"

The young woman swiped at her tear-streaked cheeks. "I must look a fright."

"You look perfectly fine," Elodie said, giving her a reassuring smile.

With a grateful look, the young woman allowed Elodie to guide her away, leaving Anthony to deal with the still-unconscious Lord Montrose. He crouched beside Montrose and gave him a firm shake on the shoulder. "Wake up, Montrose."

A low groan escaped Montrose's lips as he stirred, his eyes fluttering open in confusion. Slowly, he sat up, rubbing his reddened jaw. "Why in the blazes did you hit me, Belview?" he muttered, still groggy.

"Because you were going to strike Lady Elodie," Anthony replied without a trace of regret.

Montrose grimaced. "It was only fair, considering she hit me first."

Anthony's expression hardened. "Gentlemen do not hit women. Nor do they treat them with disrespect."

Montrose's eyes flashed with anger as he growled, "I do not need a lecture from you."

"Sadly, I think you do," Anthony responded as he stood and extended a hand to help Montrose to his feet.

Reluctantly, Montrose accepted his help, brushing off his trousers before glaring at Anthony. "You had no right to involve yourself in my business."

"If your business is hurting young women, then I am more than glad I intervened," Anthony said, taking a step back. "Now, if you will excuse me, I am at a ball and I intend to enjoy myself."

Montrose's expression darkened as he stepped closer, his breath reeking of alcohol. "You think you are better than me, don't you?"

Anthony's jaw tightened, but he kept his voice calm. "I never said that. But, yes, I think I do. I have never had to force my intentions on a young woman before."

Montrose's eyes narrowed to dangerous slits. "You will pay for this, Belview. Mark my words."

Anthony had no interest in prolonging this conversation

with a man too drunk to be reasoned with. "Goodnight, Montrose," he said curtly before turning on his heel and walking away.

As he headed back towards the townhouse, Anthony could feel Montrose's heated gaze burning into his back, but he had no regrets about what had transpired. If Montrose ever dared to repeat his actions, Anthony would gladly hit him again.

Just as Anthony reached the veranda, Bennett and Winston appeared, exiting the townhouse with grim expressions on their faces. Bennett's voice was the first to break the silence.

"Where is Montrose?" he demanded, his hands clenched into tight fists.

Anthony resisted the urge to groan. So much for not speaking about what had just transpired in the gardens. He raised a hand to calm his friend. "It is handled. There is no need for concern."

Bennett's nostrils flared as he stepped forward, the anger rolling off him in waves. "I heard, but I want my shot at him."

"*We* want our shots," Winston corrected, his voice equally as tense.

Anthony took a step closer to them, lowering his voice to a near whisper. "We do not want to cause a scene and draw unnecessary attention to Elodie. Her reputation could be at stake."

The mention of Elodie's reputation seemed to dissipate some of the brothers' tempers, though only slightly.

Winston bobbed his head. "As much as I hate to admit it, Anthony is right. We cannot afford to do anything that might risk Elodie's reputation."

Bennett still looked reluctant, his jaw clenched tight. After a long pause, he finally gave a curt nod. "You are right. But we should leave before Montrose slinks back into the ballroom."

"That would be wise," Anthony responded.

Anthony followed Bennett and Winston back into the ballroom and his eyes immediately sought out Elodie, who was standing beside her mother. Despite the crowded room and loud music, the moment he saw her, everything else seemed to fade into the background.

Elodie noticed him as well and approached, her gaze steady. "How is Lord Montrose?"

"He is alive," Anthony replied. "But you should never have hit him. His words were just words. I would never have let anything happen to you."

She pressed her lips together, her expression unrepentant. "I can protect myself."

"I know," Anthony conceded. "That was quite evident by the way you landed a solid hit on Montrose."

Elodie rubbed her right hand. "I hadn't realized how much it hurt to punch someone. It felt like I hit a brick wall."

Bennett's voice interrupted their conversation. "We should continue this conversation at home."

"We cannot leave now," Elodie argued. "If we did, it would be a grave insult to Lady Montrose, and everyone would take notice. It is not her fault that her son is a cad."

Lady Dallington nodded in agreement. "She is right. If the diamond of the Season walks out of the ball early, it will spark all sorts of rumors."

"Besides, I refuse to let Lord Montrose think he has won," Elodie said firmly. "I have done nothing wrong. Why should I slink away like the guilty party?"

At that very moment, Lord Montrose entered the ballroom, his face flushed with anger, and his gaze locked on Elodie. Anthony moved to shield her, but she placed a hand on his arm, stopping him. "He cannot touch me here. Not now," she whispered.

To her credit, Elodie met Montrose's heated stare with a fierce, unwavering look of her own. One that sent a clear message that she was not afraid. Anthony could not help but admire her strength.

Montrose's glare then shifted to Anthony, lingering for a tense moment before he finally turned and disappeared into the crowd.

Lady Dallington clasped her hands together, forcing a smile on her face. "Well, that went better than expected. Now, everyone must put smiles on their faces. We must behave as if we are having the most delightful evening."

Anthony wanted nothing more than to take Elodie far away from here since he didn't know what Montrose had planned. But by doing so, he could jeopardize her reputation. And his. No. He had to pretend that all was well for Elodie's sake.

"We need Elodie to dance another set," Lady Dallington said, looking around the ballroom.

Anthony knew precisely what to do. In a loud voice, he called out, "I daresay that Lady Elodie could use a dance partner for the next set."

His words had the desired effect. Within moments, a throng of eager gentlemen rushed towards Elodie, each vying for the chance to dance with the diamond. Lady Dallington stood next to her daughter, providing the introductions as needed.

Bennett's eyes held approval. "Nicely done, Belview."

But Anthony could barely hide his irritation as he watched the parade of suitors fawn over Elodie as if she were a prize to be won. She was so much more than that.

When Lord Westcott led Elodie to the dance floor, Anthony saw the fear in her eyes, despite her head being held high. She hated dancing, though she was not nearly as bad as she believed herself to be.

Bennett's voice pulled him from his thoughts. "I need your help with Elodie," he said, turning to face Anthony.

Now Bennett had his full attention. "What do you need?"

In a low voice, Bennett replied, "I am worried about Elodie, and I was hoping you would keep a watchful eye on her."

"Why me?"

Bennett gave him a knowing look. "You and Elodie have struck up a rather unusual friendship—or dare I say—truce of some sort. Besides, I am the annoying brother and she tends to not listen to anything I say."

Anthony's eyes followed Elodie as she danced gracefully across the ballroom. "I do believe you are overstating her regard for me. I am fairly certain she merely tolerates my existence."

"That is precisely why it is perfect," Bennett said with a grin. "You are close enough to her without being an annoyance. And you can scare off any unworthy suitors."

"You underestimate your sister. She is more than capable of handling herself."

"Perhaps," Bennett admitted. "But she trusts you, even if she does not realize it. And that is why I am asking you to watch over her. I do not want rakes or fortune hunters anywhere near her."

The truth was that Anthony did not want any gentleman near Elodie. He wanted her for himself, though he would never admit that to Bennett. Or anyone else for that matter. Maybe this request from Bennett, asking him to watch over her, was the perfect excuse to stay close. And in time, perhaps he could convince Elodie that he was the right man for her.

Anthony met Bennett's gaze, his decision made. "I will do it."

"Wonderful," Bennett replied, clapping him on the back. "I knew I could count on you."

As Anthony watched Elodie complete the set with Lord Westcott, he felt an unexpected pang of jealousy. He needed to come up with a plan to slowly, but surely, woo Elodie. They were friendly now, but he knew all too well how quickly that could change. What would it take to make her fall madly, deeply in love with him?

Love.

The word rattled around in his mind, unsettling him. Where did that thought even come from? He could not possibly be in love with Elodie... could he? The more he thought about it, the more he realized that, somehow, he had already fallen halfway in love with her.

Botheration. This would not do at all.

The music died down and Anthony watched as Lord West-cott led Elodie off the dance floor. Once they reached Lady Dallington, Westcott took Elodie's hand, lifted it to his lips, and kissed her gloved hand. Elodie smiled at Westcott in return, and it made Anthony's jaw clench. What was even worse, Westcott seemed to linger, holding her gaze a moment longer than necessary before finally taking his leave.

It was going to be a long night, Anthony realized, as he watched gentlemen line up to speak to Elodie.

7

As Elodie made her way to the dining room for breakfast, she descended the stairs and came to a halt in the entry hall. It was filled with an abundance of bouquets, in every size and color imaginable. There were flowers everywhere.

White stepped forward and informed her, "Lady Elodie, these bouquets have been arriving all morning."

"They have?" Elodie asked.

White nodded. "Yes, my lady. There are even more flowers in the drawing room. The cards are attached to the bouquets, so you can see who sent them."

Elodie remained rooted in her spot, overwhelmed by the sheer volume of flowers. Where was she supposed to even begin?

Her mother's voice rang out behind her. "Is it not wonderful?" she gushed. "It smells like a flower shop in here."

Turning to face her mother, Elodie declared, "There are too many bouquets."

"The gentlemen are simply vying for your affection, my

dear," her mother said. "Sending flowers is a small gesture to show you they are thinking of you."

"But I only danced four sets last night."

Her mother's smile widened. "You are the diamond of the Season. You must accept the fact that you will have many admirers." She gestured towards the dining room. "Come now, let us join the others for breakfast."

Elodie followed her mother into the dining room, where her brothers and their wives were already seated. As soon as Bennett and Winston saw her, they both stood and began clapping.

"Bravo, Sister," Bennett called out.

Winston grinned. "There is a glowing article about you in the Society pages this morning."

"Oh, wonderful," Elodie muttered, sinking into a chair next to Mattie.

Her brothers returned to their seats, both wearing amused expressions as they continued to observe her.

"What is it?" Elodie asked.

Winston lifted his brow. "Don't you want to know what the article said?"

Elodie reached for her napkin and placed it on her lap. "Not particularly," she replied.

Bennett cleared his throat loudly as he held up the newssheets. "'Lady Elodie was a vision of perfection last night, robbing eligible bachelors of their breath.'" He paused. "Shall I keep reading?"

"Surely, there is something else we can talk about?" Elodie asked.

Delphine placed a hand on Bennett's arm. "Leave your poor sister alone. She does not need your teasing right now."

"But, my love, that is an older brother's sacred duty," Bennett retorted. "That and stealing her buttered bread."

Elodie raised her knife, pointing it at him with a warning look. "I am starving, and no one will steal my bread today."

Their mother glanced up from her plate, clearly unconcerned. "Lower your knife, Dear. Ladies do not threaten people at the breakfast table."

A footman placed a plate of food down in front of her. Elodie reached for the bread and carefully buttered it, ensuring every corner was covered with a meticulous swipe of butter. Just as she was about to take a bite, White stepped into the room.

"Lord Danbury has come to call on Lady Elodie," the butler announced.

"Inform Lord Danbury that he arrived entirely too early, and I am still eating my breakfast," Elodie said.

Before White could leave, Lady Dallington interjected, "Kindly inform Lord Danbury that we will be with him shortly."

Elodie gazed down at her bread and sighed. "I love you, buttered bread," she murmured wistfully.

Her mother shook her head. "Hurry up and finish eating."

"But one should never rush when enjoying bread. Every bite should be savored," Elodie replied.

Bennett held his hand out. "I would be happy to eat your bread."

"I think not," Elodie said, taking an exaggeratedly large bite. "I daresay that this is the most delicious bread I have ever eaten."

Their mother pushed back her chair. "I believe you have made your point. Shall we?"

"But I am not finished."

"You can have as much bread as you like after you meet with your suitors," her mother assured her.

"Who says I will have more than one..." Elodie began but was interrupted as the butler returned.

"Mr. Thomas has come to call on Lady Elodie," White announced.

Her mother gave Elodie a pointed look. "You'd better get used to the attention."

Elodie placed the rest of her bread down onto her plate and wiped her hands together. "Why are these gentlemen calling at an ungodly hour?"

"It is almost noon, Sister," Winston pointed out.

"I stand by my statement," Elodie declared.

Winston chuckled. "What a hardship you face being loved by the *ton*."

Elodie leaned over and placed the rest of her bread onto Mattie's plate. "I hereby gift you the most delicious piece of bread you shall ever eat."

Mattie grinned. "Thank you, but the moment you leave, Winston will steal it off my plate."

"Do with it what you want," Elodie said, rising from the table. "If I die, I want all my possessions to go to Melody, except for my prized nail. I want to be buried with that so I can protect myself from the zombies."

"You aren't going to die," Winston replied with a laugh.

"We shall see, won't we?" Elodie remarked as she exited the dining room, preparing to face her eager suitors.

As Elodie started walking down the hall, her mother turned and said, "Remember to smile and do try to be pleasant."

"Aren't I always pleasant?" Elodie asked, somewhat defensively.

"Not always," her mother responded.

Elodie forced a wide smile to her lips. "Is this smile good enough?"

Her mother raised an eyebrow. "I suppose so, but perhaps you could try a little harder to make it look less like a grimace?"

"I will try," Elodie said, adjusting the sleeve of her pale blue gown. "Though I feel like a stallion being spruced up for auction."

Her mother stopped outside the drawing room and gave her a reassuring pat on the arm. "Just do your best, my dear."

Taking a deep breath, Elodie stepped into the room and saw the tall, lanky Mr. Thomas and the stout Lord Danbury in the center of the room. They both straightened as she entered, beaming wide smiles at her.

"Lady Elodie," they said in unison, bowing deeply.

Elodie dropped into a curtsy, trying to maintain the pleasant smile her mother had insisted upon.

They both eagerly approached her, and Lord Danbury was the first to speak. "You look lovely, my lady," he praised.

"Thank you," Elodie replied politely, though her smile felt more strained than ever.

Not to be outdone, Mr. Thomas quickly interjected, "I do hope I haven't called too early, my lady."

Elodie bit back her true thoughts and replied with a practiced grace. "Not at all, sir. I find that eating breakfast is vastly overrated."

Mr. Thomas let out a bark of laughter. "You are quite witty."

Lord Danbury nodded eagerly. "Indeed. After our dance last night, I told my mother the very same thing. It is rare to find a woman so beautiful and so quick-witted."

Elodie resisted the urge to roll her eyes at his blatant flattery. "Would either of you care for a cup of tea?" she offered, diverting the conversation.

"I would love one," Mr. Thomas said.

"As would I," Lord Danbury added, his gaze lingering on her.

Elodie seated herself on the settee and began pouring tea, methodically filling four cups. As she handed a cup to Lord Danbury, his gloved fingers lightly brushed against hers, and he waggled his eyebrows suggestively. Elodie ignored the touch and kept her attention on the teapot, wondering how she could survive this without encouraging either gentleman's interest.

Lord Danbury sat down next to her and asked, "May I ask what occupies your time, my lady?"

"The usual pursuits, I suppose," Elodie said with a slight shrug. "I play the pianoforte and dabble in the dark arts."

Lord Danbury nearly choked on his drink. "I beg your pardon?"

Lady Dallington rushed to smooth over the moment. "Lady Elodie was just teasing, my lord," she said with a warning glance at Elodie. "Weren't you, my dear?"

Elodie brought a smile to her face. "Of course, I was. I hope my attempt at humor did not offend you."

Lowering his cup to his lap, Lord Danbury remarked, "Not at all. I find you to be most extraordinary." His last words sounded rehearsed.

Mr. Thomas met her gaze. "Do you enjoy riding?"

Elodie knew precisely where this was headed but decided to be as truthful as possible. "I do, but I prefer to ride alone."

"And why is that?" Mr. Thomas asked, leaning forward in curiosity.

"Unfortunately, my horse does not get along with others and tries to bite them," Elodie informed him.

"I would be more than happy to lend you one of my horses for a ride, should you ever wish to go," Mr. Thomas said.

Elodie waved her hand in front of her. "I could never cheat on my horse."

"Cheat?" Mr. Thomas blinked in confusion. "How could one cheat on a horse?"

Keeping her expression serious, Elodie replied, "Oh, my horse would know. And she would never forgive me."

Mr. Thomas, now completely befuddled, tried to reason

with Elodie. "I do not think horses are capable of such emotions."

"What do you think horses care about, then?" Elodie asked, her tone innocent.

Mr. Thomas opened and closed his mouth, clearly stumped. "I have never given it much thought."

Her mother placed a hand on Elodie's shoulder. "Perhaps we can speak of something else?"

With a mischievous smile, Elodie said, "Very well. What are your thoughts on unicorns? Real or imaginary?"

Lord Danbury huffed. "They are imaginary, of course."

"Yes, that is precisely what I was going to say," Elodie said.

As she took another sip of tea, Elodie could not help but feel a small sense of satisfaction. If she was going to endure these suitors, she might as well have some fun.

Anthony sat in his study, staring at the ledgers before him, though his focus was far from the numbers. His thoughts were consumed with the impending arrival of his parents. He wished they had remained at their country estate, given his father's fragile health, but he understood their reasoning. They wanted to meet their grandchild, which was something Stephen had yet to find time for.

The door creaked open, and Percy entered, holding two squirming puppies in his arms. One was a Dalmatian puppy with its characteristic black spots, and the other was a light-silver Skye Terrier with funny-looking ears.

Percy held them up for inspection. "I have scoured London for puppies that meet Lady Elodie's stringent qualifications. Do you think either of these would suit Miss Emma?"

Anthony rose from his chair, walking around the desk to study the puppies. "They seem... fine."

"Fine, my lord?" Percy asked. "I thought Lady Elodie's instructions were quite clear—no ugly dogs."

Anthony chuckled and took the puppies from Percy. "Indeed, they were. Now, which one do you think is the cutest?"

Before Percy could respond, a footman appeared at the door. "My lord, you asked to be informed the moment Lady Elodie entered her gardens. She has just stepped outside."

"Thank you," Anthony responded. "I think I will let Lady Elodie make the decision. I trust her judgment when it comes to deciding if a puppy is ugly or not."

Cradling the puppies in his arms, he quickly made his way out of the back door and crossed the small gate that separated his gardens from Elodie's. He spotted her sitting on a bench, lost in thought.

Not wanting to startle her, Anthony called out softly, "Elodie."

She looked up, and her face instantly lit up when she saw the puppies in his arms. "Oh, how adorable!" she exclaimed, jumping to her feet.

The puppies wagged their tails enthusiastically as Elodie approached, her smile widening.

Anthony grinned. "It seems they are as eager to meet you as you are to meet them."

Elodie scooped up the Skye Terrier, laughing as it tried to lick her face. "I love dogs," she declared.

"I do hope these puppies are sufficient. I was very specific that I did not want an ugly dog," Anthony informed her.

"You did well," Elodie praised. "They are both precious."

"But if you had to choose one?" Anthony asked, though he already suspected the answer.

Elodie studied the puppies for a moment before smiling at

the light-silver-haired one in her arms. "This one. His unusual ears give him character."

Watching her bond with the puppy, Anthony felt a sudden reluctance to separate them. "You know what? I think I will keep both."

Elodie blinked in surprise. "Whatever for?"

"I am partial to the Dalmatian, and you are clearly taken with the Skye Terrier. I think it would be best for the puppies to have one another to play with," Anthony explained. "Unless, of course, your father will allow you to keep the puppy?"

"Oh, no. He is not particularly fond of animals. Though he does allow Bennett to stay in the townhouse, so perhaps there is hope," Elodie quipped.

Anthony smirked. "That was awful. I am going to tell your brother that you said that."

"Good! Perhaps it will bring him down a peg or two," Elodie said with a smile.

Holding up the spotted puppy, Anthony asked, "What names should we give them?"

She raised her eyebrows. "I thought you did not want my help in naming animals."

"I have had a change of heart."

Elodie's smile grew. "If that is the case, I think Miss Emma should name the Dalmatian since it will be her puppy."

"I think that is wise, and the Skye Terrier?"

Glancing down at the wriggling puppy in her arms, Elodie replied, "Luise, but I will call him Lulu for short."

"Lulu?" Anthony repeated. "That is an unusual name for a dog."

"It is perfect since Lulu is such an adorable puppy."

Anthony shook his head. "You are truly awful at naming animals."

Elodie laughed. "It is not easy coming up with a name on

the spot. If you had given me more time, I might have thought of something more clever."

"Like what... Bubu?" Anthony teased.

Elodie playfully narrowed her eyes. "I would be angry at you right now if I didn't have Lulu in my arms."

"Then I am grateful for the distraction."

Lulu wiggled in her arms and Elodie crouched down to set him on the ground. "How I wish I could take Lulu home with me."

"I do hope you will consider Lulu to be your puppy. The good news is that you will just have to spend more time with me," Anthony said, knowing there was truth behind those words.

"What a burden that will be," Elodie retorted.

Anthony knelt down to place the Dalmatian puppy beside Lulu. He hesitated for a moment before admitting, "My parents should be arriving soon."

The humor left Elodie's face, replaced by concern. "I hope the journey isn't too hard on your father."

"I hope so, as well. For his sake."

Elodie rose and placed a comforting hand on his sleeve. "It will be all right," she said.

"How can you be so sure?" he asked, a hint of frustration creeping into his voice. "And to make matters worse, Stephen still has not met his own daughter."

"Are you truly surprised by that?"

He let out a long sigh. "Yes... no. I don't know what to think anymore."

Elodie took a step closer to him. "Miss Emma is lucky to have you."

"I do not think so. I visit her often in the nursery, but she looks at me with such fear, like she does not trust me," Anthony reluctantly admitted.

"That is understandable," Elodie said softly. "She just lost her mother. Trust takes time."

Anthony ran a hand through his hair. "I do not know what I am doing."

Elodie met his gaze with a small, understanding smile. "Does anyone, really? You are doing the best that you can, and that is what matters."

"What if my 'best' is not good enough?" Anthony asked, his voice heavy with doubt.

Elodie's expression softened. "I have the same fear. It is always lurking in my mind, paralyzing me with doubt. But we cannot let it stop us. A little fear can be a good thing. It pushes us to be better."

Anthony felt a need to lighten the mood. "When did you get so wise?"

Elodie gave him an amused look. "I was told just this morning that I am rather clever. Lord Danbury was attempting to flatter me, though I think he was trying too hard to win my favor."

"Did he succeed in catching your interest?"

Elodie shook her head vehemently. "Good heavens, no. Lord Danbury and Mr. Thomas were just the first of many gentlemen trying to charm me with empty flattery."

"How do you know their praise was empty?"

She gave him a knowing look. "Because I am much more than a pretty face."

"Yes, you are," Anthony agreed.

For a moment, they simply stared at each other, and something unspoken passed between them. Anthony felt as if Elodie could see right into the center of him, and for the first time, he realized how badly he wanted her to see him that way.

A voice broke through the moment between them. "My lord, I do apologize for the interruption, but your parents have arrived."

Anthony turned to see a footman standing just beyond the gardens' fence. "Thank you." His gaze flickered down to the puppies nestled near Elodie. "Are you finished with them yet?"

She offered him a sheepish look. "May I have a bit more time with them?"

"You can have as much time as you like," Anthony replied. Then turning to the footman, he added, "Stay with Lady Elodie and bring the puppies in when she is ready."

The footman tipped his head. "Yes, my lord."

Anthony began to walk away, but Elodie gently placed her hand on his sleeve, halting him. "Thank you, Anthony," she said, her voice brimming with genuine gratitude.

"You are most welcome," he said.

Elodie let her hand slip away and took a small step back. "Please give my regards to your parents."

"I will," Anthony promised before turning back towards the townhouse.

As he stepped into the entry hall, Anthony's heart clenched when he saw his mother speaking softly with Percy. She looked noticeably older than the last time he had seen her. Her once dark hair was now streaked with more silver, the lines on her face deeper, undoubtedly from the toll of caring for his ailing father. It broke his heart to see her this way.

"Mother," he greeted.

His mother turned towards him, her face lighting up with a familiar, tender smile. "My boy," she said as she went to embrace him. "How are you?"

"I am well, but I am far more worried about you and Father," Anthony said, dropping his arms.

A shadow passed over her face. "The journey took quite a toll on your father," she admitted. "He is resting now."

"Why aren't you, as well?"

"I am eager to meet my granddaughter," his mother replied.

Percy stepped forward. "I regret to inform you, my lady, that

Miss Emma is napping at the moment. I will let you know the moment she wakes."

A flicker of disappointment crossed his mother's face, but she nodded in understanding. "Then perhaps I should rest for a short while, after all."

"Allow me to escort you to your bedchamber," Anthony said, offering his arm.

As they walked up the stairs, his mother asked, "Has Stephen met Emma yet?"

Anthony's jaw tightened. "No. He is far too preoccupied with other distractions."

"Well, I might be able to persuade him to do the right thing," his mother said.

"I doubt that."

She patted his sleeve lightly. "I can be very persuasive."

At the top of the stairs, Anthony came to a stop and turned to face her. "You shouldn't have come, Mother. It is too much for both of you."

"I had to," his mother asserted. "And your father, he was quite adamant as well. He wants to see at least one of his grandchildren before—" She stopped herself, her voice wavering.

"Before he dies," Anthony finished for her, his voice tight with emotion. He fought to keep his composure, but deep down, he knew she was right.

His mother reached up, gently cupping his cheek with her hand. Her touch was warm, though her eyes were clouded with sorrow. "Your father is dying. There is no use pretending otherwise. We must cherish the time we have left with him."

Anthony blinked back the tears that threatened to spill. "I refuse to accept that," he said, his voice trembling with barely contained grief.

His mother lowered her hand, her own eyes brimming with unshed tears. "It does not matter what we accept. It is the reality we face."

She gave him one final, sad smile before turning and walking down the corridor to her bedchamber. Anthony stood there, his heart heavy. As she disappeared from view, a single tear slipped down his cheek. He did not even bother to wipe it away.

The thought of losing his father filled him with an unbearable ache. How was he supposed to face a world without him? It was a day he dreaded, a day that now seemed all too close.

8

Elodie felt a strange stirring deep within her as she watched Anthony walk away. But what it meant, she could not say. It was as if her heart were softening towards Anthony. Which was ridiculous. She harbored no feelings for that infuriating man. It must have been sympathy for his current plight, nothing more. That had to be it.

Crouching down, she petted the puppies, who eagerly licked her hand with wild enthusiasm. Anthony had been thoughtful to keep Lulu for her. She had always wanted a pet, and now, in a way, she had one.

The back door to her townhouse opened and Mattie stepped out, her eyes widening at the sight of the puppies.

"Where did you get those puppies?" Mattie asked, rushing forward to kneel beside them.

Elodie moved to sit on the bench. "Anthony brought them over," she revealed. "They are for his niece, Miss Emma."

"Both of them?"

"Well, he is keeping the silver-haired puppy for me."

Mattie looked up, surprised. "For you?"

"Yes. My father would never allow a puppy inside our townhouse so Anthony will keep Lulu for me," Elodie added.

"Interesting," Mattie murmured.

Elodie picked up Lulu and placed him on her lap. "It is not interesting. I have always wanted a dog, and Anthony was kind enough to get one for me."

Mattie sat beside her on the bench. "Do you not think it is a little odd that Lord Belview will be raising your dog?"

"Well, it is not like I could keep Lulu here," Elodie pointed out, brushing a strand of hair from her face.

"True," Mattie agreed, "but it does mean you will be seeing more of Lord Belview. Is that what you want?"

Elodie shrugged. "It is not an ideal situation, but I am not opposed."

Mattie laughed as she scratched behind Lulu's ear. "He is rather cute."

"I am thinking of making outfits for him," Elodie said. "A little hat would look adorable on his head, don't you think?"

"That would require you to work on your embroidery skills."

Elodie placed the squirming puppy onto the ground. "That is true, but it is a sacrifice I am willing to make for Lulu."

Mattie shifted on the bench towards her, her expression becoming more serious. "I hate to change the subject, but there is something you should know."

"Which is?"

"Your mother wants to speak with you," Mattie shared. "I overheard her telling Winston how displeased she was by your antics earlier."

Elodie groaned. "I suppose I went too far with that comment about dabbling in the dark arts."

"The dark arts?" Mattie asked, amused.

"It sounded ominous."

Mattie shook her head. "Careful, you do not want to be branded as a witch."

"Witches aren't real, but if they were," Elodie declared confidently, "I would most definitely be best friends with one. I would help her cast spells."

"I doubt your family would let you be friends with a witch."

"They would never know. I would cast an invisibility spell on myself," Elodie quipped. "I could come and go as I please, and they would be none the wiser."

Mattie laughed. "That is genius."

Rising, Elodie dusted off her gown. "I suppose I should get this conversation with my mother over with."

"That is the spirit," Mattie teased as she stood as well.

Linking arms with Mattie as they walked back towards the townhouse, Elodie sighed. "I have missed you."

"I am right here," Mattie replied.

"You say that, but you are always so busy with Winston."

Mattie grinned. "I am his wife, after all."

"And for that, I am grateful," Elodie said. "Winston is happier than I have ever seen him."

A footman opened the back door for them, allowing them to step into the corridor. Mattie lowered her voice as they walked. "Are you happy?"

"Of course I am," Elodie responded quickly.

Mattie studied her closely. "I know that being hailed as the diamond of the Season is an utter nightmare for you."

"It is true, but I have made peace with it."

Mattie didn't seem convinced, but thankfully, she let it go. "All right. You can lie to me and yourself, but when you are ready to talk, I will be here."

Elodie patted Mattie's hand, grateful for her friendship. "Thank you, but I will be fine. I have mastered the art of fake smiles for when I must entertain callers."

"Show me."

Mustering her best smile, Elodie lifted her chin. "Do you see? Perfect, no?"

Mattie frowned. "It looks like you are in pain."

"No, this is a smile," Elodie insisted, pointing at her lips.

"I am sorry, but it is hardly convincing."

Elodie dropped her smile. "You don't need to worry about me. I would prefer if you just focused on how happy you and Winston are."

"That is not how friendship works," Mattie said.

Before Elodie could respond, her mother appeared at the other end of the corridor, her brow creased in displeasure. "Elodie, we need to talk."

"We are talking," Elodie attempted.

"Alone," her mother said.

Mattie took a step back, giving Elodie a sympathetic look. "I believe that is my cue to leave," she said, excusing herself.

As Mattie walked away, Lady Dallington crossed her arms over her chest. "The dark arts? Truly, Child?"

Elodie offered a small shrug. "I was trying to be amusing."

"Perhaps we can work on humor that isn't so controversial," her mother responded. "You know what your father would say about this."

Elodie straightened and mimicked her father's stern voice. "'Young women are not to have any true opinions.'"

Her mother uncrossed her arms. "Your father doesn't truly believe his own words. He is just trying to goad you into an argument, and most of the time, it works."

"I promise I will not bring up the dark arts again," Elodie said.

"Thank you."

Elodie went to pass by her mother, but her mother stepped directly in front of her, blocking her path. "Lord Westcott is in the drawing room waiting for you," she informed her. "I expect you to be on your best behavior, and please, for heaven's sake, do not frighten him off."

"If a gentleman is so easily frightened by a single conversation with me, is he truly the right person for me?"

Some of the tension drained out of her mother's shoulders. "Let's play a game this time, shall we? When Lord Westcott asks you a question, you will say the second thing that comes to mind, not the first."

Elodie couldn't help but grin. Her mother was genuinely trying to help her. "All right. I will agree to that."

"Good," her mother said. "Now, let us go greet Lord Westcott."

Elodie followed her mother into the drawing room, where the tall, broad-shouldered figure of Lord Westcott stood by the hearth. He was not unattractive—his dark hair framed his face nicely—but he was not as handsome as Anthony. The thought of Anthony popped into her mind suddenly, surprising her. She quickly shook it off.

As soon as Lord Westcott saw her, he stepped forward and bowed. "Lady Elodie, thank you for seeing me."

She curtsied in return. "It is my pleasure, my lord."

A warm smile spread across his face, though it was slightly awkward, as if he were not used to smiling so much. "You look beautiful," he said. "Truly a vision of perfection."

Elodie could hear the sincerity in his voice and knew that he was not attempting false flattery. "You are most kind." She gestured towards the settees. "Would you care to sit?"

"I would, thank you," Lord Westcott replied, settling into a chair opposite Elodie and her mother, his awkward but endearing smile still lingering on his face.

Elodie decided to stick to polite conversation topics to appease her mother. "It is a lovely day, is it not?"

"Yes, I even caught a glimpse of the sun peeking through the clouds for a brief moment."

"What a remarkable feat for the sun, don't you think?" Elodie joked.

Lord Westcott grinned. "Quite an accomplishment, yes."

Elodie caught her mother's glance towards the tea tray and took the hint. She reached for the teapot and asked, "Would you care for a cup of tea?"

He patted his stomach. "None for me, I'm afraid," he replied. "I have had far too much tea today."

Leaning back, Elodie teased, "You don't sound very British, declining tea like that."

Lord Westcott's eyes held a glint of amusement. "Perhaps not, but I do believe my ancient British title proves otherwise."

"You make a fine point, my lord," Elodie responded, feeling herself relax in his presence. There was something disarmingly genuine about him.

He leaned forward, his tone turning playful. "I have heard that you dabble in the dark arts," Lord Westcott remarked with a smirk on his lips.

"I see that you have spoken to Lord Danbury or Mr. Thomas."

"They were rather vocal about their meeting with you today at the club," Lord Westcott said. "But do not worry, most of the gentlemen did not pay them much heed."

"That is good because, in truth, I do not even know what the dark arts are."

Lord Westcott settled back in his seat. "I suspected as much because I think the first rule of practicing the dark arts is that you don't talk about the dark arts."

Elodie did one thing that she never thought she would do with any gentleman. She picked up the plate of biscuits. "Would you care to have a biscuit?"

"You have discovered the quickest way to my heart, my lady," Lord Westcott replied as he selected a biscuit.

Placing the plate down, Elodie asked, "Did you attend university?"

"I did," he replied proudly. "I went to Cambridge and studied psychology, though it has not been of much use running my estate."

"Not at all?"

Lord Westcott's lips twitched. "No, not once, actually. I should have studied something far more practical."

Elodie gave him a knowing look. "At least you had the good fortune to attend university."

"I was very fortunate indeed." Lord Westcott paused and shifted in his seat. "I hope I am not being too presumptuous, but would you care to join me for a carriage ride through Hyde Park tomorrow?"

The most extraordinary thing happened. Elodie found that she was not entirely repulsed by the idea of spending more time with Lord Westcott. "I would greatly enjoy that," she said.

A wide smile came to Lord Westcott's lips. "I am glad to hear that. Now that I have asked, I can finally relax."

"Are there any other pressing questions I can answer for you?" Elodie joked.

Lord Westcott's grin broadened. "Just that one. It was a very important question, after all."

Elodie had to admit there were worse ways to spend one's afternoon than with a man who seemed to genuinely enjoy her company.

———————⌒———————

Anthony stood outside of his father's bedchamber door feeling a knot of apprehension tightening in his chest. He did not know what to expect when he stepped inside. Taking a deep breath, he knocked softly.

The door opened promptly, and Randall, his father's ever-faithful valet, greeted him with a quiet, "My lord, do come in."

Anthony stepped into the room and saw his father was propped up in bed, his back supported by a mound of pillows. Despite his silver hair being slightly tousled, his father's color looked better than Anthony had anticipated.

"My son!" His father's voice was cheerful, and he opened his arms wide in welcome. "Come closer so that I may see you properly."

Randall swiftly positioned a chair beside the bed and took a step back.

Anthony sat down and managed a smile. "You are looking well, Father."

His father chuckled, though the sound was a bit wheezy. "Oh, pish-posh. I look old, and I know it. But I am grateful I survived that wretched carriage ride."

Anthony leaned forward, his brow furrowing. "Why did you even come? You should have stayed at the estate to rest."

His father's eyes crinkled around the edges. "Because, if your letter is to be believed, I have a granddaughter. That is not something a man can ignore."

Anthony sighed deeply. "But you should have considered your health—"

"You are starting to sound like your mother," his father interrupted with a wave of his hand. "I want to meet my grand-daughter before I die."

"You are not going to die anytime soon."

"Let's hope not."

Anthony settled back in his chair. "What are you going to do about Stephen? He still hasn't met Emma."

A frown creased his father's brow, and he glanced up at the ceiling as if searching for answers. "I don't know what can be done. We can't force him to do the right thing."

"We could cut off his allowance," Anthony suggested.

"What would that accomplish?" his father asked. "He would meet Emma once, then cast her aside just as easily. It is not a solution."

Frustration flared in Anthony's chest. "But Stephen is spending recklessly. If we do not curtail his habits, he could ruin us in time."

"The estate can handle his spending."

"For now," Anthony pressed. "But you must consider the future. I know you have a soft spot for Stephen, but you cannot neglect what is best for the estate or for me."

His father considered Anthony's words for a long moment before finally nodding. "You have done an admirable job managing things in my absence. I trust you will do what is best for both you and Stephen."

"Thank you, Father."

The door opened and his mother stepped into the room, her sharp gaze settling on Anthony. "I thought I might find you here." Her expression softened as she turned to her husband. "How are you feeling after your rest?"

"I am going to live another day," his father quipped with a wink.

His mother smiled, the love between them evident in the quiet look they exchanged. "That is good, considering I am rather fond of you."

Anthony spoke up. "I must assume that Mother is eager to meet Emma."

"Is it so obvious?" his mother asked with a small laugh.

His father swung his legs over the side of the bed, tossing off the covers. "I will come with you," he announced as Randall rushed to his side, assisting him to his feet.

"Are you sure that is wise?" Anthony asked.

"Perhaps not, but I did not travel all this way to delay meeting my granddaughter," his father asserted.

Anthony went to offer his father his arm. "At least allow me to assist you to the nursery."

His father accepted his arm, leaning heavily into him. "Thank you, my boy."

As they moved down the corridor at a slow pace, Anthony shared, "I acquired a puppy for Emma. A Dalmatian, to be exact."

His mother's eyes lit up. "What a splendid idea. A puppy will be wonderful for her."

They paused so his father could catch his breath as Anthony said, "I am hoping the puppy will help Emma feel more comfortable around me. She is still very shy."

The sound of barking echoed down the hall, and his mother raised a bemused eyebrow. "Am I mistaken, or do I hear two dogs?"

"I may have acquired two puppies," Anthony admitted. "One is for Emma and the other one is for Lady Elodie. Her father won't allow her to keep it, so it is staying with me."

His mother's expression shifted to one of mild curiosity. "Do you have an understanding with Elodie?"

"No," Anthony said with a shake of his head. "We are friends. Or at least I hope we are. I never quite know where I stand with Elodie."

"Yet you bought her a dog," his mother pointed out.

"It was merely a friendly gesture," Anthony said.

"Most gentlemen buy flowers, not puppies," his mother teased.

His father let out a raspy chuckle. "Leave the poor boy alone. If he wants to buy a young woman a dog, it is his right to do so."

With a knowing smile, his mother said, "I simply adore Elodie. You could do far worse than her."

"Mother..." Anthony started, already suspecting the path this conversation would take.

She laughed. "That is all I will say on the matter... unless, of course, you ask for more."

They continued down the corridor towards the nursery, the faint sound of giggles drifting through the air. When they reached the door, Anthony stepped ahead, gently opening it and standing aside as his parents passed by.

Inside, Emma sat on the floor, surrounded by the two playful puppies. Her smile was bright, a clear sign of the happiness the dogs had brought her. The nursemaid, who had been keeping watch from a chair in the corner, gave a polite bow and retreated slightly, allowing the family their moment.

Anthony crouched next to Emma. "Hello, Emma," he greeted. "Have you named your puppy yet?"

Emma's smile faltered for just a moment as she looked at Anthony, but it did not fade completely. "His name is Spot."

"Spot, hmm?" Anthony repeated, pretending to consider the name as he picked up the wriggling pup. "He certainly does have a lot of spots for a dog. I do believe Spot is a perfect name for him."

His mother lowered herself gracefully to sit on the floor with Emma, her voice warm and gentle. "Hello, my dear. I am your grandmother."

Emma studied her with cautious eyes before asking, "Did you know my mother?"

"No," his mother replied. "I did not have the privilege of meeting her, but I am sure I would have liked her very much."

"My mother was really sick, and then she died," Emma shared.

His mother's face softened with compassion. "I know, and I am so very sorry about that."

Just then, the puppies began to tumble over one another, playfully nipping at Emma's hands, drawing a bright giggle from her. "These dogs are silly."

Anthony realized that this was the most Emma had spoken

since arriving, and he had no doubt the puppies were helping her to open up.

Pointing at the silver-haired puppy, Emma said, "That one is named Lulu. He is Spot's brother, but they don't look anything alike."

"You are right," Anthony responded. "We are watching Lulu for Lady Elodie. Do you remember her?"

"I do. She was nice," Emma replied.

"Aren't people always nice to you?" Anthony asked.

Emma shook her head, her gaze dropping. "Mr. Haupt was mean to me. He would yell at my mother."

Anthony's brow furrowed. "Who is Mr. Haupt?"

"He ran the factory where my mother worked," Emma explained. "I had to be really quiet there. No talking."

Anthony's heart ached at the thought of what Emma must have endured. He placed a reassuring hand on her shoulder. "Well, you do not need to be quiet here. We want you to talk as much as possible. How else will we know what you need?"

His father, who had been leaning heavily against the wall, watched the scene with a strained expression. Anthony quickly fetched a chair and helped his father settle into it.

Once seated, his father smiled at Emma. "You are a beautiful girl, Emma. We are so lucky to have you here with us now."

Emma tilted her head. "Who are you?"

"I am your grandfather," he replied.

Satisfied with the answer, Emma turned her attention back to the puppies. As a maid entered with a tray of food, the nurse-maid quietly stood and gestured towards a table in the corner where the meal could be set.

His mother rose from the floor, brushing off her skirts. "We should let Emma enjoy her food."

Anthony offered his arm to his father, helping him stand.

"Perhaps tomorrow we can all take a turn in the gardens," he suggested.

"I would like that very much," his mother said.

The nursemaid met Emma's gaze and gave her an encouraging look. Emma stood and curtsied deeply, her eyes darting back to the nursemaid for approval.

His mother's eyes welled with tears. "What a charming curtsy, Emma. I hope you know you are most welcome here."

Emma stared up at her, puzzled. "Why are you crying?"

"These are tears of joy," she assured her, her voice thick with emotion.

"My mother only cried when she was sad," Emma murmured.

Anthony felt a lump in his throat as he watched the exchange, realizing just how much this little girl had endured, and how desperately she needed to be loved.

After they had departed from the nursery, his mother swiped at the tears that were streaming down her face. "Emma looks just like Stephen did as a child. It is almost uncanny."

His father's voice grew uncharacteristically firm. "We need to ensure that Stephen does right by her."

"I wholeheartedly agree," Anthony said.

9

E lodie was jolted awake by the incessant sound of dogs barking. Groaning, she grabbed a pillow and pressed it over her ears, hoping to muffle the noise. But it was useless. The barking was relentless. Who in the world was letting their dogs create such a racket at this obscene hour?

With a frustrated huff, she threw the pillow aside, slipped out of bed, and made her way to the window. She leaned out and immediately spotted Anthony seated comfortably on a bench in his gardens while two puppies yapped energetically around him.

Raising her voice to be heard over the barking, Elodie called, "Anthony! Can you please quiet those dogs down? I am trying to sleep."

Anthony glanced down at his pocket watch with a smile. "It is nearly ten o'clock," he replied. "I am not entirely sure what you expect me to do. I have been up for many hours working on the accounts."

"Well, unlike you, I prefer to sleep in."

Anthony chuckled, clearly enjoying her frustration. "I am afraid there is no silencing these two," he said, gesturing to the puppies at his feet, who were now yapping and chasing each other in circles. "They are a bit too enthusiastic about starting the day."

"Will you not at least try?"

With an amused glint in his eyes, Anthony turned to the puppies. He pointed a stern finger at them and commanded, "No more barking! I forbid it."

For a moment, it seemed to work. The puppies paused, their eyes wide and ears perked up, as if they understood him. But then, just as quickly, they erupted into a flurry of excited yips, their tails wagging even faster than before.

"You are making it worse!" she exclaimed, unable to suppress a small laugh despite herself.

Just then, another voice chimed in. "Do you two mind? Delphine and I are trying to get some sleep," Bennett called out from a nearby window.

Anthony's grin widened. "It is nearly ten. A perfectly reasonable hour to be awake."

Elodie leaned out further to get a better look at her brother. "Did the dogs' barking wake you up?"

"Yes, and now your conversation with Belview is not helping, either," Bennett said.

Anthony stood from the bench, still smiling. "Perhaps I will take the dogs for a walk to the park. Would you care to join me?"

"I most certainly would not," Bennett responded.

Anthony's gaze remained on Elodie. "I was not asking *you*, Bennett. I was asking Elodie."

Elodie hesitated, tucking a piece of errant hair behind her ear. "I am hardly dressed for a walk, nor have I had breakfast."

"It won't take long, I promise, and I could use the company," Anthony said.

From his window, Bennett groaned, "For heaven's sake,

Elodie, just go with him so the rest of us can get some peace and quiet."

"Fine, I will go," Elodie agreed. "But you will have to wait. I cannot rush the process of beautification."

Anthony bowed. "Take your time. I will wait for you in front."

Elodie closed the window before she made her way to the dressing table, grabbing a brush to tame her bed-tousled hair. As she worked, the door opened, and Molly bustled in with a knowing smile.

"It sounds like we are in a hurry this morning," Molly said, pulling a pale blue gown from the wardrobe.

"How did you know?" Elodie asked, pausing mid-brush.

Molly's eyes twinkled with amusement. "You are not exactly a quiet talker. The whole townhouse heard you."

"It was hardly my fault! Those dogs woke me up."

"That is what puppies do," Molly said, helping Elodie into the gown. "I have no doubt that Lord Belview will train them in no time."

"I hope so."

Once she was dressed, her hair neatly pinned back into a loose chignon, she rushed downstairs. White was waiting in the entry hall.

"Will you inform my mother that I am going on a walk to the park with Lord Belview?" Elodie asked.

"Yes, my lady. Will a maid be accompanying you?" White inquired, just as Molly appeared at Elodie's side.

"I will be joining Lady Elodie," Molly said promptly.

"Very good," White said, opening the main door.

Elodie stepped outside and saw Anthony standing there, holding two leashes. He greeted her with a warm smile. "That was faster than I expected."

"I do not know if I should be flattered or insulted," Elodie remarked.

"Flattered, I assure you," Anthony replied, stepping forward and holding out one of the leashes. "Would you like to walk Lulu?"

"Yes, but first, I have to put his hat on," Elodie said as she held up the small embroidered blue hat.

Anthony's brow furrowed. "Dogs do not wear hats."

Ignoring him, she crouched down and tied the strings of the hat under Lulu's chin. She stood up and beamed. "Is he not just adorable?"

In response, Lulu shook his head vigorously, sending the hat flying off.

Elodie picked up the discarded hat. "Oh, Lulu, do you not like your hat? I made it just *fur* you."

Anthony looked heavenward. "That joke was truly terrible," he said. "Why, pray tell, did you make a hat for a dog?"

Elodie shrugged, her fingers playing with the hat's delicate ribbon. "It is far more preferable than embroidering hand-kerchiefs."

Handing her Lulu's leash, Anthony said, "There is a reason why dogs do not wear hats."

"You are right," Elodie said, accepting the leash. "I will need to make something more manly for Lulu."

"Is that even possible with a name like 'Lulu'?" Anthony teased.

Elodie had the perfect idea. "I will make him a waistcoat. Then everyone will know that Lulu is a serious type of dog."

"A waistcoat?" Anthony repeated, incredulous. "That is just as absurd as a hat."

"I think it is a marvelous idea," Elodie said. "Lulu deserves to look distinguished."

Anthony shook his head as they strolled down the pavement. "Dogs are not meant to wear clothing or accessories."

"We shall have to agree to disagree."

He shot her a playful sideways glance. "Isn't that how most of our conversations end?"

Elodie smirked. "I can't help it if you insist on saying such dull things."

With a mock look of pain, Anthony placed a hand over his heart. "Oh, you wound me, my lady. And here I thought we were getting along so nicely."

"We are, aren't we? Which is rather strange."

"Strange? How so?" Anthony asked.

Elodie hesitated, then said, "It is almost as if we are..."

"Friends?" Anthony said, finishing her thought.

"Yes, friends."

Anthony's expression warmed. "I would like to think we are. I certainly consider you a friend."

They reached the edge of the park, the morning sun filtering through the canopy of trees, casting shadows on the path ahead. They crossed the street and started walking down a path.

Elodie cocked her head. "I suppose you are right. We are friends now that you have stopped teasing me so relentlessly."

"I tease you, but only because I care."

She let out an exasperated huff. "Did you care about me when you put worms down the back of my dress at that garden party?"

Anthony grinned. "Perhaps I got a little carried away. But I just wanted your attention."

"There were far more civilized ways to get my attention," Elodie declared.

"But none nearly as entertaining," Anthony said with a laugh.

Elodie rolled her eyes, though a smile tugged at the corner of her lips. "You are fortunate I have an unusually high tolerance for feeble-minded people."

Anthony stopped walking and turned to face her with exaggerated seriousness. "I am a viscount. You should be nicer to me."

"You wish for me to lie to you, then?"

Anthony chuckled. "You do not mince words, do you?"

"I do not see the point."

Gesturing towards a nearby bench that sat under the shade of a birch tree, Anthony asked, "Shall we sit for a while?"

Elodie went to settle onto the bench, holding Lulu's leash loosely in her hand. Her gaze drifted to the peaceful scene before them. The grass seemed to glisten in the sunlight, and she could hear the gentle rustle of the leaves in the breeze. "It really is beautiful here in the morning," she said.

Anthony sat down beside her. "It is, and it is not very crowded, either. That is one advantage of waking up so early."

Lulu gave a soft whimper, and Elodie lifted him onto her lap, stroking his soft fur. "I think dogs have a way of making everything better."

A comfortable silence settled between them. Anthony broke the silence with a soft smile. "Would you care to go on a carriage ride with me today?"

"I'm afraid my afternoon is spoken for," Elodie replied.

His lips quirked into a teasing smile. "Oh? Plans? Or are you just planning to take an impossibly long nap this afternoon?"

Elodie shrugged one shoulder, finding amusement in the fact that Anthony knew her so well. "There is absolutely nothing wrong with a long nap. But no, that is not my plan. I am going on a carriage ride with Lord Westcott."

Anthony's smile faltered ever so slightly. "Lord Westcott?"

"Yes," Elodie confirmed. "He invited me yesterday when he came to call upon me."

A hint of something unreadable crossed his features. "But you hate everything about carriage rides," Anthony remarked.

Elodie's fingers stilled on Lulu's fur, feeling a need to defend herself. "I do not *hate* them," she corrected. "I just do not enjoy the bugs. They seem to have a personal vendetta against me during this time of year."

Anthony's lips pressed into a thin line. "And yet you agreed to go with Westcott," he said, his voice holding a terseness that had not been there a moment ago.

"He asked politely, and I had no reason to decline."

"You could not think of a single reason?"

Elodie studied him for a moment. "Anthony, do not tell me you are jealous."

Anthony's eyes widened, and he let out a scoff. "Me? Jealous? Of course not," he said firmly. "I was merely pointing out your long-standing disdain for carriage rides."

With a wave of her hand, Elodie said, "I will admit that did seem rather ludicrous. Forget I said anything."

"Consider it forgotten."

"Good."

"Yes, good," he repeated, his voice sounding a touch too formal.

Elodie could not decipher what had caused the change in Anthony's demeanor, but she was not about to press the matter. Rising to her feet, she gently placed Lulu back on the ground, smoothing out her skirts as she did.

"I suppose we should continue our walk," she said, a forced lightness in her tone, "before the puppies get restless."

Anthony stood, his gaze lingering on her for a moment longer than necessary. "Yes. Let us get you home before your mother starts to worry."

As they resumed their stroll, Elodie felt a confusing mix of emotions whirling inside of her. Anthony's reaction to her plans with Lord Westcott had been unexpected, and she was not quite sure what to make of it. Part of her wanted to laugh it off, to believe that he was merely being overprotective. But another part of her could not help but wonder if there was something more behind his words.

Anthony sat in the corner of White's, cradling a drink in his hand. The low murmur of conversations and clinking of glasses filled the air, but he was in no mood to be social. His thoughts were firmly fixed on Elodie and the carriage ride she was about to take with Lord Westcott. A man he had no issue with—until now. The jealousy gnawed at him, and he hated the way it twisted his thoughts.

But what right did he have to be jealous? Elodie was not his, and she was free to do as she pleased. Yet the thought of her enjoying Westcott's company was like a thorn in his chest. Sighing, Anthony leaned forward, setting his glass on the polished table before him. He needed a clear mind, especially with the ledgers awaiting his attention back home. Drowning his frustration in a drink would not help, no matter how tempting it seemed.

When had his life become so complicated? And how could he show Elodie that he was the man for her, the one who understood her better than any other? He feared that a confession of his feelings might ruin the fragile bond they shared. If she sought nothing more than friendship, revealing his deeper affections could shatter everything. No, he could not take that risk. He would keep his feelings buried if it meant keeping her in his life, even if only as a friend.

He was about to rise when his brother appeared by his side. "I thought I might find you here," Stephen said.

Anthony was in no mood for his brother. "What is it that you want, Brother?" he asked, his tone clipped.

"I have come to talk," Stephen replied, easing himself into the brown leather armchair opposite Anthony.

"You should be at home, visiting with your daughter," Anthony remarked.

Stephen lounged back in his seat as if he did not have a care in the world. "I have already told you that I want nothing to do with that little girl."

"That little girl has a name," Anthony retorted, his temper flaring. "Her name is Emma."

"I still do not know why you brought her into our home," Stephen grumbled.

"Because she is your daughter, and my niece," Anthony stated. "I will never cast her out, no matter how inconvenient it is for you."

"You have made everything so awkward. I can hardly feel at ease in my own home anymore."

"Good gads, do you think of anyone else but yourself?" Anthony asked.

"Why should I?" Stephen shot back, completely unashamed.

Anthony decided he needed a drink after all, especially if he was going to continue this conversation. He retrieved his glass and took a sip. "What are you even doing here?"

Stephen shrugged. "This is where I come when I need to think."

He could not help a derisive snort. "Then I take it you do not come here very often."

A flash of irritation crossed Stephen's face. "I'd think you would be nicer to me since I have come bearing news."

Anthony lowered the glass to his lap. "What news?"

Stephen leaned forward, glancing around the crowded room, then lowered his voice. "Montrose has placed a wager in the betting book about Elodie."

Now Stephen had his full attention. "What kind of wager?"

"Montrose intends to 'tame the shrew.' Those were his words, not mine," Stephen said. "He is boasting that he will marry her before the Season ends."

Anthony's grip tightened around his glass, his knuckles

whitening. "Over my dead body," he growled, barely able to control the fury rising inside him. "Montrose won't even get close to Elodie if I have anything to say about it."

"His wager is causing quite the stir. Elodie is the diamond of the Season, after all. Montrose's challenge has piqued a lot of interest."

Anthony's jaw clenched. "Let them gossip all they want. Elodie will never marry that despicable man. Not while I am around."

Stephen's face grew serious. "Just be careful," he said, a rare flicker of genuine concern in his eyes. "Montrose does not take kindly to being thwarted."

"I do not care. He will not have Elodie. Not now, not ever," Anthony declared.

A tense silence stretched between them for a long moment before Stephen stood. "I believe you, but I know what Montrose is capable of. He is not a man that I would want to cross."

With those words, Stephen walked away, leaving Anthony alone to grapple with his own thoughts. He knew of Montrose's rakish ways, but he would not step aside and let the man take something that was most precious to him.

Anthony took another sip before placing his glass down. He was about to rise and leave when Bennett and Winston approached him.

"May we join you?" Bennett asked, coming to a stop next to an empty armchair.

"Of course," Anthony responded, gesturing towards the seats across from him. "I should warn you, though, I might not be the best of company."

Winston raised an eyebrow as he sat down. "And why is that?"

Anthony frowned. "Stephen just informed me that Montrose placed a bet in the book. He wagers that he will marry Elodie by the end of the Season."

Bennett's eyes narrowed. "Absolutely not! Montrose is the last man I would want anywhere near Elodie."

"I agree," Anthony said. "But you know how Montrose is. He is already spreading rumors that he intends to 'tame the shrew.'"

"The shrew?" Winston repeated, his face growing thunderous. "He dares to call Elodie that?"

Anthony nodded. "Precisely."

Winston's anger flared. He leaned back in his chair, all traces of humor gone. "What a loathsome man! We should confront him at once. This cannot go unanswered."

"Talking to him will do no good, but we should warn Elodie," Bennett said thoughtfully, his voice measured. "And under no circumstances should she be left alone with Montrose."

"That goes without saying," Winston huffed, his fingers tapping against the arm of the chair.

Bennett shifted his gaze to Anthony. "Did Stephen say what the wager was for?"

"He did not say," Anthony replied.

"I will find out," Bennett said, rising from his seat with a determined look in his eyes. "Give me a moment."

As Bennett walked off towards the betting book, Winston met Anthony's gaze. "I did not think it was possible to dislike Montrose more than I already did."

"How do you think Elodie will react when we tell her about the bet?" Anthony asked.

Winston let out a dry chuckle. "Knowing Elodie, she will probably challenge him to a duel herself."

Anthony could not help but smile at that thought. "And she would probably win."

Winston smirked. "Most likely, especially since Montrose is usually deep in his cups. He is a rakehell of the worst kind, and if the rumors are true, he has already ruined several young women this Season."

Anthony was about to respond when Bennett returned, his expression grim. He dropped down onto his seat and revealed, "Montrose wagered a thousand pounds that he would wed Elodie by the end of the Season."

"A thousand pounds?" Anthony repeated incredulously. "What a muttonhead."

"I won't disagree with you there," Bennett said with a wry smile. "I went ahead and placed a wager against him. When he loses, I will make a tidy profit."

Winston rose, his frustration barely contained. "We should warn Elodie at once."

Bennett put his hand out. "She will be safe with Lord Westcott. He is an honorable man, and he won't let any harm befall her."

At the mention of Westcott, Anthony grew tense. "Perhaps we should go to Hyde Park and keep an eye on them?"

"No," Bennett said firmly. "Elodie would be furious if she found out we were spying on her. She was not pleased when she learned we followed your carriage through Hyde Park."

"Why did you trail after us?" Anthony asked.

Bennett shrugged. "It was Elodie's first carriage ride, and we wanted to confirm it went off without a hitch."

"What did you think might happen?" Anthony inquired.

A knowing smile came to Bennett's lips. "We are talking about Elodie. Anything is possible with her."

A reluctant laugh escaped Anthony, some of the tension easing from his shoulders. "True enough," he admitted.

A server approached their table and collected their drink orders. As he walked off, Bennett asked, "Have you made any progress with Stephen? Has he shown any inclination to do the right thing?"

"No," Anthony said. "Stephen is impossible. I do not believe he feels an ounce of remorse for how he treated his wife and now his daughter."

"Did you really expect any different from him?" Winston asked.

Anthony shook his head. "Not really. But with my parents here, I hoped they might knock some sense into him. Maybe... I do not know. There is a part of me that still wishes things could be different."

Bennett offered him a look that could only be construed as sympathy. "Regardless of what Stephen does, I have no doubt you will do what is right for that girl. You have always been the one to step up when it matters."

A heavy sigh escaped Anthony. "Yes, I will do my duty, but she is not my responsibility. She is Stephen's daughter, not mine."

"That is precisely why you will make sure she is taken care of," Bennett said gently. "You have always been someone that others can rely on."

Settling back in his seat, Anthony asked, "Why do I always have to be the reliable one? Just once, I want to do something reckless. Something that is not expected of me."

Winston snorted. "No, you don't. You might talk about wanting to be reckless, but you are far too sensible for that."

A rueful grin tugged at Anthony's lips. "You are right, of course." He hesitated before he admitted, "I want what you two have."

Bennett's eyes twinkled with mischief. "You mean our good looks?"

"Or perhaps our irresistible charm?" Winston chimed in.

Anthony looked heavenward. "As insufferable as you both are, that is not what I meant."

"Then what?" Bennett asked, his tone suddenly becoming more earnest.

Tracing his fingers along the rim of his empty glass, he

replied, "I want someone who is always there. Someone who sees me—truly sees me—flaws and all. I want... love."

The word seemed to hang in the air between them, a raw and honest admission that Anthony had never dared to voice before. It left him feeling exposed, but there was no taking it back.

Winston's teasing demeanor softened. "You will find her, Anthony. When the right person comes along, you will know."

Anthony's thoughts drifted, unbidden, to Elodie. The image of her teasing smile came to his mind. There was a spark in her that had always drawn him in, a light that he could not help but be fascinated by.

Bennett eyed him curiously. "You have already found her, have you not?"

"Whatever do you mean?" Anthony asked.

"I do not know how I could make my question any clearer," Bennett replied. "It is rather obvious you are already in love. So, who is she?"

Anthony worked to keep the emotions off his face. "I am not in love," he said firmly, though the words felt like a lie even to his own ears.

Bennett didn't look convinced. "I have known you since our days at Eton. You are smitten, my friend. Anyone with half a mind can see it."

Rising, Anthony said, "Gentlemen, if you will excuse me, I have work that I must see to."

"No, stay," Bennett said.

"Don't go!" Winston attempted.

Anthony tugged down on the ends of his blue waistcoat. "I'm afraid I have neglected the accounts for long enough today."

"You can run, but you can't hide forever," Bennett advised. "Sooner or later, you will have to face your feelings for this girl —whoever she is."

Anthony gave a curt nod. "Perhaps, but that time is not now. I have other responsibilities. Good day."

As he walked away, Anthony knew Bennett's words would haunt him. Because deep down, he knew they were true. And admitting the truth—admitting his feelings—meant risking everything he had with Elodie. And he was not sure if he was ready for that kind of gamble. Not yet.

10

E lodie sat in the drawing room, her needle threading through the fabric as she worked on the waistcoat for Lulu. The fabric was delicate, embroidered with tiny blue flowers, and she tried to focus on each stitch even as her mother's voice droned on beside her. Lady Dallington, sitting primly on the settee, was in the middle of her usual lecture about the importance of conduct.

Her mother stopped speaking, and Elodie glanced up. "What is the matter?"

"You are not listening to a single word I am saying," her mother said, a trace of irritation lining her voice.

Elodie gave a slight smile, raising the embroidery to inspect her stitches. "On the contrary, I could repeat it back to you almost word for word. You warned me that one fall, even the tiniest mishap, could destroy my entire Season."

"And you must promise that under no circumstances you will lay a hand on Lord Westcott."

Elodie lowered her embroidery to her lap. "I cannot promise that. What if he tries to take liberties with me?"

"Lord Westcott has the reputation of being an honorable gentleman."

"Then I should have no need to engage in fisticuffs with him," Elodie said. "Besides, I only hit one person in my entire life, and it felt like striking a brick wall. I have no intention of repeating that mistake."

Her mother looked slightly relieved until Elodie added, "Next time, I would simply kick him."

"There will be no kicking!" her mother admonished.

"You say that now..." Elodie started.

"I say that always."

"... but if I must, I will kick like a samurai," Elodie said with mock solemnity.

With a shake of her head, her mother asked, "Pray tell, what does a samurai kick like?"

"I have no idea," Elodie admitted, lowering her voice, "but I have read about them. They are stealthy, like ninjas. There could be one in this very room, and we would not even know it."

"You are impossible, Child," her mother said, rubbing her temples.

Elodie perked up. "Do you think we could get a samurai?"

Her mother stood. "Samurai are not pets, Elodie. They are esteemed warriors in Japanese culture, and they deserve respect."

At that moment, White appeared in the doorway. "Lord Westcott, my ladies," he announced.

Elodie leaned forward and set down the unfinished waistcoat before rising to her feet. She waited as Lord Westcott was ushered into the room. He greeted them with a bow, and she returned his gesture with a graceful curtsy.

"Lady Dallington, Lady Elodie," Lord Westcott said, straightening from his bow. He glanced at the fabric and thread scattered across the table. "May I ask what you are embroidering?"

Elodie reached down and retrieved the garment. "It is a waistcoat," she said proudly, holding it up for his inspection. "For my dog, Lulu."

Lord Westcott blinked, clearly caught off guard. "For a dog? A waistcoat?"

"Yes," Elodie said, undeterred by his confusion. "I want Lulu to look distinguished when we go for our walks in the park. A puppy can be dignified, don't you think?"

His expression was one of polite skepticism. "I confess, I have never thought of a puppy as 'distinguished,' but I am intrigued by your determination."

Her mother interjected, "I do hope the two of you have a delightful carriage ride."

Elodie stepped forward, accepting Lord Westcott's outstretched arm. "Shall we, my lord?"

"Yes, of course," Lord Westcott replied, his eyes lingering on the unfinished waistcoat for a moment longer. As they walked towards the door, he added, "I do hope you have no objections, but my sister, Lady Eugenie, will be joining us."

"I have no objections," Elodie said.

Lord Westcott's eyes held approval. "Eugenie insisted on staying in the carriage. She wanted to finish reading the last chapter of her book before we set off."

"I do not blame your sister. I would not dream of inter-rupting someone during a good book."

They stepped outside through the main door, the sunlight glinting off the polished brass of the carriage. Seated inside, with a straw hat covering her blonde hair, was Lady Eugenie. Her face was partially hidden by the worn, leather-bound cover of her book, her concentration evident. As Elodie accepted Lord Westcott's hand and climbed into the carriage, Lady

Eugenie snapped her book shut, a bright smile lighting up her features.

"I have finished," she announced with triumph, tucking the book beside her.

It was then that Elodie got a proper look at Lady Eugenie, and realization dawned on her. This was the very same young woman she had seen at the ball—the one caught in a compromising situation with Lord Montrose. A flicker of understanding passed between them as Lady Eugenie's expression shifted, her eyes widening.

"It is you," Lady Eugenie said softly, her voice tinged with surprise.

Lord Westcott's brow furrowed as he glanced between them. "I had not realized you two were already acquainted."

Elodie caught the pleading look in Lady Eugenie's eyes and responded with a reassuring smile. "Yes, we met briefly at Lady Montrose's ball."

"Indeed," Lady Eugenie confirmed quickly, her expression relaxing. "It was a... memorable evening."

"Wonderful," Lord Westcott said, seemingly satisfied with the explanation. He settled back into his seat beside his sister.

Elodie seized the opportunity to shift the conversation. Gesturing to the book Lady Eugenie had set aside, she asked, "May I ask what you were reading?"

"*A Vindication of the Rights of Women* by Mary Wollstonecraft," Lady Eugenie replied. "It is a truly fascinating read."

Lord Westcott's expression tightened, and he cleared his throat. "You must forgive my sister. I do not quite approve of her choice in literature."

"And why is that, my lord?" Elodie challenged. "Is it because Mary Wollstonecraft argues that women are not naturally inferior to men, but only seem so due to a lack of education?"

Lady Eugenie's eyes grew wide. "You have read the book?"

Elodie nodded, leaning forward. "I have. But you must not tell my father. He prefers that I occupy myself with lighter novels that require far less thought."

"That sounds very much like my brother's preferences," Lady Eugenie said.

Lord Westcott crossed his arms. "I only wish to protect you. You would not want to be labeled as a bluestocking, would you?"

Lady Eugenie tilted her chin. "And what if I do? There is nothing wrong with being a bluestocking."

"I must say, I agree with your sister," Elodie said. "The world could use a few more women with a passion for knowledge."

Lord Westcott raised his hands in surrender. "I am clearly outnumbered, and a wise man knows when not to fall on his sword."

"A rare feat, indeed," Lady Eugenie said. "My brother never admits he is wrong."

Lord Westcott's mouth twisted in response. "I never said I was wrong. I merely suggested it might be better to discuss other topics," he said before turning his attention to Elodie. "Perhaps you could offer my sister some advice on navigating the *ton*. After all, you were chosen as the Season's diamond. There is no one better suited to guide her."

As the carriage wheels rumbled over the cobblestones and turned into Hyde Park, Elodie felt a slight tightening in her chest. She was not sure if she was ready to be anyone's guide, especially not a fellow bluestocking. Still, she clasped her hands in her lap. "I am not certain I am the best person to give advice on such matters," she said. "In truth, I have always felt rather out of place myself."

Lord Westcott gave her a skeptical look. "That is hardly true. You would not have been named the diamond if that were the case."

Elodie offered a slight shrug. "Perhaps the queen was simply feeling generous that day," she teased. "Nonetheless, I am happy to answer any question Lady Eugenie may have. Though I cannot promise you will like my answers."

Settling comfortably against the cushioned seat, Lord Westcott inclined his head towards his sister. "Eugenie, now is your chance. Do you have any burning questions for Lady Elodie?"

Lady Eugenie's eyes sparkled with curiosity, and she leaned forward, her voice dropping to a whisper. "I do have one."

Elodie leaned in as well. "Ask away, my lady."

Lady Eugenie hesitated for a moment, her gaze flickering briefly to her brother as if to gauge his reaction, then returning to Elodie. "I overheard you tell the queen that you intend to marry for love."

"I do," Elodie confirmed.

"But... do you truly believe that is possible?" Lady Eugenie's voice was tentative, almost wistful. "Love matches seem so rare amongst the *ton*. It is all about alliances and social expectation."

Elodie bobbed her head in understanding. "It is true, love matches are a rarity in our world. But that does not mean they are impossible," she said. "My brothers, my sister, and even my cousin managed to find love despite Society's expectations. It takes a bit of courage and a good deal of luck, but it is possible."

Lady Eugenie leaned back, her expression thoughtful. "Love feels so elusive. It is almost like a—"

"Unicorn," Elodie interjected.

With a laugh, Lady Eugenie responded, "No, not a unicorn! I was going to say an impossible feat."

Elodie grinned. "Perhaps it does seem impossible at times, but I do not believe that is the case. Somewhere out there, I truly believe there is one person meant for us. A person who speaks to our soul, who understands us in ways no one else can."

"That sounds positively romantic," Lady Eugenie said.

Before Elodie could respond, Lord Westcott spoke up. "Romantic, yes," he started, his voice laced with skepticism. "But also terribly idealistic. Love is a sentiment often found in novels and poetry, not in drawing rooms and ballrooms of the *ton*."

Elodie met his gaze. "But is that not the beauty of it, my lord? It is precisely because love is so rare that it is worth pursuing."

"And if you cannot find love?" he asked. "Would you remain unwed rather than settle for a match of convenience?"

"Yes," Elodie said without hesitation. "I would rather be alone than with someone who does not understand my heart."

Lady Eugenie's eyes shone with admiration. "That is incredibly brave."

"Or incredibly foolish," Lord Westcott murmured.

Elodie's gaze never wavered. "Perhaps a little of both. But I refuse to believe that love is just a fantasy, something we read about in books and never experience ourselves. I have seen it, so I know it exists."

The carriage rolled gently to a stop, signaling their arrival at Rotten Row. The chatter of people, the rhythmic clopping of hooves, and the hum of laughter drifted into the carriage as Lord Westcott said, "I must admit, your optimism is unexpected. In a world where most women would gladly secure a suitable match, you dare to ask for more."

Elodie knew how ridiculous she must sound to Lord Westcott, but she did not care. She would not settle for anything less than a love match. "That is because I know I deserve more," she said. "And I am willing to wait for it."

Lord Westcott held her gaze for a moment, something shifting in his eyes—perhaps respect, or a touch of envy. Then he offered a genuine smile that reached his eyes. "I do hope you find it, Lady Elodie. I truly do."

"Thank you," Elodie replied.

Just as she was beginning to relax, enjoying the lazy sway of the carriage, an image of Anthony flashed through her mind. The thought caught her off guard, and she quickly banished it from her mind. Why was she thinking of him now? It was maddening the way Anthony seemed to invade her thoughts at the most unexpected moments, lingering there like a shadow that refused to be chased away.

"Anthony!"

Anthony looked up from his ledger at the sound of his brother's voice echoing through the corridor. He had no sooner closed the ledger than Stephen stormed into the study, his face twisted with rage.

"What have you done?" Stephen demanded.

Anthony held his brother's gaze calmly, unbothered by his anger. "Would you care to be more specific?"

Stephen marched closer, slamming his hands down on the desk as he leaned over it. "I just came from meeting with Father. He informed me, in no uncertain terms, that my allowance would be cut off if I did not do the right thing by that girl."

Leaning back in his seat, Anthony asked, "And what exactly do you expect me to do about it?"

"This is all your doing!" Stephen shouted, pointing an accusatory finger. "I know you were the one who put these ideas into his head."

"So what if I did?"

"You have gone too far this time!" Stephen shouted. "You have been trying to get me to meet that girl for days now."

Anthony's tone sharpened as he stood. "That *girl* is your daughter."

Stephen waved a dismissive hand. "I do not acknowledge her, nor should you."

"Why wouldn't I acknowledge her?" Anthony asked. "You were legally married to her mother, making the child legitimate."

Stephen scoffed. "I should have realized that you wouldn't understand."

"Understand what?" Anthony demanded. "Understand how you have shirked your responsibilities with Emma or how you abandoned your wife, leaving her penniless?"

"I told you that I didn't think the marriage was legal," Stephen said, dropping down onto the chair. "That is hardly my fault for the misunderstanding."

"Misunderstanding?" Anthony's voice rose, his patience fraying. "This was not a misunderstanding. It was a scheme. You took advantage of her trust, abandoned her, and now refuse to face the consequences of your actions."

Stephen's face contorted with irritation. "And now you and Father want to punish me for not wanting her here."

Anthony took a steadying breath, reminding himself to remain calm. "Father is giving you a choice. Do the right thing or go about it all on your own."

Stephen shoved his chair back and stood, his face dark with anger. "I knew this would happen. You have always been quick to judge me, standing on your moral high ground. I will never be the golden boy. I am not the heir. I am simply the second son, the one no one ever expected anything from."

Anthony frowned. "Are you truly blaming your behavior on your position in the family?"

Stephen's expression grew defiant. "It is not an excuse. It is the truth! Growing up in your shadow, I was always a disappointment. So I stopped caring. Stopped trying."

"You have made your choices," Anthony said, frustration threading his voice. "Your position is not an excuse for abandoning your responsibilities."

Stephen jabbed a finger at Anthony. "You do not get to dictate my life. I am my own man." Anthony had finally reached his limit. "If that is true, then start acting like it. Be a man for once. Meet your daughter. It is a simple request."

His brother laughed, a bitter sound. "You mean so you and Father can feel like you did your part by making me do the 'right thing'? Spare me."

Anthony stepped closer, lowering his voice. "I fully support Father's decision. If you cannot meet her, do not expect to receive another penny. Emma is your daughter, whether you like it or not."

Stephen's nostrils flared as he glared at him. "You would not dare cut me off. I am owed that money."

"You are owed nothing. As you so often remind me, I am the heir. And if you do not take responsibility, I will see to it that you face the consequences."

A dangerous glint appeared in Stephen's eyes as he leaned closer, their faces just inches apart. "You think you are better than me, do you not?"

Anthony did not waver. "I have never thought that. But if you cannot be bothered to walk down the hall and acknowledge your own daughter, then you have no one to blame but yourself."

"This is not over!" Stephen said, taking a step back. "Do not think for a moment that you have won."

Their mother's voice came from the doorway. "Good heavens, what is all this shouting about?"

Stephen turned his attention towards their mother. "Will you kindly tell this arrogant, pig-headed brother of mine that I do not answer to him?"

She cast a worried glance between her sons, her features

creased with concern. "Perhaps we should all sit down and discuss this rationally."

"Good gads, no! I want nothing to do with Anthony!" Stephen exclaimed. "I am going out, and do not wait up for me!"

Anthony watched Stephen storm out, the door slamming behind him. He had known the conversation would be difficult, but the depth of Stephen's resentment unsettled him.

After a moment's pause, his mother stepped further into the room. "I must assume the argument was about Emma."

"It was," Anthony confirmed. "All I can hope is that someday Stephen will come to his senses... before it is too late."

With a quiet sigh, she walked over to the drink cart and poured two drinks. She handed him one with a look that held understanding. Catching the surprised expression on his face, she managed a small, resigned smile. "There is no harm in a drink or two, given the circumstances."

Anthony took a seat on the settee, rubbing a hand over his face. "What are we going to do about Stephen?" he asked, almost to himself.

His mother lowered herself gracefully onto the armchair across from him. "I do believe your father is serious about cutting Stephen off. But even if we somehow convince him to meet Emma, what then?" she asked, her voice heavy. "Do you truly think he will care for her the way she deserves?"

Anthony looked down into his glass, mulling over his words. "There is a real possibility," he began slowly, "that I will be raising her instead."

His mother's eyes glistened as she took a sip of her drink. "Yes, Anthony. I believe you might be. And Emma would be lucky for it."

"I do not know about being lucky," Anthony said. "I know nothing about raising a child."

"You will learn."

Anthony took a sip of his drink. "I daresay that this is too much. What with Father sick and me running the estate. I hardly have time for anything else."

"Life has a way of working itself out," his mother said. "You will see. Just be patient."

He opened his mouth to complain, but then he saw the sadness in his mother's eyes. He may be tired, but his mother was dealing with much more. Her husband was dying right in front of her eyes and there was nothing she could do about it.

"How are you faring, Mother?" he asked.

A small, unconvincing smile came to her lips. "I am well."

"I would prefer the truth, if you don't mind."

The smile disappeared and she lowered her gaze. "I don't know what I will do without your father. He has been, and always will be, my entire world."

Anthony moved to sit on the edge of his seat. "You will get along just fine without him," he encouraged.

"I may get by, but I will not be fine," his mother asserted. "We have been together far too long to think about a life without him."

He felt helpless as a tear fell down his mother's cheek. She swiped it away and rose. "I need to get back to your father."

Anthony rose. "Would you care for me to accompany you?"

Placing the glass down, she replied, "No, I think I need a moment alone before I face your father."

"I will be up shortly to visit with Father."

"Give him some time," his mother said. "His visit with Stephen overwhelmed him and I have no doubt he is resting."

Anthony walked over to his mother and embraced her. "No matter what happens, I will ensure you are well provided for."

She leaned back and cupped his cheek. "I know, Son."

As she walked off, Anthony returned to his desk and opened the ledger. He might as well get some more work done before dinner.

The sound of barking floated through the room, pulling Anthony's attention towards the window. He peered outside to see Spot and Lulu bouncing around Emma, their tiny tails wagging as they jumped up on her. Emma's laughter rang out as she tried to calm the puppies, her small hands gently pushing them down. Anthony's heart tightened at the sight. How could Stephen abandon this innocent child?

The accounts could wait. Closing his ledger, he made his way out the back door and crossed the gardens. He approached Emma and noticed her determined expression as she commanded, "Sit!"

Anthony crouched beside her. "How are Spot and Lulu doing today?"

A small pout formed on Emma's lips. "They won't listen to me," she replied.

"What are you trying to tell them?"

"I'm trying to teach them how to sit," Emma shared, looking at the puppies. "But they keep jumping up on me."

Anthony stifled a smile. "Do you have any treats with you?"

Emma's brows knitted in confusion, and she shook her head. "No... I did not know I needed any."

"Well, I have found that puppies, much like people, are motivated by food," he said. "If you bring a little something from the kitchen, they might be more inclined to follow your commands."

Her eyes sparkled at the idea. "I can get some treats from the kitchen."

Anthony reached down and ruffled the fur on Spot's head as the puppies calmed down. "Once you do that, I assure you that training them to sit will be much easier."

She offered him a shy smile. "Thank you, my lord."

"We are family, Emma. I would prefer if you called me Anthony. Or Uncle Anthony. Whichever you would like."

Emma looked at him with uncertainty before glancing at the nursemaid. "I was told to call you 'my lord.'"

"That is only for people who are not family or people I do not particularly care for," he said with a wink. "And I happen to like you very much, Emma."

A genuine smile spread across her face, a sight that touched him deeply. "Thank you, Uncle Anthony," she said, her voice soft. "And thank you for all the toys."

"It was my pleasure," he said, rising to his feet. "If you ever need anything else, you need only ask."

Elodie's voice drifted over the gardens' hedge, light and teasing. "Ask for a unicorn, Emma."

Emma looked up at him with a hopeful look. "Can I get a unicorn?"

Anthony chuckled. "Unicorns, sadly, are mythical creatures. But how about a pony?"

"A real pony?" Emma inquired.

"Is there any other kind?" Anthony asked.

Emma clasped her hands together. "I have always wanted a pony, but my mother said we didn't have room for one."

"Well, we have plenty of space here," Anthony assured her. "And as soon as we have everything ready, you can start your lessons."

From over the hedge, Elodie's laughter rang out. "That is the art of negotiation for you, Emma. You start with the impossible, and you end up getting exactly what you want."

Anthony looked towards her, amused. "Why don't you join us, Elodie?"

"Oh, I would not wish to intrude," Elodie said.

"Too late for that," he responded with a smile.

Moments later, Elodie hopped down from her perch and made her way to the small gate that divided their gardens. She opened it, stepped into Anthony's gardens, and approached Emma. She knelt down and wrapped the girl in a warm hug.

"You have done a wonderful job with these puppies, Emma," she praised. "I have never seen puppies so happy before."

Emma beamed. "Uncle Anthony told me that I can use treats to train the puppies to sit."

"I would listen to your uncle," Elodie said. "He sounds rather wise."

Turning towards Anthony, Emma asked, "Can I go get some treats right now?"

"Of course, but be sure to grab a biscuit for yourself," Anthony replied.

Emma dashed towards the townhouse, her nursemaid in tow. As they disappeared through the back door, Elodie turned back to Anthony. "You are very sweet with Emma."

Anthony shrugged, a mischievous smirk on his lips. "You sound surprised. I assure you, sweetness is just one of my many talents. The ladies adore me for it."

Elodie laughed, just as he had hoped. "Oh, is that so?" she challenged, a teasing glint in her eyes. "Well, you will have to put in a bit more effort to impress me."

"I am well aware, Elodie," Anthony said. His gaze lingered on her just a moment too long before he cleared his throat, breaking the spell. "Would you care to sit? It seems I have been relegated to dog-sitting duties for the time being."

"I suppose I can spare a moment or two," Elodie replied, moving past him towards the bench. The faint scent of lavender trailed in the air, striking him as utterly enchanting.

Elodie reached down and affectionately petted Lulu. For the briefest of moments, everything seemed perfect.

11

E lodie settled comfortably on the weathered bench in the gardens, her hand idly stroking Lulu's soft fur. The puppy was sitting on her lap. Anthony sat beside her, and a comfortable silence descended over them.

Anthony cleared his throat, breaking through the silence. "How was your carriage ride with Lord Westcott?"

Elodie brought her gaze up. "It was enjoyable," she replied. "Although I did discover that his sister, Lady Eugenie, was the young woman Lord Montrose was attempting to take liberties with."

Anthony's posture shifted as he turned slightly, facing her. "Did you mention to Lord Westcott how you dealt with Montrose?"

"Oh, heavens, no, and it seems Lady Eugenie did not mention it, either."

"Good. The fewer people who know, the better."

"That was my thought precisely," Elodie said, lowering her gaze to the puppy. "I cannot wait to see Lulu in his little waistcoat."

Anthony shook his head. "I contend that a dog should never wear clothing."

"You are entitled to your opinion, even if it is entirely wrong," Elodie quipped. "Lulu clearly wants to wear a waistcoat."

Anthony gave her a skeptical look. "Since when did you start speaking 'dog'?"

She lifted Lulu so their eyes met. "Surely it is not that difficult to understand," she said, only for Lulu to lunge forward, licking her face with enthusiasm.

Anthony chuckled. "I believe Lulu's interest lies more in licking you than in fashion statements."

"Perhaps we should normalize dogs wearing clothing," Elodie said.

"Be my guest," he replied, shrugging. "I have far too much on my plate already."

Elodie placed Lulu back on the ground, where the puppy quickly ran off to play with Spot. "Ah, the curse of being a lord," she teased.

Anthony sighed, his expression shadowing briefly. "True enough. My responsibilities increased tenfold when my father fell ill. Now, every detail of the estate rests on my shoulders."

"That is quite the burden to bear."

"It is, but it is my duty," Anthony said.

Elodie groaned. "I hate that word. *Duty*. It haunts me. My father is forever reminding me of my 'duty' to marry and bear sons, as if that is all I was born for."

"Your father is a good man."

"He is," Elodie agreed. "We don't always see eye-to-eye on things, but I know he has my best interests at heart."

A thoughtful look passed over Anthony's face. "An advantageous marriage would bring you security."

"Yes, but at what cost?" Elodie asked. "I want love or nothing at all."

"You deserve love," Anthony said simply.

Elodie smiled. "As do you."

For a moment, Anthony hesitated, then pressed his lips together. "I am not sure if love is in the cards for me."

"Whyever not?"

He looked away, the flicker of pain in his eyes just visible before he turned his face. "I would rather not discuss it."

Elodie caught the sadness in his tone, and it tugged at her heart. "All right. What would you care to talk about, then?"

"Anything else," he replied.

Trying to lighten the mood, Elodie shared, "I have been thinking of writing a book."

Anthony's gaze snapped back to her. "Truly?"

"Indeed," Elodie replied. "'A Lady' has already written two books. Why can't I? Though I am trying to discover the perfect way to murder someone in the story."

"That is... unnerving."

Elodie laughed, waving a hand at the gardens. "Look around you. Many of these flowers are poisonous if consumed. I need to come up with a plausible reason as to why they were consumed."

Anthony gave her a knowing look. "What would your father think of this literary endeavor?"

The humor left her face. "Oh, he would never approve. But I want to do something more with my life than sitting around."

"So, aside from novel writing, what interests you?"

"I love naps," Elodie replied.

Anthony looked heavenward. "That is neither a hobby nor a skill."

"I disagree," she replied with mock offense. "You must have your pillows arranged just so to achieve the perfect nap cocoon."

"Fine. Name another interest."

Elodie thought for a moment before saying, "I enjoy biscuits."

Anthony let out a groan. "Again, eating biscuits does not require any skill or talent."

"That is where you are wrong."

"Of course I am," Anthony huffed.

Elodie grinned. "Sometimes I have to eat biscuits quietly during church service. Bennett claims I am a loud chewer, but honestly, I think he is just jealous that I don't bring any for him."

Anthony chuckled but then grew uncharacteristically silent. After a long pause, he spoke. "Since this conversation is going nowhere, I need to tell you something of utmost importance."

The shift in his tone sent a ripple of concern through her. "What is it, Anthony?"

He took a deep breath, running a hand through his hair as though grappling with the right words. "I went to the club earlier and I learned something disturbing. Montrose placed a wager in the betting book... and it is about you."

Rearing back, Elodie asked, "Me?"

Anthony's jaw tightened. "He wagered that he would marry you by the end of the Season."

The absurdity of it stunned her, and she leaped from her seat, pacing as she processed the news. "I would never marry that man!"

"I know," Anthony said, rising. "But there is more. He is telling people that he intends to 'tame the shrew.'"

Her jaw dropped, and she spun around to face him. "And I am the 'shrew' in this scenario?"

Anthony's gaze softened with sympathy. "I'm afraid so."

A surge of anger rose from her chest, and she clenched her fists. "What a vile man! I could hit him again."

Anthony put his hands up. "No. I do not want you to go anywhere near him. Do you understand?"

Elodie resumed her pacing, her thoughts racing. The sheer arrogance of Lord Montrose's wager was appalling. She would never, under any circumstances, agree to marry him. Even if he were the last man on earth, her answer would remain an emphatic "no."

Anthony moved to block her path, gently placing his hands on her shoulders. "It will be all right, Elodie."

She looked up, her brow furrowed. "How? Lord Montrose is calling me a 'shrew.'"

Anthony's gaze was steady and warm. "There are far worse things to be called. There is no truth behind his words, only cruelty." He leaned slightly closer, and in the quiet between them, she noticed the subtle flecks of brown in his dark blue eyes. It was a detail that she had never noticed before. She realized how close he was, closer than they had ever been, and her heart beat a little faster.

"Elodie..." he murmured. "I promise I won't let anything bad happen to you."

She bit her lip, her thoughts still troubled. "But what of Lord Montrose?"

A faint smile played on his lips. Her eyes drifted to his mouth, and a strange, unfamiliar longing surged through her. It was an inexplicable urge to know what his lips would feel like against hers. Good heavens, where had that thought come from? She was stronger than this, surely.

"Let me handle Montrose," Anthony said, his voice low and reassuring. "You just focus on enjoying your naps and eating biscuits."

She frowned. "I can do more than that."

"I know. But all I want is for you to be happy, whatever it is that you pursue."

Elodie cocked her head. "Why do you care so much?"

Anthony's gaze grew intense, a depth of emotion flickering behind his eyes that she had not seen before. "How could I not care about you, Elodie?"

The words struck her like a gentle yet undeniable force, leaving her heart racing. She searched his face, her own emotions jumbled. But before she could find the right words, the sudden, gleeful shout of a child's voice broke through the moment.

"I got some treats!" Emma announced, bounding over with an excited grin and a handful of food.

Anthony dropped his hands from Elodie's shoulders, turning towards Emma. Elodie felt a pang of something. Disappointment, perhaps? She tried to make sense of his words and what they meant. He had said he cared for her before. But this time, it was different. She felt something deep down, a quiet, stirring desire, and it frightened her as much as it thrilled her.

"Elodie?" Anthony asked.

She blinked, pulling herself back to the present. "I am sorry. I was... woolgathering."

Anthony offered her a private smile. "You are missing the show. Emma is training the puppies."

Elodie turned to watch as the two puppies, Lulu and Spot, sat obediently before Emma, their eyes fixed eagerly on the treats in her hand, tails wagging in unison.

"They are sitting," Emma declared proudly, grinning ear to ear.

"That they are," Anthony agreed. "You are doing a fine job of training them."

Emma's face lit up even more. "How do I teach them to roll over?"

Anthony crouched down beside her, observing the puppies with a patient smile. "I think we should start small and focus on sitting for now."

As if on cue, Lulu darted forward and snatched the rest of

the treats from Emma's hand, gobbling them up. Emma gasped in surprise, wagging a scolding finger at Lulu. "Bad dog. You need to share with your brother."

"I think that is enough training for one day," Anthony said, standing back up. "Is it not nearly time for your supper?"

"Can the dogs eat dinner with me?" Emma asked, casting a pleading look up at her uncle.

Anthony gave her an indulgent look. "Just this once."

The nursemaid stepped forward, extending her hand towards Emma. As they began to walk towards the townhouse, Emma turned her head back and called, "Come along, Spot! Lulu!" The two puppies perked up, their tiny tails wagging furiously as they fell in line behind her.

"I wish I could eat dinner with Lulu," Elodie remarked.

Anthony turned to her, his eyes glinting with mirth. "You could, you know, but only if you agree to marry me." His tone held a teasing lilt. "Just imagine how impossibly attractive our children would be. We would be the talk of the *ton*, the most envied family in all of London. No, in all the world."

"That is quite the tempting offer, but I am afraid I will have to decline."

He sighed dramatically. "Pity. Well, I suppose you will just have to settle for less attractive children."

Elodie laughed. Yet, as the laughter faded, she felt a twinge of reluctance. It was nearing time to dress for dinner, but she was not quite ready to say goodbye to Anthony. Gathering her courage, she asked, "Would you care to join my family for dinner? I know it is a bit late notice, but..."

"I would be delighted," he said, taking a step closer.

A smile curved her lips. "Wonderful. So would I."

Anthony leaned in, his voice dropping to a murmur, his breath warm against her ear. "Careful, Elodie," he whispered. "You are making it sound as if you enjoy my company."

The closeness of him, the gentleness of his voice, sent a

flutter of nerves through her. She willed herself to remain composed, lifting her chin slightly. "Then I must have misspoken," she replied, her voice steady despite the warmth creeping up her cheeks.

Anthony took a step back and bowed. "Until later, Elodie."

Dressed in his finery, Anthony exited his bedchamber and headed down the corridor. He was looking forward to dinner with Elodie and her family. In truth, he looked forward to any time he spent with Elodie.

But first he needed to wish Emma goodnight.

He made his way to the nursery, pushing open the door quietly. Inside, the sight that greeted him made him smile. Emma stood in the center of the room, her small frame commanding the attention of two rambunctious puppies. Her fingers pointed sternly at them.

"Lay down," she ordered.

The puppies paid her no heed. They jumped up on her with excited barks, their tails wagging furiously. Emma let out a frustrated sigh, her pout deepening.

Anthony leaned against the doorframe and chuckled. "It seems bedtime training isn't going quite as planned."

Emma spun around. "I am trying to train them to lay down, but they won't listen."

He walked into the room. "Do you have any treats to encourage them?" he asked, crouching down to pet one of the energetic pups.

She offered him a sheepish smile. "I saved some scraps from my dinner."

"That is brilliant," Anthony praised. "But training can wait until tomorrow. Right now, it is time for bed."

Emma moved to the bed, patting the spot beside her. The puppies leaped onto the bed and nestled beside her.

"Shall we read more of *Little Red Riding Hood*?" Anthony asked, retrieving the book from the shelf.

"Yes, please!" Emma exclaimed.

Anthony settled on the edge of the bed, gently nudging the puppies aside to make room. As he began to read, Emma rested her head against his arm. His heart stirred at the simple gesture. Moments like these—simple, tender, and unguarded— were the ones he cherished most.

He finished the chapter and closed the book. "That is all for tonight," he said. "Goodnight, Emma."

Emma slid under the covers, her head sinking into the plush pillow. "Goodnight, Uncle Anthony."

Anthony leaned over and blew out the candle, the room falling into a gentle darkness. He tucked the covers around Emma and whispered, "Sweet dreams." Then he turned and quietly exited the nursery.

As he descended the grand staircase, the soft light from the sconces cast shadows across the marble entry hall, where Percy stood waiting, an unusual solemnity on his face. "My lord," he said, extending a folded paper towards him. "A letter just arrived. It was delivered to the back door by a street urchin."

Anthony's brow furrowed as he accepted the letter. Unfolding it, his eyes scanned the words.

I know all about Lady Elodie and Lord Montrose's tryst. Ten thousand pounds will buy my silence. Secure the money and I will be in touch.

A surge of anger coursed through him, and he crumpled the note tightly in his fist. "Where is this street urchin now?" he asked.

Percy offered him an apologetic look. "He is gone. We gave him some bread and sent him on his way. Is there a problem?"

"No," Anthony replied, forcing calm in his tone, though his mind raced. "But if another letter arrives, I want to speak with the messenger directly."

Percy nodded his understanding. "Yes, my lord."

At that moment, the main door opened with a sudden bang, and Stephen staggered into the hall, his clothes disheveled, his eyes unfocused. He met Anthony's gaze with a hazy determination. "Good. You are here. I am going to meet that chit now."

Anthony frowned. "You are drunk," he stated, shoving the crumpled note into his jacket pocket.

"That doesn't matter," Stephen slurred defiantly, his movements unsteady. "You wanted me to meet my daughter, and I am going to do it. Right now."

Anthony stepped in front of him, blocking his path. "No, Stephen. You are going to go to your bedchamber and sleep this off."

With a scowl, Stephen jabbed a finger at Anthony's chest. "You do not get to dictate my actions, Brother. You may be a viscount, but you have no right to lord over me."

Anthony held his gaze, undeterred. "You do not want to meet your daughter like this."

Stephen spread his arms wide, his body swaying. "Why not? This is the real me. A drunk, a wastrel, a cad. Is that not what you think of me?"

"This is not the time to have this discussion," Anthony responded, trying to keep his tone even.

Stephen leaned in closer, his eyes narrowing. "I am the black sheep of this family. I embarrass you. Admit it."

Anthony shook his head. "Go sleep it off, Stephen. We will talk in the morning."

"I don't want to wait until morning!" Stephen shouted. "I

want to talk about this now. It is..." He burped loudly. "...
important."

With a glance at the long clock in the corner, Anthony said,
"As much as I would love to continue this discussion, I have
dinner plans with Lady Elodie and her family."

Stephen took a step back, a mocking smile tugging at his
lips. "That is fine. I will meet my daughter without you, then."

"You will do no such thing," Anthony asserted.

"And why not?" Stephen asked, folding his arms. "Emily is
my daughter. I can see her whenever I want."

Anthony looked heavenward, stifling his frustration. "Her
name is *Emma*. And she is asleep."

Stephen moved to brush past him. "Then I will wake her
up. I am sure she will want to meet her father."

Moving to block his path, Anthony responded, "No."

Stephen raised a brow, his eyes flashing with indignation. "I
beg your pardon?"

"You are not going to see her, not like this," Anthony
responded. "She deserves better."

"I will tell her what she deserves, not you," Stephen
sneered.

As they glared at one another, their mother's voice cut
through the tension. "Perhaps you two can continue this
conversation in the drawing room."

Stephen's smirk faded, and he shrugged with feigned obedi-
ence. "Yes, Mother."

Anthony followed his brother into the drawing room,
waiting as their mother closed the door firmly behind them.
She looked at each of them in turn, her expression stern. "Have
you both forgotten yourselves? There are prying ears everywhere in this house."

Stephen straightened, adopting an innocent expression. "I
merely want to visit my daughter and Anthony is refusing to let
me do so."

Their mother leveled a steady gaze at him. "He is right. You are in no state to do so."

Stephen huffed. "I should have known you would take his side."

"I am not taking sides," their mother responded, her tone firm. "I am pleased that you want to finally meet your daughter, but she retired nearly an hour ago."

Throwing his arms up, Stephen said, "I finally decided to meet Esther, and now I am refused."

Their mother sighed. "Her name is *Emma*, not Esther. And I am not refusing you—"

"Yes, you are!" Stephen bellowed. "I do not know why I bother! Nothing I do will ever be good enough for this family."

"Stephen..." their mother started.

He headed for the door, waving off her concern. "If I cannot see her, I might as well go back out. Do not wait up for me."

"We never do," Anthony muttered under his breath, watching his brother's unsteady retreat.

Their mother made a move to follow Stephen, her face etched with worry, but Anthony gently placed his hand on her arm. "Let him go, Mother," he urged softly. "There is no point in trying to reason with him when he is in this state."

Her shoulders drooped in resignation. "You are right, of course."

Seeing the sadness in her eyes pained him. It was evident that her disappointment in Stephen weighed heavily on her, and Anthony hated that she had been forced to intervene. "I am sorry you had to step in."

She managed a weak smile, though her eyes remained filled with sorrow. "For a moment, I thought you two might come to blows over it."

"If that is what it took to keep him away from Emma tonight, I would have done it."

His mother looked out the window. "When will he learn?"

Anthony hesitated, torn between staying with his mother and honoring his dinner plans with Elodie. But before he could speak, she turned back to him and asked, "Shouldn't you be leaving for dinner?"

"Yes," he admitted, "but I can stay—"

"You will do no such thing!" she interrupted firmly. "You deserve to enjoy yourself, Anthony. This conversation can wait until tomorrow. Or, better yet, never."

He chuckled despite himself. "I think it is inevitable, Mother."

"It is the same conversation, over and over. Until Stephen wants to change, there is little that we can do for him."

Anthony leaned in to kiss her cheek. "You are a good mother. Do not forget that."

"I love you," she murmured, patting his hand. "Now, go. It is rude to be late."

He did not need to be told twice. He slipped out the main door, his steps quick and purposeful as he made his way to Elodie's townhouse. When he arrived, he knocked, and the butler promptly welcomed him, gesturing towards the drawing room.

Stepping into the warmly lit room, he found Elodie seated on the settee, focused on her embroidery. She wore a pale pink gown, her hair piled high atop her head with two curls framing her face. When she looked up, her face lit up with a smile that made warmth blossom in his chest.

"Anthony, you are here," she greeted.

He returned her smile, feeling all his worries momentarily melt away. "I am."

Elodie held up her embroidery. "What do you think?"

Anthony leaned closer, studying the delicate stitching. "It appears to be a very small waistcoat."

"Precisely," she replied, pride evident in her tone. "Do you think Lulu will love it?"

Anthony took a seat next to her. "Lulu is a dog. He has no need for clothing."

Elodie lowered the tiny waistcoat to her lap, undeterred. "Just think of how distinguished Lulu will look now. I should probably make one for Spot as well."

"Is that really necessary?"

"Yes, it is! We would not want Spot to grow jealous of Lulu's fine attire," she quipped.

Anthony chuckled. "You do realize, of course, that we are talking about dogs?"

Before Elodie could respond, Bennett's voice came from the doorway. "There is no point in trying to argue with Elodie. Once she has an idea in her head, she is determined to see it through."

Anthony stood as Bennett and his wife, Delphine, entered the room. He greeted them with a polite nod. "My lady," he said respectfully.

Delphine waved a hand. "There is no need for such formalities here. From what I hear, you are practically family."

"That is kind of you to say," Anthony said.

Delphine turned to Elodie, her eyes twinkling. "That waistcoat is adorable. I have no doubt that Lulu will love it."

Bennett leaned in, murmuring to his wife, "Let's not encourage her."

"I am merely speaking the truth," Delphine responded.

Elodie beamed with satisfaction. "Thank you, Delphine. I am glad someone understands my vision. Perhaps I should start a line of clothing for the sophisticated dog."

Bennett raised an eyebrow. "You know Father would never let you start a business."

"Why not?" Elodie countered. "Delphine runs a business, and she is quite successful."

Delphine gave Elodie an encouraging smile. "Indeed, I am.

And I do not see why you should not pursue it if it brings you joy."

"But making clothes for dogs..." Bennett began.

"*Sophisticated* dogs," Elodie interrupted with a gleam in her eyes.

"... is not a true business," Bennett finished.

Winston's voice came from the doorway. "I think it is a brilliant idea," he declared as he strode into the room.

Bennett turned to face his brother. "You do?" he asked, his tone skeptical.

Winston nodded, placing a hand over his heart with exaggerated sincerity. "And let it be known that I, Winston, wholeheartedly support our sister's dream."

"This isn't a dream. It is a passing whim," Bennett pointed out.

Elodie rose from her seat. "As much as I disagree with Bennett," she paused, casting a mock-critical glance over his attire, "and with what he is wearing, he is right. This is not my dream."

Bennett glanced down at his finely tailored clothing. "What is wrong with what I am wearing?"

Elodie gave a dramatic sigh. "If I have to tell you, you are past hope."

Delphine patted Bennett's arm. "I did try to warn you about that waistcoat color."

"It is jonquil, and I will have you know it is the height of fashion right now," Bennett defended as he buttoned his jacket.

Lady Dallington swept into the room. "Leave poor Bennett alone. He looks perfectly presentable."

"Just presentable?" Bennett muttered under his breath.

Turning towards Winston, Lady Dallington asked, "Will Mattie be joining us for dinner this evening?"

Winston's smile faded slightly. "I'm afraid not. She is not feeling well."

Lady Dallington's expression softened. "I will have a tray sent up for her at once," she said. "Shall we all adjourn to the dining room?"

Anthony stepped forward, offering his arm to Elodie. "May I have the honor of escorting you to the dining room?"

Elodie took his arm. "Did Emma manage to teach the puppies any new tricks?"

He chuckled. "No, but not for a lack of trying."

"She is a sweet girl," Elodie remarked.

"That she is," he agreed, leading her towards the dining room.

As they walked, Anthony felt the weight of the crumpled letter in his jacket pocket, the reminder of its contents casting a faint shadow over his mood. He knew he needed to speak to Elodie about it soon, but he did not want to ruin the evening. Perhaps it would be best if he spoke to Bennett and Winston first. They needed to know about the threat. Together, the three of them could determine the best course of action to ensure Elodie's safety without alarming her unnecessarily.

Elodie glanced up at him. "Is everything all right?"

He forced a smile to his lips. "Of course. Perfectly."

"You seem bothered," she remarked. "Or perhaps you are just overwhelmed by Bennett's jonquil waistcoat."

Anthony's lips curved into a genuine smile. "It is certainly... bright."

Elodie bobbed her head. "It could probably guide ships safely into port."

Up ahead, Bennett turned his head and said, "I can hear you, Sister."

"Good," Elodie replied, stifling a laugh. "At least the brilliance of your waistcoat has not affected your hearing."

They stepped into the dining room, and Anthony guided Elodie to her seat. Once she was situated, he sat down next to her. He leaned closer and whispered, "You look lovely this evening."

Rather than deflect the compliment, her cheeks tinged with the faintest blush. "Thank you."

He tilted his head. "What? No witty retort?"

Elodie laughed softly. "I cannot risk becoming too predictable, now can I?"

Anthony leaned back, a satisfied grin on his face. "I can assure you, Elodie, you are the least predictable person I know."

And he meant it.

That was one of the many things he loved about her.

Love?

The realization struck him. He was not halfway in love with her. No, not anymore. He had fallen for Elodie—deeply, irrevocably. Every laugh, every clever retort, every smile that lit up her face had slowly but surely woven its way into his heart, leaving him with a certainty he could not ignore.

He loved Elodie. And there was no going back.

12

E lodie leaned out of her bedchamber window, watching as Anthony tossed sticks across the lawn for the puppies. She laughed softly as the energetic pups eagerly fetched the sticks but, time and time again, failed to return them. Instead, they darted off, sticks clamped in their tiny jaws, forcing Anthony to chase them down with playful exasperation.

As she watched him, Elodie felt a strange, unexpected warmth blossom in her chest. Anthony was truly remarkable. He had a kindness to him, a natural ability to make her laugh and lift her spirits. Though he still vexed her at times, she was beginning to see him in a different light. But being attracted to Anthony would not do, especially when what she wanted desperately was to dislike him.

At that moment, Anthony glanced up at her window, catching her gaze. A bright smile spread across his face as he raised a hand in greeting. Elodie's cheeks flushed, and she waved back, feeling oddly flustered at having been caught staring. Quickly, she took a step back from the window, retreating from his view just as a soft knock sounded at the door.

"Good morning, my lady," Molly greeted as she stepped inside. "A guest has arrived to see you."

"A guest? At this hour?"

Molly grinned. "You overslept this morning and missed breakfast."

"Oh, I had not realized," Elodie said.

Molly walked over to the wardrobe and pulled out a pale green gown with a delicate net overlay. "This should be perfect for today," she said, draping it across the bed.

Elodie took a seat at her dressing table as Molly removed her cap and began brushing her long blonde hair, quickly but skillfully arranging it into an elegant chignon. "Who has come to call?" she asked as Molly pinned the last of her curls in place.

"A Lady Eugenie."

Shifting in her chair, Elodie asked, "And what of Lord Westcott?"

Molly gave her a blank look. "What of him?"

"Did he not accompany his sister?" Elodie inquired.

Her lady's maid shook her head. "Lady Eugenie and her maid arrived only moments ago," she informed her. "Were you expecting Lord Westcott?"

"No, but I am just surprised that Lady Eugenie is here to see me. We barely know one another."

"Well, perhaps you two will become the best of friends."

Elodie smiled at that thought, though it struck her as unlikely. "I do not think we should get ahead of ourselves. She has only come to call."

Rising, Elodie approached the bed and removed her night-gown. She slipped the gown on, and Molly started the ardent task of fastening the buttons on the back of Elodie's gown.

With a final, gentle tug on the gown, Molly finished fastening the last buttons. "Will there be anything else, my lady?"

"No, but thank you. I am going to meet with Lady Eugenie," Elodie said as she walked over to the door.

As she descended to the main level, Elodie's thoughts lingered on Lady Eugenie's unexpected visit. She reached the drawing room and found Lady Eugenie seated comfortably on the settee, deeply engrossed in a book. Her finger marked her place, her brows knitted in concentration.

"Lady Eugenie," Elodie greeted.

Lady Eugenie held up one finger, her eyes never leaving the page. "Just a moment."

Elodie took a seat beside her, waiting patiently. After a few long moments, Lady Eugenie turned the page with a nod of satisfaction and looked up. "I apologize, but I had to finish that page."

Elodie smiled. "Is that the same book from yesterday?"

Lady Eugenie laughed. "Oh, heavens, no. I finished that one yesterday. Now I am nearly done with this one. I do so love reading."

"As do I," Elodie replied, "though it takes me several days to truly absorb a good book. I do not read as quickly as you do."

Lady Eugenie slipped the book into her reticule and leaned in, her expression growing solemn. Lowering her voice, she said, "I wanted to thank you for not telling my brother the true story of how we met."

Elodie waved her hand. "Your secret is safe with me."

"I cannot tell you how much I appreciate it," Lady Eugenie said. "I also never did have the chance to properly thank you for saving me from Lord Montrose."

"There is no need to thank me."

"Oh, but there is," Lady Eugenie asserted. "I would have been ruined and it would have been entirely my fault."

Finding herself curious, Elodie asked, "If I may ask, why did you agree to go into the gardens with Lord Montrose?"

Lady Eugenie looked away, embarrassment coloring her

cheeks. "I fell for his charm. The way he spoke to me—it made me feel... seen, in a way I had not felt in a long time."

"Do not be too hard on yourself," Elodie reassured her. "From what I have heard, lots of women have been fooled by his 'charming act.'"

Lady Eugenie sighed. "But I knew of his reputation and still followed him blindly into the gardens. I should have been more sensible."

Elodie offered her a reassuring smile. "Well, it all worked out and no one else is the wiser."

"That is not entirely true," Lady Eugenie replied. "My brother informed me of Lord Montrose's wager in the betting book at White's."

"I would not give that wager much heed."

"I try not to, but it bothers me that Lord Montrose has been calling you a 'shrew.'" Lady Eugenie fidgeted with her hands, guilt flickering in her eyes. "You may be the diamond of the Season, but no one is untouchable."

Elodie poured tea from the service on the table, offering Lady Eugenie a cup. "Would you care for some tea?"

"Tea?" Lady Eugenie repeated. "How can you even think of tea at a time like this?"

Elodie let out a small laugh. "It is rather simple. I pour, I sip —it is a very easy process."

Lady Eugenie pressed a hand to her forehead, visibly frustrated. "I am sorry. I feel terrible for putting you in this position. It is entirely my fault that Lord Montrose turned his attention to you."

"None of this is your fault," Elodie said, handing her the cup. "Now, let us drink our tea, shall we?"

"I do not think I can," Lady Eugenie admitted, lowering the cup to her lap. "I am feeling too discombobulated."

Elodie met Lady Eugenie's gaze. "One little mishap is not

going to define me. Lord Montrose's words are just that... words."

"But he is a very convincing man."

As Elodie lifted her teacup to take a sip, White stepped in with a small, formal bow. "Lord Westcott has come to call, my lady."

Lady Eugenie's eyes went wide. "My brother must not know that I am here."

"I think it is a bit late for that," Elodie said.

Glancing frantically around the room, Lady Eugenie's eyes landed on the large windows. "I will slip out through the windows. He would be none the wiser."

Elodie gave her a bemused look. "I do not think that is wise. Surely, he saw your maid in the entry hall."

Lady Eugenie's shoulders slumped. "You are right. But how are we to explain my presence here?"

An idea formed in Elodie's mind, and she gave Lady Eugenie an encouraging nod. "Leave that to me. Just follow my lead." She turned to White, who had been waiting patiently for her response. "Please, send in Lord Westcott."

Moments later, Lord Westcott entered, looking polished in a blue jacket and buff trousers, his confidence slightly dimming when he spotted his sister. "Eugenie," he greeted, his tone laced with surprise. "What are you doing here?"

Before Lady Eugenie could respond, Elodie spoke up. "I invited her," she said. "We both share a love of books, and I thought it would be wonderful to discuss them together."

Lord Westcott's surprise softened into a smile. "My sister does have rather strong opinions on books."

Gesturing to a nearby chair, Elodie asked, "Would you care to join us, my lord?"

"I would be delighted," he said as he sat down on the proffered chair.

Elodie reached for the teapot. "Would you care for a cup of tea? Or perhaps you have already had your fill for the day?"

Lord Westcott chuckled. "No, tea sounds wonderful. Thank you."

She poured the tea, extending the cup to him, and he accepted it with a nod of gratitude, taking a sip. A brief silence followed as they sipped their tea, the room settling into an unexpectedly awkward quiet. Elodie's mind scrambled for a topic, and she blurted the first thing that came to mind. "The weather is rather lovely this morning, is it not?"

Elodie felt like a simpleton. Good heavens. Who actually cares about the weather?

Fortunately, Lord Westcott seemed to take pity on her. "Yes, indeed. It was a beautiful morning."

Just then, Lady Eugenie abruptly rose. "Well, I should be returning home now. I have much that needs to be done today."

Elodie stood as well. "Must you leave so soon?"

"Yes," Lady Eugenie replied, casting a fleeting glance at her brother. "I do not wish to intrude any longer."

"Nonsense," Elodie assured her. "I have enjoyed our time together. You need not rush off."

Lady Eugenie offered her a grateful smile. "I shall call upon you again, assuming you have no objections."

"I have none."

"Good," Lady Eugenie said, a hint of playfulness returning to her voice. "Next time, I will talk your ear off about books." She turned to her brother with a smile. "Brother, I shall see you at home."

Lord Westcott tipped his head as his sister departed. "I am not quite sure why she was in such a hurry to leave."

A maid stepped into the room for propriety's sake and hurried over to a chair in the corner.

Elodie leaned forward, setting her teacup onto the table. "Your sister is delightful."

"That is one word for her," Lord Westcott muttered.

She tilted her head, curiosity piqued. "Are you two not close?"

Lord Westcott's smile turned rueful. "I love my sister dearly, but we are quite different. She is a self-proclaimed bluestocking, and I worry that she will end up a spinster without a second thought about it."

"Do you take issue with her being a bluestocking?"

Lord Westcott sighed, a hint of resignation in his expression. "No, not at all. Our mother instilled in us a love of learning. But we each have a duty—"

Elodie groaned, interrupting him. "I detest that word. My father is constantly reminding me of what my 'duty' is to myself and this family."

"We were born into this gilded life, and with that comes a responsibility to abide by Society's contract."

"I prefer to live my life the way I see fit," Elodie replied firmly.

"That is a dangerous way to live," Lord Westcott remarked.

Elodie smirked, her gaze steady. "Is it, though?"

Lord Westcott gave her an amused look. "You are the diamond of the Season. All the debutantes are looking to you on how to act."

Her eyes widened in mock horror. "Dear heavens, then they are in serious trouble," Elodie quipped. "Because, quite frankly, I have not the faintest idea what I am doing."

Lady Dallington entered the room, and Lord Westcott immediately stood, offering her a respectful bow.

"Lord Westcott," her mother greeted. "What a pleasant surprise."

He inclined his head. "My lady."

Her mother settled beside Elodie, her attention turning to Lord Westcott with keen interest. She launched into a flurry of questions.

Elodie could not help but smile as her mother took hold of the conversation. Taking advantage of the chance to sit back, she sipped her tea, enjoying the warmth of the cup in her hand. This allowed her a moment to observe Lord Westcott as he gracefully answered each of her mother's questions, his responses measured and polite, with a hint of charm.

She had to admit that Lord Westcott was not awful. But that is all she was willing to admit... for now.

Anthony sat in the dimly lit corner at White's, holding a drink as he waited for his friends. The club was quieter than usual, a handful of gentlemen scattered across the room, speaking in low tones or reading the newssheets. The calm suited him. He needed discretion, and White's offered the perfect mix of privacy and familiarity.

He had informed Bennett and Winston that he had to speak to them at once but wanted to do so in private. Although he knew he should tell Elodie about the threat he had received, he dreaded her reaction.

Bennett and Winston entered the club together and made their way to the corner of the hall. Bennett was the first to speak. "Now, what is so urgent that you had to speak to us immediately?"

Anthony gestured to the chairs across from him. "Have a seat, and I will explain."

As Winston settled in his seat, he raised an eyebrow. "And why here, of all places? Could you not simply walk a few feet to our townhouse? We are neighbors, after all."

"I wanted this conversation to be in private," Anthony replied with a glance around the hall. Bennett smirked. "You know, we do have doors at home."

Anthony set his glass down and leaned forward. "I received a threatening letter last night. It concerns Elodie."

All traces of humor left Bennett's face as he asked, "What did it say?"

Reaching into his jacket pocket, Anthony removed the crumpled letter, handing it over. "See for yourself."

Bennett's eyes narrowed as he read the letter. "Blazes," he muttered under his breath before passing it to his brother.

Winston's face turned grave as he read, then looked up. "Do you have any idea of who sent this?"

Anthony shrugged slightly. "It could be anyone."

Bennett leaned in, his voice low. "Did anyone witness your altercation with Lord Montrose in the gardens that night?"

"Not that I am aware of," Anthony replied. "However, I was rather preoccupied with handling an unconscious Montrose. There could have been someone nearby. Someone that did not make themselves known."

Winston dropped the crumpled letter onto the table. "Could Montrose himself have sent it?"

"To what end?" Anthony asked. "Besides, he does not seem the type to advertise his own disgrace."

"What of the young woman that Lord Montrose was trying to take advantage of?" Winston inquired.

"Lady Eugenie," Anthony said. "If her involvement were revealed, her reputation would be in tatters. I doubt she is playing a part in this."

Bennett pressed his lips thoughtfully. "I think it would be in Elodie's best interest if we paid them off."

Anthony's jaw tightened. "Ten thousand pounds is no small sum."

"No," Bennett agreed, his voice steady. "But I do not want to risk having Elodie being ruined."

Winston shook his head. "If you bow to this blackmailer now, what is to stop him from demanding more? I suggest hiring a Bow Street Runner to investigate. Fortunately, I know just the man."

Anthony arched a brow. "You are acquainted with a Bow Street Runner?"

Winston nodded. "Yes, Grady. He helped me with a delicate matter before. He is discreet and effective."

Anthony had to admit that Winston had a point. If they paid the ransom, it could lead to more demands, a never-ending cycle. "Very well, I would like to speak to this Bow Street Runner."

"I will arrange it," Winston said.

Bennett regarded Anthony with a curious expression. "Why was the letter sent to you? Why not to us, her family?"

"That is a good point," Anthony admitted. "It is strange. I am not quite sure why I was singled out."

A lanky server approached the table and took their drink orders. Once he was out of earshot, Winston asked, "Does Elodie know about the letter?"

Anthony winced. "No, I have not told her."

"I think that is for the best," Winston replied.

"You do?" Anthony asked.

Winston bobbed his head. "There is no need to alarm her, not until we have got this sorted out."

Anthony picked up his glass, swirling the contents. "I am not sure that is the right approach. Elodie is no wilting flower. She does not need to be coddled."

"Why worry her unnecessarily?" Winston asked.

Bennett interjected, "I agree with Winston. Let's keep this from her, at least for now. If we can solve it quietly, then she will be none the wiser, and her reputation will remain intact."

Anthony took a long sip from his glass as he considered their words. Though a part of him bristled at the idea of withholding this from Elodie, another part recognized the sense in it. Why worry her when this could be dealt with?

His thoughts were interrupted by Winston muttering, "Speak of the devil."

Anthony turned and saw Montrose striding towards their table, a smug smirk stretching across his lips.

"Good afternoon, gentlemen," Montrose greeted, his voice laced with mock civility. "How are you on this fine day?"

Anthony barely concealed his irritation, refusing to entertain Montrose's forced pleasantries. "What do you want, Montrose?"

"Nothing but the pleasure of your company," Montrose remarked.

Bennett shot up from his seat. "Go away. No one wants you here."

Montrose placed a hand over his chest with dramatic flair. "That is disappointing since we will be family soon enough."

"Elodie will never marry you," Bennett growled, his hands balling into tight fists.

"Should we not let *her* decide whom she will marry?" Montrose asked, his voice laced with amusement.

Bennett took a threatening step forward, but Winston's hand shot out, stopping him. "He is not worth it," Winston cautioned.

Montrose chuckled dryly, turning his gaze to Anthony with a glint of challenge. "What say you, Belview?"

Anthony's jaw tightened, anger simmering beneath his calm exterior. "Elodie will never be yours."

Leaning in, Montrose lowered his voice. "I will let you in on a secret. I always get what I want. Lady Elodie will be no exception."

"Not this time," Anthony asserted.

A taunting smile came to Montrose's lips. "Ah, so you want Lady Elodie for yourself? I have seen the way you look at her. It is rather revolting, if you ask me."

"No one asked you," Anthony said firmly.

Montrose's lips quirked, as if savoring every ounce of irritation he provoked. "You and your brother are no different. Both yearning for things you can never have."

Anthony rose from his chair, meeting Montrose's gaze with steely resolve. "I am nothing like my brother."

"Your actions suggest otherwise," Montrose replied.

Through clenched teeth, Anthony said, "I imagine you would know all about poor choices, considering your long history with Stephen."

Montrose's smirk faltered momentarily. "That is in the past."

"Were you not his second at that infamous duel?" Anthony pressed.

Montrose scoffed, his tone defensive. "I had little choice."

"Everyone has a choice," Anthony shot back. "You simply chose poorly."

Montrose moved closer until he was mere inches away, his voice a low snarl. "And I suppose you know plenty about choosing poorly?"

"And what is that supposed to mean?" Anthony demanded, fighting the urge to recoil as Montrose's foul breath lingered uncomfortably close.

"Stephen is a scoundrel, and yet you do nothing to rein him in. Word has it he even has a daughter hidden away."

"Stephen is his own man," Anthony responded.

Montrose shook his head, his tone mocking. "You are weak, Belview. And that will not serve you well in the House of Lords."

Before Anthony could reply, Winston interjected. "You are causing a scene, both of you."

Anthony glanced around, realizing that several club members were watching the exchange with keen interest. Reluctantly, he took a step back. "Leave, Montrose. If I had my way, you would be blackballed from White's."

Montrose adjusted the lapels of his jacket with exaggerated indifference. "Good thing your opinion means little to me." He gave a brisk nod. "Good day."

With one final, self-satisfied smirk, Montrose turned on his heel and strolled out.

As Anthony returned to his seat, he said, "I cannot abide that man."

"At least you had the pleasure of hitting him," Bennett remarked with a half-smile.

The server approached the table with a tray of drinks in his hand. He set them down, quickly excusing himself.

"We need to ensure that Montrose stays far away from Elodie," Anthony said.

"I have already instructed White to deny Montrose entry into our home," Bennett informed them.

Winston reached for his glass, his expression resolute. "And Bennett and I have already formed a plan on keeping Elodie away from Montrose at social events."

"That is good," Anthony responded.

Bennett met Anthony's gaze. "You are nothing like your brother, Belview. Do not let Montrose's words dig at you."

Anthony rubbed a hand over the back of his neck. "I know I am not like Stephen, but Montrose was right on one thing. I have done nothing to rein Stephen in."

"Stephen is not the type of person to be reined in," Bennett said. "He will always do exactly as he pleases, regardless of what anyone else thinks."

"That is precisely it," Anthony said with a sigh. "By standing idly by, I am as good as condoning it. Perhaps I am part of the problem."

Bennett moved to sit on the edge of his seat. "You are doing the best that you can, considering the hand that you have been dealt."

"It is not enough, not anymore," Anthony said, rising. "By allowing his behavior, I am complicit."

Winston followed suit and rose. "You are being too hard on yourself. Stay and have a drink with us."

Anthony clasped a hand on Winston's shoulder. "You are both good friends, but I have a few things I need to see to at home."

Winston looked as if he had more to say, but instead, he simply nodded. "Very well. Just remember, you can run, but you can't hide. We will finish this conversation someday."

"Hopefully not," Anthony said as he lowered his hand.

Leaving White's, Anthony had an immense desire to speak to Elodie. Somehow, she had a way of understanding him without needing to say a word. Her presence was a quiet balm he craved more than he cared to admit.

Perhaps calling upon her was not the worst idea.

13

A fter an endless stream of gentlemen callers that afternoon, Elodie was exhausted and longed for a nap. How did anyone function without one? She had asked herself that question several times over, particularly as she endured the endless drivel coming from her suitors.

Her mother, seated beside her on the settee, patted her hand approvingly. "You did well, Dear."

Elodie gave a weary sigh. "If I hear one more comment about the weather, I might actually die from boredom," she muttered. "Thank heavens it is finally over."

But no sooner had the words left her lips than White stepped into the room. "Lord Danbury and Mr. Thomas have come to call upon Lady Elodie."

Elodie resisted the urge to groan. She wanted to send them away, but a glance at her mother told her that such a thing would never be permitted.

As she anticipated, her mother said, "Please, send them in."

"There is no point," Elodie whispered. "I would never consider either of these men to be my suitor."

Her mother gave her a gentle but firm look. "We must not be rude."

White departed, and moments later, Lord Danbury and Mr. Thomas entered, bowing in unison with murmured greetings.

Elodie forced a polite smile onto her lips. "Please, join us."

Lord Danbury took the seat beside her and offered her a private smile. "You are looking particularly lovely this afternoon, my lady."

"Thank you," Elodie replied, not knowing what else she could say. Or even wanted to say. She did not want to encourage Lord Danbury.

Mr. Thomas, meanwhile, sat across from her and waggled his eyebrows. "I must agree with Lord Danbury. You are indeed looking lovely today."

"That is kind of you," Elodie murmured, wondering how long she would have to endure their company.

Lord Danbury settled back in his seat, his expression turning thoughtful. "As I walked here, I could not help but notice the weather. Quite lovely, is it not?"

Elodie stifled the urge to roll her eyes, knowing a lecture on her manners would surely follow if she did. She replied with mock enthusiasm, "Oh, do tell me more about the weather."

In response, Lord Danbury gave her a baffled look. "Pardon?"

"I do so love speaking about the weather. It is my favorite," Elodie said, feigning interest.

"Well... it was cloudy, but I did see the sun peeking through for a moment," Lord Danbury continued.

Elodie clasped her hands together, maintaining her act. "How delightful! Such a rare and special sight in London, especially this time of year."

Mr. Thomas seized the opportunity to contribute. "I rather enjoy the sun myself," he said, puffing up as though he had made a profound statement.

"And what, exactly, do you enjoy about the sun?" Elodie asked.

Mr. Thomas scratched his chin thoughtfully. "I suppose it is because it is so... bright and round."

Elodie had to bite back a laugh, struggling to maintain her composure. *Bright and round?* Did he truly think that would impress her? She kept her voice steady as she replied, "The moon is bright and round, too."

Mr. Thomas bobbed his head. "Yes, I suppose it is. I do enjoy round balls."

A giggle escaped her, and she quickly brought her hand up to her mouth. "My apologies. I am just delighted to know you enjoy round balls."

Her mother shot her a warning look, swiftly intervening. "Would anyone care for a cup of tea?"

"Yes, please," Mr. Thomas replied, seeming unruffled.

Knowing what was expected of her, Elodie retrieved the teapot, pouring tea for everyone before reclaiming her seat.

Lord Danbury took a sip of his tea and lowered the cup to his lap. "Have you finished the waistcoat that you were making for your dog?"

Elodie smiled proudly. "I have, indeed."

He gave a slight nod, though his tone held a note of disdain. "Personally, I think it is rather foolish to put clothes on a dog. But if it amuses you, then so be it."

"That is kind of you, but I do have other interests," Elodie said. "Russian literature among them."

Lord Danbury bristled. "Russian literature is far too dark and carries an overwhelming depressive tone."

"True," Elodie conceded. "But I find it reflects more honesty than most novels. At least, the parts I understand."

Mr. Thomas perked up, leaning forward. "Have you read *Sermons to Young Women* by James Fordyce? My sister devours it."

Elodie nodded. "I have, but I must say, I find it dreadfully dull."

"Dull?" Mr. Thomas repeated in disbelief. "Perhaps you are not reading it correctly."

"Ah, that must be it," Elodie said, her tone dry. "I do tend to misread books."

Her humor was lost on Mr. Thomas, who simply smiled. "Women's minds are easily distracted. It is not really your fault. It is more of a weakness of the gender, would you not agree?"

Elodie tried to maintain her composure at that idiotic remark, but she felt her patience was stretched perilously thin.

Fortunately, at that precise moment, White stepped into the room and announced, "Lord Belview has come to call, my ladies."

Relief flooded through Elodie, and a genuine smile came to her lips. "Please send him in," she said eagerly, perhaps too eagerly.

Moments later, Anthony stepped into the room with a smile on his lips as his gaze sought out hers. She felt a sense of calm settle over her, an ease she had not realized she had been missing all afternoon.

He bowed. "Lady Dallington. Lady Elodie," he greeted.

Elodie tipped her head. "Lord Belview."

Anthony took a seat next to Mr. Thomas. "I fear I may have missed a riveting discussion on the fine weather we are having this Season," he said with a wink.

"You did, my lord," Elodie replied.

"Then I shall endeavor to introduce a topic of equal fascination," Anthony mused. "Perhaps a detailed analysis of the state of your gardens."

Elodie smiled into her cup as she took a sip of her tea. "I prefer if we discussed something else. Truly, any other topic would suffice."

Anthony feigned consideration, tapping a finger against his

chin. "Well, I could regale you with the latest developments in agricultural trade. Did you know the price of a bushel of hay has increased significantly? Though I suspect you might find that somewhat boresome."

"A bushel of hay? How fascinating," Elodie joked.

Her mother gently nudged her shoulder, a subtle reminder of her hostess duties. "Elodie, dear, will you not offer Lord Belview a cup of tea?"

"Of course," Elodie replied, setting her teacup down and reaching gracefully for the ornate silver teapot. "Would you care for a cup of tea, my lord?"

"Yes, thank you," Anthony said.

After she poured the tea, she extended the cup towards him, their gloved fingers brushing ever so slightly. A subtle jolt of warmth coursed through her at the contact, catching her off guard. She glanced up, searching his face for any sign he had felt it, too, but Anthony's expression remained the same.

What was wrong with her?

Elodie quickly looked away, chiding herself silently. It was just a simple touch, hardly something to dwell on. Attempting to regain her composure, she retrieved her own teacup and took a sip.

Mr. Thomas rose from his seat, placing his empty teacup onto the tray. "Pardon me, but I must be leaving. Thank you for the tea."

"You are most kindly welcome," Elodie said.

He hesitated for a moment, his gaze lingering on her. "Lady Elodie," he began, "would you care to join me for a carriage ride during the fashionable hour tomorrow?"

Elodie blinked, momentarily caught off guard. Her mind raced as she searched for a reason to decline—any reason—but for once, words escaped her.

Before she could formulate a response, Anthony smoothly interjected, "Unfortunately, Lady Elodie has already agreed to accompany me tomorrow," he said, turning to her with a small, conspiratorial smile. "Is that not right, my lady?"

"Yes... I did already commit to Lord Belview," Elodie rushed out. "I apologize, Mr. Thomas."

Mr. Thomas's expression faltered, disappointment flickering across his features. "I see. Well, perhaps another day then."

After Mr. Thomas departed from the drawing room, Lord Danbury addressed Anthony with a sly smile. "How is your brother?"

Anthony grew tense. "He is well."

"Rumor has it that he has a child," Lord Danbury said. "Is there any truth to that?"

Elodie noticed Anthony's grip tighten on his teacup, his knuckles whitening. A flicker of irritation passed over his features. "That is neither here nor there," he answered in a curt voice.

Lord Danbury's lips curled into a knowing smirk as he pressed on. "It is a straightforward question, is it not? Though, considering your brother's reputation as a rakehell of the highest order, it would not be surprising."

"This is neither the time nor the place to discuss such things," Anthony said, his eyes narrowing ever so slightly.

Sensing the rising tension, Elodie decided to intervene. She set her cup down gently and spoke to Lord Danbury with a composed smile. "I fear that such topics are ill-suited for polite company. My delicate constitution does not favor discussions of scandal."

"My apologies, my lady," Lord Danbury said, though sincerity was notably absent from his tone. "I was merely attempting to make conversation."

"Well, I do think you should work on refining your conversational skills to suit the company you keep," Elodie suggested.

A flicker of surprise crossed his face at her candidness,

quickly replaced by a frown. "I do not wish to overstay my welcome." Rising abruptly, he placed his teacup down with a decisive clink. "Good day, my ladies. Lord Belview."

Once he had departed, Elodie turned her attention to Anthony. "Are you all right?"

Anthony exhaled, releasing some of the tension from his shoulders. "I am, thank you. But sadly, this was not the first time I have fielded questions about Stephen today."

She offered a sympathetic smile. "Well, I do think you could use some good news," she said, reaching for her embroidery. "I finished the waistcoat."

Anthony's eyes held amusement. "Dear heavens, do I even want to see this masterpiece?"

With a flourish, Elodie held up the tiny dark blue waistcoat. "What do you think?"

He leaned in to examine it, a smirk tugging at the corners of his mouth. "It is indeed... a tiny waistcoat."

"Is it not spectacular?" Elodie asked.

Anthony chuckled. "I believe we have different definitions of 'spectacular.'"

She traced a finger over the delicate embroidery. "I do think Lulu will love it. He will look so sophisticated."

"Shall we find out?" Anthony asked, rising from his seat and offering his hand.

Elodie beamed. "I think that is a fine idea," she agreed, placing her hand in his as she stood. "Though it is a shame I have not made one for Spot yet."

"I am sure that Spot will be all right."

Her mother rose as well. "Do not tarry too long in the gardens. I need to speak to Elodie about her questionable behavior with our guests just now."

"Yes, Mother," Elodie said, knowing there would be no escaping the inevitable lecture. But despite what awaited her, she felt no hint of remorse. She had defended Anthony, and she would do it again without hesitation. That is what friends do for one another.

Friend.

The word seemed to catch strangely in her mind. It felt wrong, somehow, to use that word when she thought of Anthony. There was something more there, something that made her heart race. But she pushed the thought away.

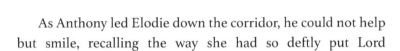

As Anthony led Elodie down the corridor, he could not help but smile, recalling the way she had so deftly put Lord Danbury in his place. He had not needed her to defend him, but the gesture was thoughtful, nonetheless.

Elodie's voice broke through his thoughts. "You are smiling."

"Am I?" he replied, the smile still lingering on his lips. "I was just thinking about how you brought Lord Danbury down a peg or two."

She shrugged lightly. "That was easy. That man is a half-wit."

"I won't disagree with you there," Anthony said. "But I can handle myself. You do not need to risk your reputation for me."

Elodie looked over at him. "You would have done the same for me."

"I would have," Anthony said without hesitation. "In an instant."

"Friends look out for one another, do they not?"

The word "friends" tugged at Anthony in a way that made his heart ache, but he held his tongue. Now was not the time to bring up what he truly felt. Her friendship was precious enough, though it did little to silence the longing for something more.

A footman opened the back door for them, and they stepped into the gardens. Elodie dropped her arm from his but remained close.

Anthony turned to face her. "How was your afternoon?"

Elodie huffed dramatically. "It was awful. It felt like every eligible gentleman in Town was parading through my drawing room."

"Well, you are the diamond of the Season," he teased.

"Yes, but must everyone remind me of it?" Elodie asked. "I daresay that most of my callers seem more interested in the title of 'diamond' than in me."

"I doubt that."

Elodie frowned. "No, it is true. I am nothing special."

Anthony stared at her in astonishment, stepping closer until she looked up to meet his gaze. "Elodie, that is the most absurd thing I have ever heard. You are captivating, unpredictable, and beautiful. Any man would be lucky to call you his own."

A hint of vulnerability appeared in her eyes. "Do you truly believe that?"

"With my whole heart," Anthony replied.

She offered him a weak smile. "You are kind."

Anthony smirked. "That is better than what I was called earlier. Montrose said Stephen and I were two of a kind."

Elodie's eyes went wide. "You are nothing like your brother," she asserted. "You are one of the most honorable men I know."

"You must not know many people," Anthony joked.

She laughed, just as he had intended. "Ignore Montrose. He is a muttonhead."

"Indeed," Anthony said. "Promise me you will stay far away from that infuriating man. He is still hell-bent on marrying you."

"Then he is in for a rude awakening. I have no desire to be known as 'Lady Muttonhead,'" Elodie said.

Without thinking, Anthony reached out, his hand gently resting on her arm. "Thank you, Elodie. You always know precisely what to say to make me feel better."

"That is because I know you."

"And I you," Anthony replied, his voice low. "In fact, I might know you better than I know myself."

Elodie's eyes sparkled with mischief. "That almost sounds like a challenge."

"Not a challenge," Anthony responded. "Just an observation. For instance, when you are happy, truly happy, the faintest dimple appears on your left cheek."

"You have noticed that?"

Anthony nodded, holding her gaze. "I have noticed many things about you over the years."

She bit her lower lip, and his gaze dropped, lingering on her mouth. Her perfectly formed lips. He wanted nothing more than to lean forward and kiss her. But would she welcome it?

Just then, the sound of barking filled the air, breaking the spell. Anthony turned to see the puppies bounding through the gardens.

Elodie's eyes lit up. "It is time for Lulu to try on his waistcoat."

Anthony took a step back, gesturing towards the gate that connected their gardens. "After you, my lady."

Following her through the gate, he watched as Elodie's gaze found Emma playing nearby. She hurried over, crouching down beside the girl with a gentle smile.

"How are you, sweet Emma?" Elodie asked.

Emma grinned up at her. "I am well."

Elodie tilted her head, her tone playful. "Have you taught the puppies any new tricks yet?"

"Not yet," Emma responded.

Holding up the dark blue waistcoat, Elodie asked, "Do you think Lulu will like this?"

Emma giggled. "It is so tiny!"

"Well, Lulu is only a puppy," Elodie pointed out.

Anthony stepped forward, gathering the squirming Lulu in his arms. "Shall we see if Lulu likes the waistcoat?" he asked, holding the pup out to Elodie.

Elodie carefully slipped the waistcoat over Lulu's head and guided his little paws through the openings. Once the waistcoat was in place, Anthony set him down, and Lulu wasted no time pouncing on Spot, tail wagging wildly.

"He doesn't seem to mind it at all," Anthony noted.

Clasping her hands together, Elodie gushed, "Just look at him! Is he not the cutest thing?"

Elodie had barely finished speaking when Stephen staggered out of the townhouse, his sharp gaze landing on Emma. His eyes narrowed, a flicker of something dark crossing his face.

"Is that her?" Stephen asked, his tone dripping with disdain.

Anthony immediately moved to block his path. "Not now, Stephen. Do not do this here." Stephen scoffed. "You wanted me to meet the chit, did you not? Well, I am here."

"You are drunk... again," Anthony remarked.

Stephen leaned in, his breath reeking of whiskey. "Here is a little secret for you, Brother. I am always drunk. It is the only way I can tolerate you."

"Is this really the impression you want to leave on your daughter?"

"Does it matter?" Stephen asked, shoving past him.

Ignoring Anthony's warning, he strode towards Emma, his gaze perusing over her with a cold, appraising look. Elodie quickly stepped behind Emma, placing a protective hand on the girl's shoulder.

"Stephen," Elodie greeted.

He tipped his head at her in acknowledgment, then looked down at Emma. "Hello, Child. I am your father," he announced, his tone devoid of warmth.

Emma's gaze fell to the ground, her posture shrinking under his scrutiny.

"Look at me when I am talking to you," Stephen barked.

Anthony rushed forward, positioning himself between his brother and Emma. "That is enough. You have met her. Now go."

Stephen's lips curled in disdain. "I would like to talk to my daughter, if you do not mind."

"You are frightening her," Anthony responded.

Stephen's eyes flashed with irritation. "Perhaps I should buy her a puppy like you did to win her favor. Predictable, as always."

"You made your point," Anthony said. "Now leave."

Taking a threatening step towards him, Stephen asked, "Why is it you think you can tell me what to do?"

Anthony held his ground, enduring the stench of his brother's whiskey-laden breath. "You give me little choice. You will not treat her this way."

"She is *my* daughter!" Stephen exclaimed, pointing at the child. "I will treat her however I see fit."

Anthony kept his voice calm, though his patience was thinning. "No. You will treat her with respect and kindness."

"Her mother was a whore," Stephen declared.

Elodie gasped. "That is a terrible thing to say," she shot back. She knelt beside Emma. "Come, Emma. Let us go inside and play."

As Elodie led the girl away, Anthony turned back to his brother. "Was that your intention all along?"

Stephen shrugged, unbothered. "All you said was that I had to meet her. Nothing more. I do not need—or want—a child. They are useless creatures."

Anthony stared at his brother in disbelief, struggling to comprehend Stephen's cold-heartedness. "Fine. Do not worry about Emma. Mother and I shall see to her needs."

His brother's mouth twisted into a mocking smile as he shouldered past Anthony. "Finally, you are seeing reason."

Watching Stephen stumble away, Anthony couldn't, in good conscience, let him treat Emma so callously. The girl deserved better, and he would ensure she got it.

His mother emerged from the townhouse, pausing briefly as Stephen brushed past her with only a slight acknowledgment. She approached Anthony, a hopeful look softening her features. "I saw Stephen speaking to Emma. Did it go well?"

"What do you think?" Anthony muttered.

A frown creased her brow. "That is unfortunate news," she said. "You will have to tell me what happened. But first, someone is here to see you."

"Whoever it is, send him away. I am not in a mood to converse with anyone," Anthony said.

"I would," she responded with a hint of apprehension, "but I do not dare. He claims that Lord Winston sent him, and he is wearing a red waistcoat. I believe he may be a Bow Street Runner."

Anthony grew solemn. "I will speak to him."

His mother eyed him, concern in her eyes. "Why is a Bow Street Runner seeking you out, Anthony?"

"There is no need to worry yourself, Mother."

"Are you in some kind of trouble?" she asked, her voice laced with worry.

He offered her a reassuring smile, hoping to ease her fears. "Me? Of course not. Remember, I am the one who always follows the rules."

His mother did not look convinced. "Very well. If you won't tell me, then I won't press. But do be careful, whatever it is you are involved in."

Anthony leaned in and kissed his mother's cheek before he headed inside. In the study, a tall, broad-shouldered man stood waiting, his stance confident and alert. Anthony shut the door, regarding the man with interest.

"You must be Grady," he greeted.

Grady turned, giving him a polite nod. "I am. Lord Winston mentioned you are in need of my services."

Reaching into his jacket, Anthony retrieved the crumpled letter, extending it towards the Runner. "A street urchin delivered this to my door yesterday."

Grady read the letter before handing it back. "Who do you think could have sent this note?"

"I have no idea," Anthony admitted.

Grady studied him carefully. "Lord Winston informed me on the situation. I understand the need for discretion, but it seems someone is intent on blackmailing you."

Anthony walked over to the desk, dropping the note onto it. "I agree. But how do we find who wrote this letter?"

"Leave that to me," Grady replied, moving towards the door. "I will be in contact."

Anthony's brows knitted in concentration. "And how do I reach you?"

Grady smirked. "You don't. But rest assured, I will be close by."

As the Bow Street Runner left the study, Anthony felt a mixture of hope and unease. If Grady was as capable as Winston claimed, he might be the answer they needed. However, ten thousand pounds was a substantial sum. But if it protected Elodie's reputation, it was a price he would gladly pay.

14

E lodie sat at her dressing table as Molly skillfully gathered her hair into a loose chignon, the soft tendrils framing her face. She had managed to avoid her mother's impending lecture by spending the last few hours at Anthony's townhouse.

Molly took a step back and asked, "Do you like your hair, my lady?"

Elodie turned slightly, admiring her reflection in the mirror. "It is lovely," she replied. "You have truly outdone yourself."

"Shall we dress you now?" Molly asked, moving towards the gown draped across the bed.

As Elodie rose from her seat, the door to her bedchamber opened, and her mother slipped inside with her usual grace. "Good, there you are. I need a word with you."

Elodie held back a sigh, bracing herself for the lecture she knew was inevitable.

Her mother sat down on the bed. "How is Miss Emma?"

That brought a smile to Elodie's lips. "She is well. Stephen said something rather harsh to her, but Anthony and I managed to distract her with toys and games."

Her mother's brow knitted. "What did Stephen say this time?"

Elodie's smile faded. "He called Emma's mother a whore."

"Wasn't he married to this woman?"

Elodie nodded, a note of sadness in her voice. "Yes, but I believe he was only trying to hurt Emma. He was terribly unkind."

Lady Dallington frowned. "How terrible. Well, I am glad you and Anthony were there for her."

"Emma is a delightful girl." Elodie stepped into her gown, and Molly began fastening the buttons down her back. "I do believe Anthony intends to raise her himself, given Stephen's behavior."

"How do you feel about that?"

Elodie shrugged, feigning indifference. "Why should it matter to me?"

Her mother gave her a knowing look. "I can't help but notice you and Anthony seem to be growing rather close."

Elodie made a face. "We are friends, Mother. Just as we always have been."

"He did buy you a puppy."

"Only because he thought it best to get two dogs so they would not be lonely."

Her mother's lips curled into a small smile. "Ah, I see."

Molly stepped back to tidy the room as the dinner bell rang. Rising from the bed, Lady Dallington extended Elodie a hand. "We should go down to dinner."

Elodie tilted her head, studying her mother's expression. "Is that all you wanted to discuss?"

"No," her mother replied, linking her arm with Elodie's as they walked out into the corridor. "But we can discuss the rest on our way to the drawing room."

"Oh, wonderful," Elodie muttered under her breath.

As they moved down the hall, her mother glanced at her.

"First and foremost, I want you to know I am proud of you for standing up for Anthony with Lord Danbury."

Elodie's surprise showed plainly. "You are?" That was the last thing she had expected to hear.

Her mother bobbed her head. "Yes, but as your mother, I would be remiss if I did not caution you to wield that sharp tongue with care. There are always consequences to our words."

"Lord Danbury is a muttonhead."

Her mother's lips twitched, though she quickly composed herself. "True, but he is also quite influential in the House of Lords. Crossing him could spell trouble for your father."

Elodie offered a contrite smile. "I'm sorry. I had not considered that."

"I know," her mother replied, patting her hand. "Which is why I am ending this lecture here."

"Truly?" Elodie asked. "Your lectures usually go on for much longer."

Her mother laughed. "Consider it my gift to you. And I am proud of how you handled the situation. But do not tell your father that."

"I would not dream of it."

Coming to a stop at the top of the stairs, her mother turned to face her fully. "You are truly shining as the diamond this Season. But remember, love can often be found in the most unlikely of places."

"I will not marry for anything less."

Her mother's expression softened, and she placed a hand on her arm. "I have been blessed to love two men in my life. True love is not something to take for granted. When you find it, hold on to it with everything you have. Never let it go."

"I promise."

Her mother's gaze grew thoughtful. "And I do not believe you will have to look very far to find that kind of love."

Elodie pressed her lips together as she tried to hide her surprise. Did her mother think she harbored feelings for Anthony? Or... perhaps even loved him? No, that could not be. Anthony was—well, what was he exactly? More than a friend, certainly, but the rest was too uncertain to consider.

Thankfully, her mother seemed to sense her unease and did not press further. Instead, she dropped her arm with a warm smile. "Shall we join the rest of the family for dinner?"

Bennett's playful voice echoed from the entry hall below. "Are you two engaged in subterfuge?" he joked, a mischievous glint in his eyes as he looked up at them.

"Not at all," her mother replied. "Elodie and I were just talking."

Bennett arched an eyebrow. "And what subject were the two of you so deeply engrossed in discussing?"

Her mother grinned. "Aren't you being rather nosy?"

As Elodie descended the stairs with her mother, Delphine emerged from the drawing room. Delphine smiled at her. "Good evening, Elodie. I haven't seen much of you today."

"That is because she was at Anthony's townhouse," Bennett announced with a slight smirk.

Delphine's eyes widened with surprise. "Alone?"

Elodie quickly shook her head. "No, I was visiting Anthony's niece, Emma. We were playing games with her."

"Still, were you alone?" Delphine pressed.

"No," Elodie replied firmly. "Lady Kinwick was there with us the entire time. I assure you, we were properly chaperoned. But even if we weren't, Anthony is a family friend. Being alone with him would not ruin my reputation."

Delphine exchanged a telling glance with Bennett. "I am not entirely sure if that is true."

"Whyever not?" Elodie argued.

Bennett stepped forward, lowering his voice in a conspiratorial tone. "You see, Elodie, when a man and a young woman, such as you, begin to develop certain feelings—"

Elodie cut him off with a huff. "I do not have feelings for Anthony."

"Don't you?" Bennett asked, his tone full of implications.

Elodie rolled her eyes. "It is entirely possible for two people of the opposite sex to be friends, you know."

Before her brother could respond, their father entered the entry hall. "Let us all go into the dining room."

With a glance over her shoulder, Elodie asked, "Are Winston and Mattie not joining us this evening?"

"They went to the theatre," Bennett informed her. "You would have known that if you were not spending all of your time at Anthony's townhouse."

Elodie sighed. "It was only for a few hours."

Bennett offered his arm to his wife. "I understand you are going on a carriage ride with Anthony during the fashionable hour tomorrow."

"I am, but do not read too much into it," Elodie said as they moved towards the dining room.

When they arrived, she took her seat across from Delphine, hoping Bennett would let the matter drop. But luck was not on her side.

Bennett settled into his chair beside his wife. "You do realize this is the second time you will be seen in Hyde Park with him during the fashionable hour?"

"Well done, Brother. You can count up to two," Elodie quipped.

Bennett placed his hand up. "I am only saying that the gossips' tongues may start wagging."

Elodie retrieved her napkin and placed it on her lap. "This is ridiculous. Anthony and I are merely friends. Can we please change the subject?"

"All right," Bennett relented. "What shall we discuss instead?"

Turning towards her mother, Elodie said, "I would like to commission a portrait of myself and Lulu."

"Whatever for?" her mother asked.

Elodie leaned forward. "Lulu looks so distinguished in his waistcoat. I think it should be memorialized."

Her father let out a quiet scoff. "A dog has no business wearing a waistcoat. And as for the portrait, you may have one commissioned once you are betrothed. That is the tradition in our family."

"Can Lulu at least be part of it?" Elodie asked.

Her father's response was swift. "No. A portrait is no place for a dog."

She leaned back, undeterred. "But the queen has many portraits of her with her dogs."

"Well, when you are the queen, you can do whatever you want," her father said, reaching for his glass.

"Fine," Elodie remarked. "Perhaps I will marry a prince and live far, far away in a tall tower. You may never see me again, but I will be surrounded by my dogs."

"At least, in this scenario, you would have a husband," her father retorted.

Lady Dallington shot her husband a warning look. "Dear, leave poor Elodie alone. She will find a husband when she is good and ready."

"I hope she does not take too long," her father said.

Elodie lifted her brow as she tried to keep her voice light. "Are you in such a hurry to be rid of me, Father?"

"On the contrary," her father replied, his tone gentle. "I only wish to see you cared for, even when I am no longer around to look after you."

"You are going to live a long life since I forbid you to die," Elodie stated.

"Then I shall heed your command," her father replied with a wink.

Her mother interjected, breaking the somber mood with a cheerful note. "Enough of this morbid talk. Let us eat before our soup grows cold."

———————

The sun was high in the sky as Anthony stepped out of his townhouse and strolled the short distance to Elodie's main door. He knocked, and the door was promptly opened by the butler. Before he could step inside, Elodie slipped out, bonnet in hand, her eyes bright with anticipation.

"Shall we go?" she asked, her voice almost too eager.

He eyed her curiously. "Why the urgency?"

Elodie flashed him a sweet smile. "I am just anxious to spend time with you," she said as she batted her eyes.

"The truth, if you please."

Her smile faded, replaced with a sigh of resignation. "My mother is driving me mad," she admitted. "She is insisting I perform a piece on the pianoforte at Mrs. Fletcher's soiree tomorrow."

Anthony looked at her, bemused. "And why is that such a problem? I happen to know you are an excellent player."

Elodie turned her head slightly, though not before he caught a flicker of vulnerability in her gaze. "I do not enjoy performing in front of large groups. Playing for a small gathering is one thing, but an entire roomful of people?" She shuddered. "It is unnerving."

A playful smile tugged at his lips. "I never thought I would see the day that you would admit to being nervous."

She shot him a look. "You are not helping."

Anthony grinned. "I am not trying to. I am merely trying to

understand. Besides, you are the diamond of the Season. People will expect you to perform at the soiree."

"Well, I never asked to be the diamond," Elodie declared. "What if I make a mistake? One that I cannot recover from?"

With a gentle hand, Anthony touched her arm. "You won't."

Her brows knitted as she looked at him, her eyes unguarded. "How can you be so sure?"

"Because everything will work out in the end," he replied. "I don't know how. But I trust that it will."

Elodie frowned. "I have never heard someone say so many wrong things, one after another, in a row."

Anthony chuckled. "You just don't like hearing the truth."

Placing the bonnet on top of her head, Elodie tied the ribbons under her chin. "What if I trip and fall on the way up to the pianoforte? I would be utterly ruined."

He shrugged, as if his next words were inconsequential. "Then I would marry you."

Elodie huffed. "Me? A ruined woman? I do think you need to set your sights a little higher, my lord."

Anthony offered his arm. "Perhaps I already have. As we have discussed before, our children would be extraordinarily beautiful. The envy of the *ton*."

She arched a brow. "Is beauty all you care about? What of love?"

"Oh, I have no doubt that if we wed, you would fall desperately in love with me, given time. I am quite likable, you know."

"So say you," she teased.

"Furthermore, I am a wealthy viscount," he added, puffing out his chest with an exaggerated air. "You could do much worse."

Elodie considered him for a moment. "What else do you seek in a marriage?"

Anthony hesitated, the truth lingering on the tip of his tongue. What he wanted to say was that he sought her as a wife.

She was everything he had dreamed of, but he did not dare say that.

Instead, he met her gaze steadily. "That is easy. I want someone I can laugh with—every single day."

"Well then, you would best find yourself someone hilarious because you, my lord, are remarkably unfunny," she quipped.

Anthony shook his head, though his voice held amusement. "Why must you constantly insult me?"

"I suppose it is my way of keeping you humble."

"That you do," Anthony said as he helped her into the carriage.

As the coach slowly moved forward, merging into the flow of bustling carriages on the road, Elodie looked over at Anthony. "How is Emma doing today?"

"She is well," he replied. "I feel as if I should apologize for my brother... again—"

Elodie interrupted him gently. "There is no need, Anthony. You seem to forget that I know Stephen, and I know what he is capable of."

Anthony clenched his jaw. "But to say something so cruel to Emma about her mother... it is unfathomable."

"I agree," Elodie said. "He was entirely wrong in doing so."

Anthony let out a slow, frustrated breath. "Everything out of my brother's mouth is wrong. It is as if he can't help himself."

Elodie turned to face him more fully on the bench. "You have done all you can for him."

"Then why do I feel as if I haven't done enough?" His voice was barely more than a whisper, but the weight of his words filled the space between them.

She grew silent. "What is it that *you* want?"

He furrowed his brows. "What do you mean?"

"If you could do anything in the world, what would it be?"

With a blank look, he replied, "I don't have time to think

about such things. There is the estate to manage, meetings to attend, tenants to look after..."

She reached out, placing a hand on his arm, quieting his words. "But is that what you want to do?"

"I do what is expected of me."

A rueful smile came to her lips. "I know you. You have always valued duty above all else. But humor me, just for a moment. What is it that you want out of this life?"

After a brief pause, he replied, "I suppose I would buy up land. Try to become one of the largest landowners in England."

She yawned, a spark of mirth in her eyes. "That is your grand wish? Forgive me, Anthony, but that is dreadfully boring. Try again."

Anthony grinned. "All right... I would travel. See the world. There are so many places I have only read about. Sometimes I think I would like to experience them firsthand."

"That is my wish as well," Elodie said softly.

"Then let us travel together," Anthony declared. "We will buy a ship and sail off to distant lands, far from London's endless demands."

Elodie gave him a wistful look. "If only it were that simple."

His gaze fell to her hand, still resting on his arm, and she quickly withdrew it, a faint blush coloring her cheeks as she turned her head. Perhaps she was not entirely immune to his charms, after all.

The carriage reached Hyde Park and began rolling down Rotten Row. But coming towards them in the opposite direction, Anthony noticed Lord Montrose riding on horseback. His mood darkened instantly.

Elodie must have noticed his reaction because she asked, "What is wrong?"

"Lord Montrose," he muttered, not bothering to hide his disgust.

Montrose had a smug smile on his lips as he reined in his horse beside their carriage.

"Lady Elodie. Lord Belview," he greeted, tipping his hat with exaggerated politeness.

"Do not address Lady Elodie," Anthony growled.

But Elodie placed a calming hand on Anthony's sleeve, her voice a whisper. "It is all right. I do not wish to cause a scene."

Montrose's smile widened, his gaze lingering on Elodie. "You are looking especially lovely on this fine day, my lady."

"Is it fine?" Elodie asked, glancing up at the gray sky. "It is rather cloudy and drizzly, do you not think?"

"Ah, but seeing you has brightened my day considerably," Montrose said.

Elodie met Montrose's gaze. "How is your nose, my lord?"

Montrose's smile faltered for a brief second, his eyes narrowing. "It seems you are determined to dwell on unfortunate incidents from the past."

"I suppose I am allowed a bit of honesty, considering I am a shrew," she replied with an innocent look. "Is that not what you called me, my lord?"

"A beautiful shrew," Montrose replied. "Would you care to—"

"No."

Montrose's eyes flashed with annoyance. "You do not even know what I was going to ask."

"Does it matter?" Elodie asked. "I have no desire to associate myself with you. In fact, every word you speak only reminds me of how thoroughly vapid you are."

"Careful, my lady, or I will start to think you disapprove of me," Montrose mocked.

Elodie straightened, fixing him with a withering stare. "I know very little about you, but everything I do know leaves me utterly unimpressed."

Montrose tightened the reins in his hand. "One day, we will

recount this amusing story to our children, and we will all laugh at it."

Elodie visibly tensed. "I will never marry you."

"You say that now..."

"I will say that always," Elodie said firmly.

With a smirk, Montrose inclined his head. "We shall see about that," he said before clicking his horse forward, trotting off with an arrogant tilt of his chin.

Elodie watched Montrose's retreating figure with a look of utter disdain. "What an audacious man. He has some nerve."

"That goes without saying, but you must never be alone with Montrose," Anthony said. "I do not trust that man."

"Neither do I. How he could ever think I would consider marrying him is beyond me," Elodie declared.

Anthony leaned back in his seat. "I do not think he cares if you are willing."

"Perhaps I should challenge him to a duel myself."

"Absolutely not!" Anthony exclaimed. "Ladies do not fight duels."

"Why? Are men afraid that we would actually win them?" Elodie asked.

Anthony cast an exasperated look at the sky. "Duels are not a matter to joke about," he said, his voice coming out much harsher than he had intended.

Elodie's voice softened. "I am sorry. I should not have brought up such a sensitive topic, knowing Stephen's past involvement in a duel."

"Stephen is an idiot," Anthony grumbled.

"I do not dispute that."

Anthony ran a hand through his hair. "Let us talk about something other than my brother or Montrose."

Elodie's eyes sparkled with mischief as she gestured towards two gentlemen seated on a nearby bench, both wearing solemn expressions. "Very well. What do you think those two are discussing?"

He glanced over, raising an eyebrow. "Likely something important."

"Pudding, perhaps?" she guessed.

"Pudding?" he repeated with a laugh. "They are far too serious for that."

Elodie tapped a finger against her lips. "You made a good point. What do serious gentlemen discuss when they are gathered together?" Her eyes lit up. "I have got it—whist. They are reliving every detail of their card game from last night."

"You are terrible at guessing."

"Oh? Do you think you can do better?" Elodie challenged.

Anthony studied the gentlemen with mock seriousness. "If I had to guess, I would wager they are discussing the state of the government."

"I stand by my theory," Elodie said. "And there is only one way to know for certain. You will just have to ask them."

Anthony looked at her, half-amused, half-bewildered. "Why must I be the one to ask?"

"Because," Elodie started with a wave of her hand, "you are seated closest to them. It is just practical."

Anthony gave a resigned smile, settling back in his seat. "As entertaining as that would be, I am not going to approach them. Why don't we enjoy the rest of the carriage ride in quiet?"

Elodie adjusted the brim of her bonnet. "I quite agree. I do prefer it when you are not speaking."

"Of course you do. And to think, I did you a favor by taking you on this carriage ride," Anthony said. "I'd think you would be nicer to me."

"But it is so difficult to be nice to you," Elodie retorted.

15

The carriage rocked to a halt in front of Elodie's townhouse, and Anthony quickly stepped out, offering his hand to help her down onto the cobbled street.

Once she was on the pavement, he didn't let go of her hand but instead guided it to the crook of his arm. "Allow me to escort you inside."

"That is not necessary," Elodie attempted.

"I am trying to be a gentleman," he said with a smile.

Elodie couldn't help but tease him. "Why start now?"

He chuckled. "You, my lady, are a minx."

"Thank you," Elodie said as they walked up to the main door, her hand still resting on his arm. The door promptly opened, and White stood back to admit them.

"Lady Eugenie is waiting for you in the drawing room," White announced with a small bow.

Elodie slipped her hand from Anthony's arm. "Lady Eugenie is here?"

"Yes, my lady," White replied. "She asked to wait when she heard you were out."

"I wonder what she wants," Elodie mused.

Anthony gestured towards the door. "Shall we find out together?"

Elodie gave him an appraising look. "What makes you think I want you to join me in greeting Lady Eugenie?"

In a low, flirtatious voice, Anthony replied, "Because you are not ready to say goodbye to me just yet."

She huffed, feigning irritation. "You are a nuisance."

"A handsome nuisance?" Anthony asked, his eyes twinkling with amusement. "I cannot help but notice you can't take your eyes off me."

Elodie shook her head. "That is only because it is polite to look at someone when you are speaking to them."

Anthony leaned closer. "Or perhaps... just humor me here... you are wondering what it would be like to kiss me."

Her mouth dropped open, and she felt a blush rise to her cheeks. "I would never kiss you."

"Never say never, Elodie."

To her dismay, she could not stop the blush from deepening. The thought had indeed crossed her mind, albeit briefly. But she would never admit that to him or to anyone.

Anthony raised an eyebrow, a small smile playing on his lips. "So, shall we go speak to Lady Eugenie or are you tempted to test this theory of mine?"

"You are impossible."

His smile grew. "I did not hear a 'no' in there."

Elodie was not going to dignify that with a response. She turned on her heel and strode into the drawing room, grateful for the excuse to avoid his gaze. Inside, she found Lady Eugenie sitting on the settee, a pensive expression on her face.

"Lady Eugenie," Elodie greeted.

Lady Eugenie stood abruptly, holding a letter in her hand. "Forgive me for arriving unannounced, but I had to see you."

She held out the letter, her fingers trembling slightly. "A street urchin delivered this to my townhouse this morning."

Elodie took the paper, quickly reading over the note.

I know all about Lady Eugenie and Lord Montrose's tryst. Ten thousand pounds will buy my silence. Secure the money and I will be in touch.

Her eyes widened in shock. "This... this was sent to you?"

Lady Eugenie's expression grew downcast. "It was sent to my brother, but I intercepted it. He will be furious when he sees this. He knows nothing of that night with Lord Montrose."

"He will understand," Elodie assured her.

Lady Eugenie let out a nervous laugh. "Perhaps, but he may very well send me to a convent for such a disgrace. Tell me honestly, did you mention what happened that night to anyone?"

"I confided in my family, but no one else," Elodie replied.

Anthony, who had been watching silently, stepped forward. "May I see the note?"

Lady Eugenie gave a small nod, and Elodie passed the note to him. As he read it, Elodie guided her new friend back to the settee. "Would you care for some tea?"

"Tea won't mend this," Lady Eugenie said with a dismissive wave of her hand. "I am ruined. No one will have me once this gets out."

"You do not know that," Elodie attempted.

Lady Eugenie bobbed her head. "I do know that," she asserted. "I am not the diamond. I am a nobody."

Reaching for her hand, Elodie said, "You are not a 'nobody.' You are a lady."

"A lady foolish enough to trust a rake like Lord Montrose. And now someone is blackmailing my brother over it," Lady Eugenie said.

Elodie noticed Anthony's silence, his jaw clenched as he studied the letter. "Is something the matter?"

Anthony looked up, his attention directed at Lady Eugenie. "You are not the only one to receive a note like this."

Lady Eugenie furrowed her brow. "What do you mean?"

Anthony's frown deepened. "I received a similar letter a few days ago, only it mentioned Lady Elodie."

Elodie pursed her lips together. "Truly? And you are only telling me about this now?" she asked, her voice rising.

Anthony offered her an apologetic look. "Your brothers and I decided it was best not to worry you unnecessarily."

Elodie stared at him in disbelief. "And you decided this without me?"

"Only because we wanted to protect you," Anthony replied, his tone measured. "I have already hired a Bow Street Runner to investigate, and I am prepared to pay the blackmail fee to keep your reputation safe."

Elodie felt her anger surge as she placed a hand on her hip. "You would pay ten thousand pounds for my reputation?"

"Without a second thought," he replied, his voice resolute.

"That is absurd," Elodie replied. "I won't allow you to spend such a fortune on this."

Taking a step closer, he held her gaze, his voice low. "I would do anything to protect you, Elodie. You must know that."

"Except be honest with me?" Elodie challenged.

Lady Eugenie rose from her seat, glancing between them. "Perhaps I should leave. It seems the two of you have much to discuss."

"No need," Elodie replied, her gaze locked on Anthony's. "Lord Belview was just leaving."

"Elodie..." Anthony started.

Elodie put her hand up, stilling his words. "How could you have kept something like this from me?" she demanded, her voice wavering between anger and hurt.

"It was for your own good."

Elodie let out a disbelieving huff. "My own good?" she repeated. "You don't truly believe that, do you?"

Anthony shifted, visibly uncomfortable under her gaze. "At the time, yes. I thought it was the best way to protect you."

Gesturing towards the door, Elodie ordered, "I think you should go."

A heavy silence lingered between them, stretching awkwardly before he finally conceded. "Very well. I will go... for now. But I hope you will allow me to explain more later."

Elodie tilted her chin. "Maybe. That is all I can promise for now."

"Then I shall take that," Anthony said before departing from the room.

Lady Eugenie moved closer, placing a hand on Elodie's sleeve. "Are you all right?"

"Yes... no... I don't know," Elodie replied as she lowered herself down onto the settee. "I thought Lord Belview and I were friends."

"It is evident that you two are more than friends."

Elodie met her gaze, uncertain. "I do not know what we are. Regardless, he should have told me about the letter."

"I agree, wholeheartedly. However, I do think he was trying to protect you, in his own way."

"That does not make it right," Elodie said.

"No, it does not," Lady Eugenie agreed, "but it does show how deeply he cares. Your brothers and Lord Belview seem determined to look after you."

Elodie turned her attention towards the window. "I do not like it when others decide what is best for me."

Lady Eugenie leaned back against the settee. "At least your brothers won't ship you off to a convent."

Bringing her gaze back to meet Lady Eugenie, Elodie insisted, "Your brother would not do such a thing."

"No, but I know he will be disappointed in me. I cannot bear that thought," Lady Eugenie said, her expression growing somber. "I never should have followed Montrose into the gardens."

"What's done is done. Now, we must move forward," Elodie asserted. "And with any luck, the Bow Street Runner that Lord Belview hired will uncover the blackmailer."

"But even if he does," Lady Eugenie began, "the damage could still be done. Our reputations could be ruined."

Elodie's lips curled into a mischievous smile. "Then we will run off and join the circus! I can juggle. What hidden talents do you have?"

Lady Eugenie thought about it for a moment. "I can ride backward on a horse."

"You can?"

Laughing softly, Lady Eugenie said, "Yes, much to my brother's horror. He always dreaded my riding tricks. But," she continued with a sigh, "I suppose it is time to go home and show him this note."

"I think that is wise."

Lady Eugenie straightened in her seat. "What if you come with me?"

Elodie gave her a skeptical look. "For what purpose?"

With a wry smile, Lady Eugenie said, "I would be blind if I did not notice my brother's infatuation with you."

"We are merely friends," Elodie said.

Lady Eugenie fixed Elodie with a knowing smile. "Just like you and Lord Belview?"

Elodie rose, smoothing her skirts with a feigned sigh. "I'm beginning to like this circus idea more and more," she quipped, attempting to deflect the conversation. "But first, I think I will need to take a much-needed nap."

"Very well," Lady Eugenie said, rising. "If you do run off to join the circus, it was a pleasure knowing you."

Elodie managed a smile, some of her earlier irritation
fading. "You will be fine," she assured her. "Just speak with your
brother honestly, and it will be all right."

With a quick glance at the doorway, Lady Eugenie lowered
her voice. "I would not be so hard on Lord Belview or your
brothers. Misguided as they may have been, their actions came
from a place of care."

Elodie knew Lady Eugenie had a point, even if she was
not ready to fully concede. "Perhaps you are right," she admitted. "But that does not mean I am not upset with them right
now."

"Of course. Just remember, it is not every day you have
people willing to go to such lengths to protect you, even if they
bungle it a bit," Lady Eugenie stated. "Now, get some rest. And
if you do decide to run away to the circus, let me know. I might
just join you."

"It is a deal," Elodie said as she escorted Lady Eugenie to
the door.

Anthony paused outside of his father's bedchamber door,
exhaling a slow, steady breath. He never knew quite what to
expect on the other side. But his father was dying, and he could
not bear to waste a moment with him.

He knocked softly, and the door opened as the valet
ushered him inside. His mother sat dutifully at his father's
bedside. She offered Anthony a weak smile, though her own
weariness showed in the faint lines on her face.

"Good evening," she whispered.

He hesitated, feeling almost intrusive. "Perhaps I should
return later."

"Nonsense, I am awake," his father said, forcing himself up

in bed with stubborn determination. "I was just resting my eyes."

His mother gave a small, knowing smile. "You were snoring."

His father leaned his back against the wall, exchanging a loving look with his wife. "Your mother exaggerates. I do not snore."

"How would you know?" she teased gently. "You are asleep."

His father shifted his attention to him, observing him with a keen gaze. "You look troubled, Son. Is it lady troubles?"

Anthony shook his head. "No trouble. Not... exactly."

His father chuckled, though the sound quickly turned into a cough. "You are a terrible liar. I do not have time for lies and half-truths. I am dying."

His mother gasped. "You should not say such things."

"It is merely the truth," his father said. "Now, sit, and let me impart my great wisdom upon you about women."

"This should not take long," his mother quipped.

Anthony fetched a chair and positioned it near the bed. Settling down, he waited, giving his father his full attention as he watched the man take a sip of water.

"Now," his father began, setting the glass down with deliberate slowness. "I assume this is about Elodie?"

Anthony's jaw tightened in surprise. "How could you possibly know such a thing?"

"Because, my dear boy, I sit by this window a great deal, watching the world beyond. I have observed you both walking those gardens more times than I can count," his father replied.

"Well, I am afraid that may change," Anthony admitted, looking away. "Elodie's rather upset with me at the moment."

His father's eyebrows lifted, his tone pointed. "And what did you do to incur her wrath?" Anthony decided he needed to choose his next words carefully so as not to worry his father. "I received some troubling news about Elodie. I met with her brothers, Bennett and Winston, and together, we thought it was best not to tell her. At least, for her own peace of mind."

His mother gave him a chastising look. "Elodie is no simpering miss. I must assume that she did not take it well."

Anthony's shoulders sagged. "No. Not well at all."

"As well she should not," her mother said, folding her arms. "Why should you decide what is best for her?"

His father nodded in agreement. "Indeed. You should have told her."

Anthony leaned back in his chair. "At the time, I felt like I was protecting her."

"And now?" his father prodded.

Running a hand through his hair, Anthony said, "Now, I wonder if I only made things worse. She is angry, and I do not know how to make things right."

His father let out a soft chuckle. "The age-old question of men everywhere. But I am sure that you will figure out what to do."

Anthony gave him a doubtful smile. "You have far more faith in me than I do."

A servant entered the room carrying a silver tray laden with food. He placed it carefully in front of Lord Kinwick, whose face immediately twisted in distaste.

"I should go and let you enjoy your meal," Anthony said, standing.

His father grimaced, eyeing the food as if it were poison. "Enjoy? This food is inedible."

"It is what the doctor ordered," his mother reminded him patiently.

"I might as well be eating a boiled shoe," his father grumbled.

His mother frowned. "It is not as bad as all that."

"I notice that you do not eat this slop," his father pointed out. "If the cancer does not take me, this food just might."

Anthony shared a smile with his mother, appreciating the rare lighthearted moment. He touched his father's shoulder. "Rest, Father. And do not worry. I will figure this out."

His father's eyes sparkled with humor as he leaned in conspiratorially. "One more thing. Next time you come, would you be so kind as to smuggle me a few biscuits?"

"Absolutely not!" his mother cut in, feigning a stern tone. "The doctor has forbidden sweets. They are not good for your stomach."

His father sighed, bobbing his head in a show of reluctant compliance. "Fine, no sweets," he agreed, but a wink followed, aimed squarely at Anthony.

His mother sighed. "I saw that, Dear."

"Oh, did I wink?" His father put on an innocent face, one hand half-covering his grin. "Anthony knows better than to bring me sweets." And then he winked again.

"Now you have winked twice," his mother chided, a soft laugh escaping despite her effort to scold him.

"Did I?" his father asked. "I might have something in my eye."

Anthony chuckled. "I will leave you both to it before any more winking accusations fly," he said, heading to the door.

His father's voice stopped him. "I appreciate you visiting. Perhaps, next time, you could bring Stephen with you?"

"I will ask him," Anthony said before stepping out and closing the door behind him, hoping he could make good on that promise.

Anthony descended the stairs, his gaze settling on Percy, who stood waiting in the entry hall with a solemn expression. "A Mr. Kingsley awaits you in the study, my lord."

"I do not believe I know a Mr. Kingsley," Anthony said.

Percy stepped closer, his voice lowered. "I daresay that he is not the sort of gentleman you would associate with. He is the solicitor for a gambling establishment in Hampstead."

Anthony felt a pang of dread. Stephen. What had he done this time? "Very well," he said. "I shall speak to Mr. Kingsley."

He made his way down the hall, moving deliberately, each step heavier with a suspicion of what awaited him. Entering the study, he found a short man with slicked back black hair, clad in a brown suit that was finely cut, though his boots betrayed their wear with a dull, unpolished finish.

"Mr. Kingsley," Anthony greeted. "What brings you here at this hour?"

The short man gave a quick bow. "Lord Belview, I wish I could have come under better circumstances."

Anthony came around his desk and gestured towards a chair. "Please, have a seat."

Mr. Kingsley lowered himself into the chair, his posture stiff. "I am afraid I must discuss an unfortunate matter about a debt your brother, Mr. Stephen Sackville, has incurred at our establishment. He has frequented our fine hall for several years and, in doing so, has amassed a rather significant debt of nearly eleven thousand pounds."

His brow shot up. "Eleven thousand pounds?"

"Yes, my lord," Mr. Kingsley said.

Anthony clenched his jaw as he processed the staggering amount. "Why in the blazes would you permit him to accumulate such a debt?"

Mr. Kingsley smiled. "It is not our policy to turn away customers."

"Perhaps it should be," Anthony retorted. "Stephen does not have those kinds of funds."

The solicitor's expression turned steely. "No, but you do."

Anthony crossed his arms over his chest. "That may be so, but I fail to see why I should pay for my brother's reckless gambling."

Mr. Kingsley leaned in, his voice dripping with a thinly veiled threat. "Because, my lord, if you do not settle this debt, we will have no choice but to see him thrown into debtor's prison."

"That is a matter between you and my brother."

A smug look glinted in Mr. Kingsley's eyes. "What will Society say, then? The whispers will spread quickly. Your brother will rot away in debtor's prison while you continue to live comfortably in this extravagant townhouse. Some might even say it is unbecoming of a man of your station."

Anthony rose. "My brother made his choice, and I am making mine. Good day."

Mr. Kingsley rose as well, tugging his waistcoat into place, his expression sharp. "Are you truly willing to let your own brother waste away in prison? Have you no decency?"

"Eleven thousand pounds is no small sum," Anthony responded. "Those funds are necessary to maintain our estate and to ensure the wellbeing of those who depend on it."

"Perhaps we could come to an understanding. Nine thousand pounds to settle the debt, and we both walk away happy."

Anthony's eyes narrowed. "How, precisely, would I be 'happy' with this arrangement? You are asking me to pay off my brother's debts."

The solicitor leaned forward, his tone pressing. "I understand your father's health is... delicate. How would he take the news of his son's disgrace?"

Anthony held his gaze, unmoved. "My father is used to Stephen disappointing our family by now."

A twisted smile formed on Mr. Kingsley's lips. "But think of his daughter. Would you deny this child her father?"

Gesturing towards the door, Anthony said, "I have had quite enough. You may see yourself out."

Mr. Kingsley straightened, his mouth tightening. "I believe you are making a grave mistake."

"No, for once, I am doing what is right for my family, and my brother," Anthony remarked.

The solicitor's lips pressed into a hard line. "When the newssheets learn of this, they will have quite the story to tell."

"I care little about what is written about me," Anthony replied, crossing the room and holding the door open.

Mr. Kingsley scoffed, a sneer twisting his face. "You think yourself better than your brother, do you not?"

"I never said that."

"Imagine how different your life would have been if you had been born second, the spare," Mr. Kingsley said.

Anthony's gaze remained resolute. "But I wasn't. I was born first, and I have a responsibility to my family and all who depend on us."

"My establishment is not the only one that your brother owes money to," he taunted.

Turning his head, Anthony shouted, "Percy!"

His butler appeared almost instantly. "Yes, my lord?"

"Please see Mr. Kingsley out. He is no longer welcome here."

Percy nodded before holding his hand out. "This way, sir."

As the butler escorted him out, Anthony went around his desk and heard a low voice drifting in from the open window.

"That went well, all things considered."

Startled, Anthony turned his gaze towards the window to see Grady leaning nonchalantly against the frame. "What are you doing here?"

"Isn't it obvious?" Grady replied. "I was ensuring you were protected."

"I can handle Mr. Kingsley."

Grady tipped his head. "Oh, I do not doubt that, but what about the men who came with him?"

"There were others?" Anthony asked.

A smirk came to Grady's lips. "Indeed. Two unsavory fellows loitering by the carriage. Nothing I could not handle, but it tells me Mr. Kingsley's threats might not end at polite demands."

"So, the man truly intended to intimidate me?"

Grady climbed through the window, brushing off his coat. "Not just intimidate. I would wager he came with every intention of leaving with some of your money, one way or another," he said. "But Mr. Kingsley was not entirely wrong about one thing. By my calculations, your brother owes nineteen thousand pounds to many disreputable establishments."

"Botheration!" Anthony muttered, his voice filled with frustration. "What was my brother thinking?"

"I cannot answer that, but I would be leery of him," Grady said. "Desperate men tend to do desperate things."

Anthony clenched his fists, his gaze shifting to the flickering fire casting shadows across the room. If he settled Stephen's debts, it would drain the coffers, leaving him with barely enough to support the estate. And what of the tenants and workers who depended on him for their livelihood? Could he let them down?

He dropped onto the settee, rubbing his hands over his face as he leaned back and let his gaze drift to the ceiling. Despite the trouble with his brother, his thoughts kept straying back to Elodie. What could he do to show her how truly sorry he was?

A thought suddenly came to him.

He knew precisely what he needed to do to get back into Elodie's good graces.

16

E lodie descended the stairs, her white wrapper tied tightly around her. She had planned to sneak down to the kitchen for one of the biscuits the cook had left out for her. It was a small indulgence that she often enjoyed late at night. But as she reached the bottom step, she noticed a soft light glowing from the parlor. Who could possibly be up at this hour?

Her curiosity got the best of her, and she shifted her path towards the parlor. Stopping just outside of the door, she could hear her brothers' familiar voices. Bennett and Winston seemed to be discussing their recent outing to the opera. It was a conversation that was so utterly dull that she nearly turned back. But she had a few things she wished to say to her brothers, so she decided to make her presence known.

She slipped into the room, and Bennett, sitting comfortably on the settee, was the first to notice her. A grin spread across his face. "Good evening, Sister. To what do we owe this grand honor of you visiting us from on high?"

She crossed her arms, giving them both a stern look. "I am still quite upset at you, both of you."

"Whatever for?" Bennett asked.

"You know very well what for," Elodie said. "Anthony told me about the note—the one that threatened to ruin my reputation. And he also told me about your grand decision to keep it from me."

Not looking the least bit repentant, Bennett responded, "It seems Anthony was rather chatty."

Winston spoke up, his tone apologetic. "We were only trying to protect you."

"By hiding things from me?" Elodie retorted.

Bennett just shrugged. "It had to be done."

With a resigned sigh, Elodie took a seat beside her brothers. "And the worst of it is that Anthony lied to me as well."

"Do not be too hard on him," Winston said. "Anthony's intentions were good. He was only trying to protect you."

"I do not need anyone's protection," Elodie insisted.

Bennett leaned forward, giving her a pointed look. "Yes, you do. Life is not all sunshine and fairy tales. Sometimes, bad things happen to good people, and you need someone to look out for you."

Elodie frowned. "I think I would like you more if I had a biscuit in my hand."

"I wager you are only angry because, somewhere inside, you know we were right to keep this from you," Bennett said.

"Oh? And what part of me knows that? My elbow?" Elodie quipped.

Bennett chuckled. "Perhaps. Go, have your biscuit, and we will discuss this tomorrow."

"Wonderful. I have something to look forward to, then," Elodie said, rising with mock enthusiasm. "Though I assure you, I will still be cross with you tomorrow."

"It is a chance that I am willing to take," Bennett said with a wry smile.

Turning to Winston, she asked, "And what say you?"

Winston met her gaze earnestly. "What Bennett should be saying is that we are genuinely sorry for keeping this from you."

Her expression softened. "Thank you, Winston. You have now firmly secured your place as my favorite brother."

Bennett gasped, placing a hand over his heart. "How dare you, Sister! You take that back!"

"No," Elodie responded with a smile. "My statement stands. Now, if you will excuse me, it is time for a delicious biscuit... or perhaps two."

As she turned to leave, Bennett called after her, "Oh, by the way, Father mentioned he would like a word with you."

Elodie stopped, glancing over her shoulder. "Why did he not say so at dinner?" Bennett shrugged. "I cannot say, but if I had to guess, he is probably going to suggest you move up to the attic."

"And why, pray tell, would he suggest that?" Elodie asked.

Bennett's eyes sparkled with amusement. "Delphine requires more room for her clothes. I recommended your bedchamber as a suitable wardrobe extension."

Elodie shook her head. "You did no such thing."

"We must all make sacrifices to ensure Delphine is happy. And the attic would not be so bad. You could knit some waist-coats for all the rats that are running about," Bennett said, his smile growing.

Elodie rolled her eyes. "You are impossible to like," she said. "Does Father even wish to speak to me?"

Reaching for his glass, Bennett responded, "That much is true. But think some more about the attic. It would be the perfect solution... for me, at least."

With an exasperated sigh, Elodie left the parlor. She noticed a faint light under the study door as she made her way down the corridor. Her father's late-night work habits were notorious, and it seemed tonight was no exception. She wondered what he wanted to discuss. Had he somehow heard of her mishap with Lord Montrose?

Reaching the study door, she knocked softly. When there was no answer, she slowly turned the handle and slipped inside. Her father sat in his favorite armchair, head drooping, and he was snoring softly. But what truly caught her attention was the black cat curled up contentedly in his lap.

Where had the cat come from? She noticed the open window and realized that the cat must have snuck in while her father dozed off. A surge of panic hit her. Her father absolutely despised cats. She needed to remove it before he woke up.

But as she took a step forward, the floorboard creaked under her weight. Her father stirred, raising his head groggily. "Elodie?" he murmured, his voice thick with sleep. "What are you doing here?"

"Father," she began, striving to keep her voice calm, "I do not mean to alarm you, but there is a cat on your lap."

To her utter amazement, instead of pushing the cat off his lap, her father stroked its soft fur. "It is all right."

"How can it be all right?" Elodie asked. "You hate cats."

"I do not *hate* cats. I have always thought cats were best suited for the barn, where they catch the mice."

Elodie gestured towards the cat. "Then how do you explain this one? And on your lap, of all places?"

Her father simply smiled, as if this was all perfectly normal. "The first night we arrived in Town, this cat slipped through the window. He has been coming back every night since."

"And you... you let him?"

"Of course." He looked almost amused by her astonishment. "I even leave out a little food for him. It is the least I could do."

Elodie blinked, wondering if she was dreaming.

The cat started purring loudly and her father settled back

in his chair. "It is good that you are here. I did need to speak to you about something."

"Hold on," Elodie said before she pinched herself. "Ouch."

Her father gave her a bemused look. "Why did you just pinch yourself?"

"To make sure I was not dreaming," Elodie replied. "I never thought I would see a day that you would take a cat for a pet."

"This is not my pet. He just comes in at night to keep me company."

Elodie went to sit across from him. "It seems like a pet to me."

"Well, it is not," her father replied. "And we have more important matters to discuss."

"But it is so unlike you, Father. Does anyone else know about this... arrangement?"

Her father's lips twitched. "You are making more of this than it deserves."

She had an idea. "Can I have a pet, then?" she asked, seizing her chance.

"No."

Elodie started to protest, but her father's expression turned serious, interrupting her. "I wanted to speak with you on another matter. Lord Westcott came to see me yesterday. He asked for your hand in marriage."

"What did you say?" she asked.

Her father gave her an indulgent smile. "I told him that I would leave that choice to you."

Relief flooded her, and she leaned back. "Thank you. But... what am I to do?"

"That is for you to decide," her father replied. "Do you even want to marry Lord Westcott?"

Elodie grew quiet. She thought of her time with Lord Westcott. He was kind, an earl, and respectable. But she hardly knew him. A future with him seemed possible, but did she truly want it? In her heart, she knew she wanted more than just a respectable match.

An image of Anthony came to her mind, and she realized something. It was easy with him. She loved spending time with him, and he made her laugh. That is what she wanted in a marriage. Friendship. Love.

Her father's voice broke through her thoughts. "You are smiling."

"Am I?" She quickly schooled her expression, trying to conceal her thoughts.

"Were you thinking about Lord Westcott?"

Her smile faded, and she looked away. "No... not exactly." She did not dare reveal the truth. Then her father would think she had developed feelings for Anthony. Which she had not. She could not. If she developed feelings for Anthony, and they were unrequited, she would risk losing him. And that was a risk she was not willing to take.

"Then who were you thinking about?" her father prodded.

Taking a deep breath, she clasped her hands and said decisively, "I do not wish to marry Lord Westcott."

"Whyever not? He is an earl, and such a marriage would be advantageous for both of you."

Elodie held her head high. "I want more out of marriage, Father. I want... love. Someone who makes me laugh. I want what you and Mother have."

He nodded, his gaze warm with understanding. "Very well. But be sure to let him down gently. And be prepared, I doubt he will be the last man to offer for you."

"You are not angry with me?" Elodie asked, surprised by his response.

"Why would I be?" her father asked. "I only want what is best for you."

Elodie gave him a grateful smile. "Thank you, Father."

He turned his head towards the crackling fire, his expression distant but content. "Marrying your mother was the best decision I ever made. I love her now more than I did on the day we wed." A wistful smile came to his lips. "I waited my entire life to find someone that I could sit with in silence, feeling wanted and loved, and when it finally happened, I knew why it was worth the wait."

Her father turned to her, his gaze steady. "That is what I want for you. To marry someone that you love with all of your heart."

Her heart swelled at his words, but a familiar doubt crept in. "What if I do not find that?"

"You will," her father asserted. "It is no less than you deserve."

Elodie was touched by her father's rare show of emotion. "You do not speak of love often. I thought you would have married me off to Lord Westcott without a second thought."

Her father gave her an amused look. "Your mother would never permit me to do such a thing."

"Well, it is a good thing for Mother, then," Elodie said.

The humor left his expression. "Tell me... when you think of your future, is there someone you think of?"

Anthony.

But Elodie could not say that. "No one comes to mind," she lied.

Her father did not look convinced. "Well, when that someone does come to mind, hold on to them."

Rising, Elodie said, "It is late. I should go to bed."

"Goodnight, my dear," he replied.

As she left the study, a quiet truth settled over her. She cared for Anthony, far more deeply than she had let herself realize. But this would not do. She could not fall for him. But the more she dwelled on it, the more it did not seem like such a terrible idea, after all.

———————⌇———————

Anthony sat at the head of the long, rectangular dining table, the morning light filtering softly through the windows as he attempted to read the newssheets. But his mind wandered, mostly back to Elodie and how she had looked hurt when she learned of the note he had kept from her. He'd had the most restless night between dwelling on Elodie and his brother's gambling debts. The only bright spot in the morning was the surprise he had arranged for Elodie, which he hoped would arrive soon.

The door swung open and Stephen staggered into the room, looking all the worse for wear. "Good morning, Brother," he mumbled.

Anthony offered a curt nod. "Good morning."

Stephen winced, placing a hand on his forehead. "Must you be so loud? I am a little bottle-weary this morning."

"A little?" Anthony questioned, folding his newssheets and regarding his brother with a raised brow.

Stephen stopped by a chair and waited expectantly for the footman to pull it out for him. "I am in no mood for your sense of humor today," he muttered, settling into his seat. "The most humiliating thing happened last night."

"I am almost afraid to ask, but do tell?"

Reaching for a glass of water, Stephen replied, "My favorite gambling establishment refused me entry. Me? Can you imagine such an insult?"

"I can, actually," Anthony said dryly. "By any chance, was this gambling hall in Hampstead?"

"It was, yes. But I have no desire to ever return there after such treatment."

Setting aside the newssheets, Anthony decided to drop the news he had been withholding. "Mr. Kingsley visited me last night."

Stephen's brow knit together. "What did that bloke want?" he asked, casting an impatient look towards the footman. "I need coffee. Immediately."

As the footman hurried off to fulfill his demand, Anthony replied, "Mr. Kingsley informed me that you have racked up an impressive debt of nearly eleven thousand pounds."

Stephen waved a hand, dismissing the matter. "I've had a bit of bad luck lately. Things will turn around."

Anthony fixed him with a hard look. "Mr. Kingsley made it quite clear. If you don't pay, he will throw you into debtor's prison."

His brother scoffed, entirely unconcerned. "A mere scare tactic. It would be terrible for business if they tossed the son of an earl into prison."

"Nevertheless, you do owe them a staggering sum of money, and they intend to collect."

Stephen shrugged. "Then settle it and be done with it."

Anthony shook his head. "Not this time."

"Pardon?"

Keeping his gaze steady, Anthony responded, "There is talk of you owing as much as nineteen thousand pounds. That is an amount that could drain the coffers. Most of our funds are invested in land and other assets. There is no extra to spare."

Stephen's face twisted in irritation. "You would truly let your own brother be sent to prison over this?"

"I have responsibilities beyond you, Stephen," Anthony said, keeping his tone calm though anger simmered beneath. "I have hundreds of tenants and staff relying on me."

His brother's voice grew louder. "You speak of duty, yet you would abandon your own brother. You are nothing but a hypocrite!"

Unruffled, Anthony leaned back in his chair. "Perhaps, but I am also the one trying to secure the future of our family's estate and honor."

"What would Father or Mother say about this?" Stephen demanded, his nostrils flaring.

"That does not matter," Anthony said. "You are five and twenty years old and have received the finest education. What have you done with your life?"

"What can I do with my life?" Stephen asked. "I am the spare. My only purpose is to ensure Father has an heir if something happens to you."

Anthony glanced heavenward. "You are your own person. It is perfectly acceptable for you to have a profession."

"I do not want to be a vicar or a barrister."

"There are other professions you could have," Anthony said.

A footman stepped into the room and placed a cup in front of Stephen. He reached down and took a sip. "Blast it!" he shouted. "It is too hot. Tell the cook that she is incompetent at best."

Anthony turned towards the footman. "Do not tell Mrs. Franks that."

Placing the cup down, Stephen said, "I do not know why you protect Mrs. Franks. You should have hired a French cook by now."

"Mrs. Franks has been our cook since we were young."

"That does not mean she is any good," Stephen countered.

Anthony pushed back his chair and rose. "This conversation is over. I have work that I need to see to."

"But what about me?" Stephen asked.

"What about you?"

Stephen looked up at him, his eyes narrowing. "You would truly let me rot in prison because you wish to lord over me?"

Anthony lifted his brow. "I am not lording over you. There are consequences to your actions and it is time that you learned that."

"Father will not let you do this to me," Stephen asserted.

"Perhaps not. But I am responsible for the purse strings now."

Stephen shoved back his chair and moved to stand in front of Anthony. "What of my inheritance?"

"What of it?" Anthony asked, ignoring his brother's foul breath. "You spent that ages ago."

"I did not. You must have kept it for yourself," Stephen seethed.

Anthony pursed his lips together. "I have kept a record of your spending. You have been a drain on our finances for far too long."

"You think you are so much better than I am, do you not?" Stephen asked.

Anthony gave a tired sigh. "Why do you insist on asking that question over and over?"

Stephen inched closer, a sneer on his lips. "You are the golden boy, the heir. You have been given everything and I have been given your crumbs."

"You have been given plenty of opportunities, and you have squandered every single one."

At that moment, Percy stepped into the dining room and announced, "My lord, it has arrived."

Stephen glanced over his shoulder at Percy. "What has arrived?"

Anthony looked past his brother, addressing the butler. "Wonderful. Is it in the gardens?"

Percy nodded. "Yes, my lord. And I took the liberty of attaching the bow as requested."

Stephen gave him a bemused look. "What exactly did you buy, Brother?"

"Something for Elodie," Anthony said. "Now, if you will excuse me..."

Stephen's face twisted with anger. "You claim we have no funds to spare, yet you are lavishing gifts on Elodie?"

"It is a modest token of my affection, and a far cry from the sum you owe."

Before Stephen could launch into another tirade, Anthony excused himself and made his way to the gardens. There, sporting a red bow on its mane, was a chestnut miniature horse. It was even more perfect than he had imagined. Elodie would be thrilled.

The groom approached, offering the rope, but Anthony held up his hand. "Would you mind stepping out of sight for a moment? I want to surprise Lady Elodie myself."

"Yes, my lord," the groom said, leading the horse to a more concealed spot.

Anthony reached down, gathering a few small pebbles, and aimed for Elodie's window. The first rock missed. So did the second. He had not realized how difficult it would be to hit a window on the second level. Finally, on the third attempt, the pebble tapped against the glass.

After a long moment, Elodie opened her window and looked out at him in confusion. "Did you just throw a rock at my window?"

"I did," he replied, unable to suppress a grin. "I was hoping you might join me in the gardens."

Elodie frowned. "Did you forget that I am still angry with you?"

"I do recall that," Anthony said, rocking back on his heels. "But I think I have something here that might change your mind."

Her eyes roamed over the gardens. "And what is that? There is nothing there with you."

"Ah, but there is," Anthony insisted. "You will just have to trust me on this one."

Elodie held his gaze for a long moment before sighing and disappearing from the window. A few moments later, she emerged from her townhouse in a pale blue gown, her expression curious yet guarded. "All right. I am here. What is it you wanted to show me?"

Anthony smiled. "Thank you for coming, even though I know you are still upset with me."

"*Very* upset," she corrected.

"Noted," he replied, trying to contain his excitement. "I thought about what I could do to show you how truly sorry I am, and I believe I have found just the thing." He extended his hand towards the side of the gardens where the groom had led the horse.

Nothing happened.

Elodie gave him a puzzled look. "I am not seeing anything."

Anthony held up a finger. "Wait here." He walked briskly to the side of the townhouse and cleared his throat, drawing the groom's attention away from the horse.

"My apologies, my lord," the groom said sheepishly.

Anthony reached for the rope. "No harm done."

As he rounded the corner back to Elodie, he saw her eyes widen, her expression lighting up with joy. She practically danced in place as she spotted the miniature horse.

"It is a miniature horse!" she exclaimed, rushing forward to meet them.

"It is, and it is yours," Anthony said, extending her the rope.

Elodie's mouth dropped open. "You are giving me a miniature horse?"

"I am. Do you like it?"

Without warning, Elodie threw her arms around him,

hugging him tightly. "I love it so much!" she exclaimed, her voice full of emotion.

He wrapped his arms around her in return, breathing in the warmth of the moment. "I am glad."

She took a step back, eyes sparking with mirth. "I was planning to make you my sworn nemesis after that note incident, but I think you have officially redeemed yourself."

"I do want to apologize again for not telling you," Anthony said. "It was wrong of me to do so."

"Yes, you should have. But I know you meant well. Just do not let it happen again."

He performed a small bow. "I can agree to that."

"Good," Elodie said, turning back to her horse. "What should I call him?"

"I thought you had already decided that you would call him Henry."

Elodie's face grew thoughtful as she looked at the horse. After a moment, she said, "I did, but I think I shall call him Lord Henry."

"Why 'Lord'?" Anthony asked.

Gesturing towards the horse, Elodie replied, "Just look at him. He has the air of a proper lord."

"I do not think miniature horses can be proper."

"It is just one of the many things that we can agree to disagree on," Elodie joked.

Anthony chuckled. "I am pleased that you like Lord Henry."

Elodie laughed, stroking Lord Henry's mane. "I don't just like him, Anthony. I adore him." Her expression grew serious as she looked up at him. "Thank you, truly. This gift means the world to me."

He held her gaze, feeling his heart swell with unspoken words. "You are very welcome, Elodie. You must know all I want is for you to be happy."

A bright smile came to her face. "I am happy," she started,

then hesitated, glancing at the miniature horse, "but I must admit I am much happier with Lord Henry."

"Then my work here is done," he said, pretending to tip an imaginary hat.

A throat cleared from behind them, and they turned to see Bennett regarding them with a curious expression. "What is this?" he asked, his brow raised.

Elodie turned to face Bennett. "This, Brother, is a miniature horse," she said, her tone matter-of-fact. "It is smaller than a regular horse, but it is still a horse."

"Yes, I can see that," Bennett replied with a huff. "But what is it doing in Anthony's gardens?"

"Anthony was kind enough to gift Lord Henry to me," Elodie explained.

"Did he, now?" Bennett asked, crossing his arms. "Well, your 'gift' has left a mess on Anthony's ground. Perhaps he would be better suited to the stables."

Anthony held his hand out. "Allow me, my lady."

Elodie relinquished the rope. "Thank you, kind sir." She turned back to the horse, giving Lord Henry a parting pat on his neck. "I will come later to visit you."

As she disappeared back inside, Bennett stood there, a knowing smirk tugging at his lips. "I see exactly what you are doing."

"And what might that be?" Anthony asked.

Bennett took a step closer to him. "Let us just say it would be far less costly—and considerably easier—if you simply told her how you felt."

Anthony held his gaze, his expression guarded. "I have no idea what you are talking about."

"Of course you do," Bennett said. "And it is insulting for you to pretend otherwise."

Fearing Bennett would press him further, Anthony cleared

his throat and held up the rope. "I should get Lord Henry settled in the stables."

"While you are there, perhaps you can gather a bit of courage," Bennett called after him, his voice laced with humor.

Anthony moved towards the stables, grateful for the reprieve from Bennett's keen eyes. His friend wasn't wrong. He needed the courage to tell Elodie how he felt. But what if his feelings were not reciprocated? Would he lose her?

And that fear is what kept him quiet.

17

Elodie entered the dining room, joining Mattie and Winston at the large table. Her mother and father sat at either end, with Delphine seated directly across from her.

Mattie gave her a warm smile. "Good morning, Elodie."

"Good morning," Elodie responded, unfolding her napkin and setting it on her lap.

Her father gave her a pointed look. "It is good of you to join us, Daughter."

"Better late than never," Winston teased.

As a footman placed a plate of food in front of her, Bennett entered and took a seat beside his wife, casting Elodie a knowing glance. "Our dear friend, Anthony, has bought Elodie a rather unique gift. Is that not right?"

Elodie tilted her chin. "Indeed, he did. I found it very thoughtful of him."

Her mother leaned forward with interest. "Well, do not keep us in suspense. What did he give you?"

Elodie hesitated, then replied, "A miniature horse."

Mattie's eyes widened with delight. "How wonderful! You

have wanted a miniature horse since you were a little girl. I am thrilled for you."

Winston leaned towards his wife, his expression less enthused. "It seems a bit forward for a friend to give such a gift."

"He is a family friend, is he not?" Elodie countered, defending Anthony's gesture.

Bennett crossed his arms and gave her a quizzical look. "And what exactly do you plan to do with this miniature horse?"

Elodie beamed. "Lord Henry and I will be the best of friends."

"You intend to befriend a horse?" Bennett asked.

"Why not?" Elodie asked. "Lord Henry is the perfect friend. He is quiet and does not criticize."

Bennett shook his head. "A miniature horse will only take up space in our stables. They serve no real purpose."

"Perhaps I can bring Lord Henry inside..." Elodie started.

Her father quickly interrupted her, his tone firm. "Absolutely not! I am still debating if I will even allow you to keep this horse."

Elodie's face fell. "Please, Father. Do not make me return Lord Henry."

Her father's eyes held compassion. "You must consider the implications of such a gift. Such gestures are usually reserved for a fiancé."

"He is just a friend, Father," Elodie insisted.

Her mother reached out and gently squeezed her hand. "I am not opposed to you keeping this miniature horse, but let this be the last gift from Anthony."

A bright smile broke across Elodie's lips. "I can agree to that. Thank you, Mother."

Just then, White stepped into the room and announced, "Lord Westcott has come to call on Lady

Elodie." He met her gaze. "Are you accepting callers at this time?"

Elodie pushed her chair back. "I am."

Her mother stood as well. "I will accompany you—for propriety's sake."

Clearing his throat, her father said, "Do let Lord Westcott down gently, assuming it comes to that."

She nodded. "I will, Father."

As she walked with her mother to the drawing room, a pang of apprehension settled in her stomach. She rather liked Lord Westcott, but only as a friend. She hoped he was here simply for a social call and nothing more.

Stepping into the drawing room, she saw Lord Westcott standing by the window, his back to them. His tall figure was framed by the morning light filtering through the glass, and for a moment, Elodie admired his handsome profile.

After a moment, Elodie thought it was best to make their presence known. "Good morning, my lord."

Lord Westcott turned to face her, bowing deeply. "Lady Elodie. Lady Dallington."

Elodie gestured towards the tea service on the table. "Would you care to join us for tea?"

He paused, shifting uncomfortably in his stance. "Actually, I was hoping for a private word, if I may."

She exchanged a look with her mother, who nodded discreetly. "Would you care to tour the gardens with me?"

A flicker of relief crossed his face, and he managed a faint smile. "I would be honored."

Lord Westcott stepped forward, offering his arm, and they made their way outside in comfortable silence. Elodie knew why he was here, and she knew this impending conversation was going to be most difficult. She may care for Lord Westcott, but not enough to marry him.

Once they reached the gardens, she gently slipped her hand from his arm, turning to face him. "How is your sister?" There. That was a safe question.

"She is well, thank you," he replied, but his tone was unmistakably serious. "Though, to be honest, I did not come here to speak about her."

"The weather, perhaps?" she suggested, half-teasing, trying to hold off his next words.

He shook his head. "No, not the weather, either," he said with a quiet sigh. "Lady Elodie, I was hoping that you might consider—"

Suddenly, Anthony's voice boomed from the other side of the gardens' gate, louder than necessary. "Westcott! What brings you here?"

Westcott turned, clearly frustrated by the interruption. "Belview," he greeted, his voice terse. "I was calling upon Lady Elodie."

Anthony opened the gate and stepped in. "You picked a fine day to do so," he remarked, glancing skyward. "I expect we might even see the sun soon."

"Lord Westcott would prefer not to discuss the weather," Elodie said. "And what, pray tell, brings you here?"

"I was on my way back from the stables and realized you were without a chaperone. I thought I would offer my services," Anthony replied.

Elodie was not fooled by his explanation. What was Anthony up to? "My mother is watching from the parlor," she pointed out.

"Of course she is," Anthony said. "I should have suspected. Lady Dallington is quite diligent in her chaperoning duties."

But Anthony made no move to leave, and Elodie felt her patience fray. "Do you not have work to see to?" she pressed, hoping he would take the hint.

He shrugged. "Nothing that cannot wait."

Elodie decided to try another tactic but stopped herself. Why was she in such a rush for Anthony to leave? The longer he was here, the less likely that Lord Westcott would offer for her.

Lord Westcott was not as patient, though, and fixed Anthony with an irritated stare. "I was hoping to speak to Lady Elodie *alone*."

Anthony tipped his head. "I completely understand," he said, though he did not budge an inch. "I often enjoy speaking with Elodie alone myself. You know she is quite fond of miniature horses. You should ask her about it sometime."

Lord Westcott's irritation deepened. "I had something else in mind."

"Ah, yes," Anthony replied with a smile. "Mind if I do a bit of gardening while you talk? I noticed a few weeds that need pulling."

Lord Westcott looked at him, bemused. "Surely you have gardeners for that task?"

"Indeed, but there is a certain satisfaction in handling it myself." Anthony cast Westcott a pointed look. "I do not mind getting my hands dirty. Do you?"

Lord Westcott frowned. "Gardening is hardly my pastime."

Anthony looked disappointed. "Well, you cannot be good at everything. We all have our strengths."

Elodie stifled a smile, watching as Anthony casually picked at weeds in his gardens. She had never seen him take an interest in gardening in all the years she had known him. Why now the sudden interest?

Lord Westcott sighed in defeat and turned to her with a determined look. "Perhaps we could continue this conversation indoors?"

"Very well," she replied, and as she took his offered arm, she cast a final, curious glance at Anthony. He winked at her, and she felt warmth rise to her cheeks. Dear heavens, why did he have such a profound effect on her? It was maddening.

As Lord Westcott escorted Elodie into the corridor, he cast a glance over his shoulder, muttering with a touch of impatience, "Does Lord Belview often linger outside, loitering about like that?"

"I must admit, it is rather unusual for him."

With a dismissive shake of his head, Lord Westcott led her into the drawing room, where he finally released her arm, his voice dropping to a murmur. "At last, we are alone—"

"Not quite," came a calm, familiar voice from across the room. Bennett sat comfortably in an armchair, one leg casually crossed over the other, a book open in his hand as if he had been there all afternoon.

Elodie raised an eyebrow, surprised. "What are you doing here?"

Bennett held up his book. "I am reading."

"You never read," Elodie remarked.

"I read all the time," he replied. "And perhaps I shall write a book myself someday. Surely there are countless people eager to learn from my vast knowledge."

Elodie laughed. "Oh? And what wisdom could you possibly impart, Brother?"

Bennett shrugged. "I shall have to dwell on that. Though Delphine seems to hang on my every word."

"She is your wife," Elodie teased.

"Yes, she is," Bennett said, rising from his seat. "And on that note, I will grant you two some privacy. But I am not far. I will be just on the other side of this door, ever watchful."

Once Bennett left the room, Lord Westcott turned back to Elodie, running a hand through his neatly combed hair. "It seems as if everyone is conspiring against me today."

"Whatever for?" Elodie asked, feigning ignorance.

Taking a breath, Lord Westcott reached for her gloved hand. "Lady Elodie, I was hoping that you would consider being my wife."

Elodie stared back at him, her heart quickening despite her previous suspicions of his intentions. "Your wife?" she repeated.

"Yes, my wife," he affirmed, his tone steady.

Elodie glanced down at their intertwined hands, her mind racing. "Surely you do not want to marry me."

"I do," he replied. "You are the Season's diamond, and I am thought to be among the most eligible bachelors in London. A union between us would make sense."

She withdrew her hand sharply. "Is that why you are offering for me? Because I am the diamond?"

Lord Westcott's brow creased slightly. "Not entirely. I also find you to be a delight."

"But, what else?"

He faltered, grasping at words. "Well, you are extraordinarily beautiful, of course, but—"

"Do you love me?" she asked bluntly.

Lord Westcott blinked, visibly taken aback. "Love?" he stammered. "Good heavens, what does love have to do with marriage?"

She took a small step back, her voice resolute. "I want to fall desperately, hopelessly in love, my lord," Elodie said.

There was a faint urgency in his eyes as he said, "I am not saying that we would not find love in time. But isn't what we have enough?"

"Not for me," she asserted. "I'm sorry, but I must decline your offer."

Lord Westcott gave her a perplexed look. "Are you certain? I know you say that you want love, but perhaps with more time to think..."

She spoke over him. "I am quite certain, my lord."

He hesitated, then gave a slow, accepting nod. "Very well. I shall see my way out."

After he had gone, Elodie sank onto the settee, releasing a long, weary sigh. She had no desire to hurt Lord Westcott, but she could not in good conscience marry the man. They were friends, nothing more.

Moments later, Bennett appeared in the doorway, his expression thoughtful. "I may have overheard your conversation, and for what it is worth, I think you made the right choice."

"I know I did. But I did not want to hurt him."

"Westcott will manage," Bennett reassured her. "I am much more concerned about you."

Elodie forced a smile to her lips. "Do you not have a book to write?"

He grinned, his playful arrogance restored. "I do. The world awaits a literary masterpiece by 'A Lord.'"

"'A Lord'?"

Bennett gave her a smug smile. "Yes, because my book will be so popular that I need to use a pseudonym for my own sanity."

Elodie felt her spirits lift with this ridiculous exchange. "You are utterly delusional."

"Come, let us return to breakfast," Bennett said, lifting his hand. "I could use another piece of bread. Do you mind buttering it for me?"

"Butter your own bread, Brother," Elodie retorted, rising.

The late afternoon sun streamed through the windows, casting a warm glow across the study as Anthony sat at his desk, reviewing his accounts. Despite his attempts to focus on the columns of numbers before him, his mind kept drifting to thoughts of Elodie. He would have the opportunity to see her tonight at Mrs. Fletcher's soiree.

Percy stepped into the room and announced, "My lord, there is a Mr. —"

Before Percy could finish, Grady entered the room, his expression grave. "I need to speak to you."

Anthony gave Percy a nod, signaling him to leave and shut the door. Once they were alone, Anthony leaned forward, concern in his voice. "What has happened, Grady?"

Grady approached the desk and produced a folded piece of paper, holding it out to Anthony. "I intercepted this message from a street urchin that was meant for you."

Anthony's brow furrowed as he took the note, unfolding it with unease. His eyes scanned the message.

The time is up. Place ten thousand pounds in a sack, leave it in the back alley on Grantham Street tonight at dusk and walk away. If you fail to follow my instructions explicitly, Lady Elodie's reputation will be ruined.

Anthony looked up at Grady. "What are we to do?"

Grady's eyes were sharp and steady. "I have a plan."

"Good, because I am at a loss as to what to do," he admitted.

Grady took a seat across from him, leaning forward. "We will put a hundred pounds in the sack and fill it with papers to make up the weight. At first glance, it will appear to be the full amount. Then I will follow the person who picks it up and find out who is behind this."

Anthony gave him a doubtful look. "What if they notice you following?"

A sly smile crossed Grady's face. "They won't. I have become rather skilled at going unseen. Have you even noticed me watching you these past few days?"

"You have?" Anthony asked.

"Yes," Grady replied. "And I must say, your exchanges with Lady Elodie are rather telling." Anthony did not want to discuss Elodie with Grady, much less anyone. "All right. I will go to the bank and secure the funds."

"No need," Grady said. "It is already done. I forged the necessary documents, withdrew the funds, and left it with Percy. Though perhaps you might reconsider your choice of bank in the future. It is not quite secure."

Anthony frowned, both grateful and perturbed. "Once the blackmailer realizes we have shorted him, what is to stop him from following through on his threat?"

"Once I have identified him, I will have him thrown into Newgate," Grady said. "A few nights there will have him eager to cooperate."

"And if he does not?" Anthony pressed, unwilling to leave anything to chance.

Grady grinned, as if he found Anthony's question to be very amusing. "He will. My methods of persuasion are quite effective."

Anthony leaned back in his chair, studying Grady. "But why demand the money in an alley, and why at dusk?"

"Dusk is when the laborers flood the streets on their way home. Grantham Street will be crowded, a perfect cover for an escape," Grady explained. "But I will have no trouble moving through a crowd. You, however, would draw attention."

Anthony inclined his head, acknowledging the point. "Do you have any ideas on who this blackmailer could be?"

"I have my suspicions," Grady replied. "But I would prefer to confirm them before sharing."

A knock interrupted them, and Percy reappeared. "Lord Westcott requests a moment of your time, my lord."

"Send him in," Anthony said.

A moment later, Lord Westcott entered, his gaze darting

from Anthony to Grady, tension evident in his posture. "I need to speak with you alone," he said tersely.

Anthony closed the ledger on his desk. "You may speak freely in front of Grady."

Lord Westcott hesitated. "What are your intentions towards Lady Elodie?"

"Pardon?" Anthony asked. He had not been anticipating that question. He thought Lord Westcott was here to discuss the blackmailer.

"I believe my question was clear," Westcott said, his voice firm.

Anthony met Lord Westcott's gaze. "Why, may I ask, are you asking me this?"

Lord Westcott stepped closer to the desk. "Lady Elodie declined my proposal of marriage, and I believe it is because of you."

"Me?" Anthony asked. "Lady Elodie and I do not have an understanding."

"That is apparent, but I suspect you desire one," Lord Westcott countered.

Anthony rose from his seat, struggling to keep his temper in check. "Not that it concerns you, but even if I did, Lady Elodie has not indicated she wants anything of the sort."

"Have you even bothered to ask her?"

"No," Anthony replied.

Lord Westcott let out an exasperated sigh. "Perhaps you should spend less time gardening and recognize what is right in front of you."

Anthony walked over to the drink cart. He needed a drink. He no more wanted to discuss Elodie with Lord Westcott than he wanted to chew glass. He picked up the decanter and poured three glasses.

He offered them each a glass before retaking his seat. "Is Lady Elodie the only reason why you are here?"

Lord Westcott glanced down at the drink in his hand, visibly conflicted. "No. I also received a blackmail letter, demanding ten thousand pounds to protect my sister's reputation."

Anthony nodded. "I received the same instructions."

Lord Westcott placed his glass onto the desk. "It took some time, but my sister did confess to what happened that night. She also mentioned you enlisted a Bow Street Runner."

"I did." He gestured towards Grady. "This is Grady. He is investigating the matter."

Lord Westcott's brow furrowed. "Am I truly to leave a sack of money in some alley and hope for the best?"

Grady rose. "You will do nothing. I will follow the black-mailer and deal with him myself."

"And by 'deal with him,' you mean…" Lord Westcott's voice trailed off.

Grady's smile grew grim. "It means I will arrest him and send him to Newgate until I convince him to remain quiet."

"How will you convince him?" Lord Westcott pressed.

Grady placed his full glass onto the drink cart. "Have you had rats crawl across your skin at night as you lay on the cold ground that reeks like the inside of a chamber pot?"

Lord Westcott shuddered. "I have not."

"Trust me. Newgate can break even the toughest of men," Grady said. "Now, it is almost time for Lord Belview to make the drop in the alleyway."

Lord Westcott stood up. "And what if you are wrong on this?"

"I am not," Grady replied.

"But humor me for a moment," Lord Westcott started. "I cannot have my sister's reputation ruined."

Grady's eyes held understanding. "Trust me, my lord. I know what I am doing. This blackmailer is no match for me."

Anthony interjected, his tone calm but resolute. "Trust Grady. He is our best hope."

With a solemn nod, Westcott walked over to the door and stopped. "I love my sister and I would do anything to keep her name out of the newssheets."

"I feel the same way about Lady Elodie," Anthony replied.

As Lord Westcott left, Grady watched him go, his expression shadowed by something unspoken. "My own sister once trusted the wrong man, and her life was ruined," he said softly. "I will not let that happen to Lady Elodie or Lady Eugenie."

Anthony could hear the pain in Grady's voice, and he said, "I believe you."

Grady's gaze shifted to him thoughtfully. "But Lord Westcott is right about one thing. You should tell Lady Elodie how you feel."

"She is not ready yet. If I said anything, it would scare her off."

Grady's expression softened with understanding. "My profession is a lonely one. I work long hours, leaving me little time for a wife. But if I ever found someone who looked at me the way Elodie looks at you, I would never let her go."

Anthony dropped down onto the settee. "She only looked at me that way because I bought her a miniature pony."

"Do you truly believe that?"

Glancing up at the ceiling, Anthony replied, "I do not know what to believe. Not anymore. I just want her to be happy."

Grady came to sit down across from him. "And you do not believe you could be the one to make her happy?"

Anthony looked away. "Why does this matter to you?"

"Lord Winston mentioned you might need encouragement to share your feelings," Grady replied with a slight smile.

He let out a long sigh. "Enough of this. We have a black-mailer to catch."

Grady put his hands up in mock surrender. "I will drop it...

for now. But Lord Winston did pay me extra to offer relationship advice."

With a glance at the long clock in the corner, Anthony said, "We should depart if we want to arrive at dusk."

"You go first, and I will trail behind," Grady said.

Anthony walked over to the door. "I wish you luck."

Grady's expression grew serious. "I would much rather catch a blackmailer than go to a soiree. It is I that should be wishing you luck."

As Anthony exited the study to go in search of Percy, he hoped that this evening went well. The weight of the blackmailer's threat bore down on him, but deeper still, he realized how much Elodie meant to him. That is when he realized something. He had once wondered how long Elodie had been on his mind, but it occurred to him that since they were young, she had never left.

As he entered the entry hall, Stephen spotted him and raised an eyebrow. "Where are you off to in such a rush?"

"I have an errand to take care of before the soiree," Anthony replied.

Stephen's expression soured with mild irritation. "Do not make us late. I have every intention of joining my friends in the cards room, and I will not miss my chance because of you."

"Good heavens, I would never be so monstrous as to delay your reunion with the card tables," Anthony mocked. "If you are that concerned, why not take the other coach?"

Stephen huffed. "Maybe I will."

At that moment, Percy stepped into the entry hall, a small sack in his hands. "As per Mr. Grady's instructions, my lord," he announced, holding it up.

"Excellent work, Percy," Anthony replied.

Stephen's gaze dropped to the sack, his expression turning suspicious. "What are you mixed up in, Brother?"

"Nothing that concerns you," Anthony replied dismissively.

Tossing up his hands, Stephen said, "I do not know why I bother even speaking to you. I shall see you at the soiree. Do try not to embarrass me this evening."

Anthony watched his brother turn on his heel and leave. He glanced down at the sack in his hand and hoped tonight it would all go according to plan.

18

E lodie sat at her dressing table as she hummed the melody of the piece she was set to perform tonight at the soiree. The very thought of standing before a crowd, playing the pianoforte under their critical gazes, made her stomach churn. How she hated feeling like a performing monkey for the amusement of Society.

Behind her, Molly took a step back, a satisfied smile on her face. "Is your hair to your liking, my lady?"

Elodie turned her head to examine the elegant coiffure in the mirror. "Well done, Molly," she praised.

"Thank you. Shall we dress you now?"

Instead of answering directly, Elodie spun in her chair and fixed Molly with a mischievous look. "Grab a trunk and fill it with my gowns. If we leave now, we can escape unnoticed."

Molly laughed, playing along. "And where would we go?"

"To the woodlands," Elodie replied with a dramatic flair. "We will learn to live off the land and our friends will be the charming creatures."

"And where would we live in this idyllic woodland existence?"

Elodie tapped a finger to her chin, feigning deep thought. "We will build a cottage by the river and have picturesque views. It will be perfect."

Molly's smile grew. "Do you know how to build a cottage?"

"Well, no, but we can figure it out."

Shaking her head, Molly crossed the room and picked up the pale pink gown with its delicate net overlay from the bed. "As tempting as that sounds, I think it would be best if we stay here. Besides, if we left, we could not take Lord Henry with us, and I know how much you adore that horse."

Elodie sighed, her shoulders slumping. "You are right, of course. But I truly do not want to perform tonight. Everyone will be watching me... judging me."

"You are the diamond of the Season—" Molly began.

Elodie interrupted her with an exasperated groan. "Why does everyone insist on reminding me of that? I am nothing special."

"The queen seemed to think otherwise," Molly pointed out. "You made her laugh, which was a feat no other debutante has managed."

Elodie made a face. "Why must I be so likable?"

"What a dreadful burden you must bear," Molly teased.

The door opened and her mother entered the room. She gave her a disapproving shake of her head. "Why are you not dressed, Child? We are leaving soon."

"Molly and I have decided that we are going to run away to the woodlands and befriend the creatures there," Elodie said with mock seriousness.

Her mother barely reacted, smoothing a hand over her skirts. "You may do so *after* the soiree. Not before."

"You have no objections?" Elodie asked.

"I have many, but we do not have time to debate them. You need to look your best tonight."

Elodie rose and retrieved the gown from Molly. She slipped

it on while Molly began the painstaking task of fastening the countless buttons down the back.

Her mother nodded in approval. "That gown is perfect for this evening. You will be the envy of the *ton*."

"Can I bring Lord Henry with me?" Elodie asked.

"Absolutely not!"

Elodie shrugged, undeterred. "It was worth a try. Perhaps I will teach Lord Henry how to play the pianoforte."

"Horses cannot play the pianoforte," her mother replied.

"No, but *miniature* horses might. They have smaller hooves. I wonder why no one has tried it before."

Her mother pressed her lips together. "It might be best if you avoid speaking to people this evening."

"That is my goal every time I attend a social event."

Molly fastened the last button and stepped back. "Will there be anything else, my lady?"

"No, thank you." Elodie walked back to her dressing table and picked up her reticule. "I am bringing my bent nail this evening."

"Dare I ask why?" her mother asked.

"In case someone abducts me."

Her mother looked unimpressed. "And why would anyone abduct you?"

"It has happened before," Elodie replied matter-of-factly.

Walking over to the door, her mother opened it. "I will not argue with you, but it is a foolish idea."

Elodie followed her mother into the corridor and they made their way down to the entry hall, where Winston and Mattie were waiting.

Mattie's eyes lit up when she saw Elodie. "You look lovely, Elodie."

"Thank you," Elodie said.

Winston gave his sister a pat on her shoulder. "Do try not to embarrass the family this evening."

Elodie shot him a dry look. "Thank you for that vote of confidence. Any other words of advice you wish to share before we leave?"

"Do not trip on the way to the pianoforte," Winston quipped, withdrawing his hand.

Mattie swiped her hand at Winston's sleeve. "Leave your sister alone. You know she does not like to perform in front of people."

"I do not," Elodie agreed. "Which is why I am puzzled as to why Mother accepted the invitation on my behalf."

"It is expected of you," her mother said.

"You know who does not expect anything from me? Woodland creatures," Elodie declared with a flourish of her hand.

Just then, White entered the hall and bowed slightly. "The coaches are out front."

"Thank you, White," Lady Dallington acknowledged, ushering them towards the door.

Elodie glanced back at the stairs. "Should we not wait for Bennett and Delphine?"

"They are running late. They will arrive as soon as they can," her mother shared.

"I would be happy to wait for them—" Elodie attempted.

Her mother placed a firm hand on her shoulder. "You need to be on time."

"Why does it matter?"

"Because you have no husband," her mother said. "Once you are married, you can arrive as late as you please."

Elodie smirked as they stepped outside. "You may have just convinced me of the benefits of marriage."

As they stepped inside the coach, Elodie moved to sit beside her mother on the bench, while Winston and Mattie took their seats across from them.

The coach jerked forward, the cobblestones below causing

a mild jostle. Mattie leaned forward, her expression curious. "What piece will you be performing tonight?"

"It is one of Melody's compositions," Elodie replied. "It is one of my favorites. I only wish she were here to accompany me."

Her mother gave her a light nudge on the shoulder. "Well, Melody has a husband now, and you, my dear, are still husbandless."

"Thank you for the reminder... again," Elodie muttered under her breath. "Where is Father?"

Her mother sighed. "He is still at Parliament. I do believe that man will work himself into an early grave."

Elodie turned her attention towards the window, where the fading light of day danced on the passing buildings. The streets of London bustled with activity, but her mind was miles away, consumed by her own dread. What if she stumbled over the notes tonight? Despite countless hours of practice, she had never performed this piece before an audience.

How she wished that Melody were here. Her sister had a knack for soothing her nerves, for reminding her what truly mattered. But tonight, Elodie would have to manage on her own.

The coach came to a halt in front of Mrs. Fletcher's grand townhouse. Winston stepped out first, offering his hand to assist the ladies. Elodie accepted his help, though as soon as her feet touched the pavement, she withdrew her hand.

She glanced up at the townhouse, its pristine white façade glowing softly in the evening light. The crowd outside was buzzing with excitement. Elodie took a deep, steadying breath. *I can do this.*

Inside, the entry hall gleamed with polished black and white marble floors and soaring white columns that gave the space a sense of grandeur. Elodie admired it briefly, but she became so lost in thought that she collided with the gentleman in front of her.

Startled, she stepped back quickly. "My apologies—" Her words caught in her throat when Lord Westcott turned to face her.

His steady hand reached out to her. "Are you all right?"

"Yes," Elodie stammered. "I was just distracted. I did not mean to run into the back of you."

"No harm done," he said, his expression composed, though his tone carried a gravity that was hard to ignore.

Before Elodie could say more, Lady Eugenie appeared at her brother's side. "I am so relieved that you are here. Are you performing tonight?"

"I am," Elodie confirmed.

Placing a hand to cover her mouth, Lady Eugenie lowered her voice. "My brother is vexed with me because I refuse to play tonight."

Elodie gave her a rueful smile. "I wish I had that choice."

Lady Eugenie's expression softened as she lowered her hand. "I am sure you will play spectacularly."

She managed a small laugh. "Let's hope so. I have been given strict instructions not to embarrass the family tonight."

As she spoke, Elodie was very aware of Lord Westcott's gaze lingering on her. She wished they could return to the way it was before he offered for her. Now their conversation felt awkward and strained.

Lord Westcott cleared his throat. "If you will excuse me, I need to secure our seats for the performance."

Lady Eugenie watched him walk off before saying, "My brother informed me that you turned down his offer of marriage."

Elodie winced. "I did and I am sorry if—"

Lady Eugenie cut her off with a shake of her head. "Do not apologize. It was for the best. Do not get me wrong, I would have loved for you to become my sister, but my brother approached it all wrong. He was looking for a wife with logic, not his heart."

Elodie felt a wave of relief wash over her. "I was worried you would be upset with me."

"Upset?" Lady Eugenie repeated. "Heavens, no. Why would you even think such a thing?"

Before she could reply, her mother tapped her on the shoulder. "We should take our seats, Dear."

"Yes, Mother," Elodie said, offering Lady Eugenie a brief smile before following her mother.

As they walked towards the rows of neatly arranged chairs, Elodie's gaze swept the room. She spotted Winston speaking with Stephen near the back. If Stephen was here, could Anthony also be in attendance? Her heart gave a small, hopeful flutter, but as her eyes scanned the crowd, she felt a stab of disappointment when she did not see him.

Why should it matter if he was here tonight? It shouldn't. But, as much as she tried to convince herself otherwise, it did.

Her mother leaned closer to her, her voice low. "Who are you looking for?"

"No one," she lied.

Her mother arched a skeptical brow but said nothing, much to Elodie's relief. They found their seats near the front, and as Elodie sat down, a small part of her could not help but hope for a glimpse of Anthony before the evening was through.

The coach lurched to a halt outside Mrs. Fletcher's grand townhouse, and Anthony wasted no time. He pushed the door open before the footman could reach it and stepped out onto the pavement, his boots crunching softly against the gravel.

The evening air was crisp, but he barely noticed as he ascended the steps to the main door.

The butler promptly opened the door, and he stepped inside. The strains of a pianoforte drifted through the entry hall, a beautiful melody that drew Anthony forward. He followed the music and found a seat near the back of the room just as the piece concluded.

The applause was polite but brief, and then the tall, long-faced Mrs. Fletcher stepped forward, her hands clasped primly in front of her. "And now, we have the privilege of hearing from Lady Elodie," she announced, her voice carrying easily over the murmurs.

Anthony straightened, his eyes fixed on Elodie as she rose from her seat. Her movements were graceful but hesitant, and he could sense her unease. He knew how much she dreaded performing in front of an audience, and he wished there was some way to ease her nerves, to offer her the quiet reassurance he knew she needed.

As she walked towards the pianoforte, her eyes swept over the room and, for a fleeting moment, landed on him. Something flickered in her expression. Was it relief? Hope? Whatever it was, Anthony's breath caught as Elodie captured his soul with her gaze. He winked, and her lips curved into a brief smile before she turned to the pianoforte.

Elodie sat on the bench and rested her hands lightly on the keys. When she began to play, the room seemed to hold its breath. Anthony had heard her play many times before, but tonight, there was something different, something extraordinary. Her fingers moved with precision and passion, pouring life into the melody in a way that stirred something deep in him.

He leaned forward, sitting on the very edge of his seat, his attention wholly captured. At first, he felt her tension as though it were his own, silently willing her to hit every note perfectly.

But as the music flowed, he relaxed, letting the sound wash over him. By the time she struck the final chord, he realized his worry had been for nothing. Elodie's performance had been flawless.

The room erupted into applause, and Anthony joined in, though he noted how uncomfortable Elodie seemed with the attention. She hurried back to her seat, and Lady Dallington leaned over to whisper something to her. Judging by her mother's pleased expression, it was undoubtedly praise.

Mrs. Fletcher rose once more, her voice cheerful. "Thank you to all of tonight's performers. That concludes the musical portion of the evening."

As the guests began to shift and mingle, Anthony stood quickly. He wanted to reach Elodie, to congratulate her, to speak to her. But before he could make his way through the room, a group of gentlemen blocked his path to her, their idle chatter forming an impenetrable wall. Frustrated, Anthony accepted a glass of champagne from a passing server, taking a small sip as he waited for an opening. He had no patience for waiting, but for now, it was all he could do.

Lord Westcott joined him. "Lady Elodie played exquisitely, did she not?"

"She did," he confirmed, glancing briefly towards her. She was smiling at the crowd of gentlemen, but it did not quite reach her eyes.

Lowering his voice, Lord Westcott asked, "How did the drop-off go?"

Anthony met his gaze, his tone matching the seriousness of the question. "I followed the instructions precisely. The sack was left in the alleyway. Now, we wait."

"Do you trust this Bow Street Runner?"

"I do," Anthony said with conviction. "Grady knows what he is doing."

Lord Westcott sighed, his composure briefly giving way to

worry. "There is so much at stake, I do not know what I would do if Eugenie's reputation were ruined. She has already endured so much with the loss of our parents. I cannot bear the thought of her facing more pain."

"You are a good brother."

"It depends on the day, I'm afraid," Lord Westcott retorted.

Before the conversation could continue, Stephen appeared, his nearly empty glass dangling precariously from his fingers. "Brother, you were late," he drawled, his tone laced with mockery. "I was worried you would miss Elodie's performance."

Anthony did not have time for his brother. Not now. "I had an errand I had to attend to."

"An errand more important than Elodie? Shocking," Stephen stated.

He frowned. "I thought you planned to be in the cards room."

"I am on my way," Stephen said, downing the last of his champagne. "Do not wait up."

"I never do."

As Stephen sauntered away, Lord Westcott's expression turned grim. "I have heard rumors about your brother's gambling debts."

"They are all true," Anthony admitted. "It is only a matter of time before his creditors catch up with him and he ends up in debtor's prison."

"Good. A stint in prison might do him some good," Lord Westcott said. "At least the mothers of young ladies will sleep easier."

Anthony shook his head. "My brother is a blackguard."

"That is putting it politely," Lord Westcott muttered. "How is your father? I heard he came into Town."

"He did, and he is doing much better than expected. I visit him often."

A shadow passed over Lord Westcott's face, his expression

unreadable. "It is difficult watching your father wither away in front of you."

"It is," Anthony said. "I'm sorry. I did not mean to bring up painful memories—"

His friend raised a hand to stop him. "The memories are painful, but they are mine. And I treasure them."

Anthony placed a comforting hand on Lord Westcott's shoulder. "I am glad that you have your sister."

Lord Westcott's voice was low, almost a whisper. "She is lucky to be alive after her accident." He paused. "Forgive me. I need a moment alone."

Anthony watched as Lord Westcott walked away, his posture heavy with unspoken burdens. He wished there was a way to help the man, but he found himself at a loss. Some pain could not be eased with words alone.

Just then, movement in the crowd caught his attention. Elodie emerged from a horde of gentlemen, her steps hurried and her expression one of mild exasperation. She came to a stop in front of him, her voice low as she murmured, "Goodness, they are relentless."

A server passed with a tray of champagne, and Elodie swiftly took a glass. She raised it to her lips for a tentative sip, only to grimace. "This is awful," she declared, eyeing the glass.

"It is an acquired taste," Anthony offered.

"Well, I do not think I will be acquiring it anytime soon," Elodie said, placing the glass on a nearby table. "I think I will stick to lemonade."

Anthony's gaze shifted to the group of gentlemen still hovering nearby, their eyes fixed on Elodie as though waiting for another opportunity to approach. He leaned closer and suggested, "Shall we take a tour of the gardens?"

With a glance over her shoulder, Elodie replied, "That would be much more pleasurable than having to endure polite conversation with those nick-ninnies."

Anthony offered his arm with a faint smile. "They are just waiting for their chance to win your affection. Is that not a good thing?"

"They are only interested in me because I am the diamond," Elodie replied, slipping her hand into the crook of his arm.

"I do think you are selling yourself short," Anthony said as they made their way towards the open French doors leading to the gardens.

"You are kind, but I want to be loved for who I am, not because I am the diamond of the Season," she admitted.

The gardens were softly lit by lanterns, their glow casting shadows across the pathways. When they reached the iron railing overlooking the manicured hedges below, Anthony dropped his arm and looked up at the stars sparkling in the clear night sky. He had a plan, one that he had just cultivated, to win Elodie over. He just hoped he knew Elodie as well as he believed he did.

"I am glad that we have a moment to speak alone," Anthony began.

She grinned, glancing around at the other couples milling about. "Well, not entirely alone. There are plenty of people out here."

"True, but none of them are listening to our conversation." Anthony hesitated as he turned to face her. "I wanted you to know that I am done trying to win you over."

Her smile faltered. "I beg your pardon?"

This was it. If his plan did not work, he could lose Elodie. But he could not keep going on as he had been, pining after her without her knowing.

"I care for you," Anthony confessed, his voice steady but filled with emotion. "More than I probably should. It has always been that way. But it is clear to me now that you do not feel the same."

Elodie opened her mouth to speak, but Anthony held up a

hand to stop her. "Please, you do not need to say anything. I think it is best if we remain friends."

Before she could reply, a mocking voice interrupted them. "Look at what the rubbish dragged in."

Anthony stiffened, stepping protectively in front of Elodie as Lord Montrose sauntered towards them, his smirk as infuriating as ever. "What do you want, Montrose?"

Lord Montrose's gaze flickered to Elodie, his tone dripping with false charm. "Nothing but the pleasure of Lady Elodie's company." He extended a hand towards her. "Would you care to take a stroll with me, my lady?"

"Absolutely not!" Anthony exclaimed.

Lord Montrose's smile widened, clearly enjoying himself. "I do believe the young lady can speak for herself."

Elodie stepped out from behind Anthony. "I would rather chew on a boot than spend time in your company."

Lord Montrose raised an eyebrow. "How very specific. Do you often chew on boots?"

Anthony's patience snapped. "Lady Elodie is not interested in your company. Move along."

Lord Montrose's expression darkened as he turned his attention to Anthony. "And what do you think would happen if certain rumors about Lady Elodie's actions in the gardens were to spread? She would be ruined. Who would want her then?"

"I would," Anthony said firmly.

Lord Montrose took a threatening step closer, his sneer replacing his smug smile. "You? You are not man enough for Elodie!"

"But you are?" Anthony shot back.

Elodie placed a hand on her hip. "Why are you two speaking about me as if I am not standing right here?"

Lord Montrose reached out towards her, but Anthony slapped his hand away. "Do not touch her."

"You will pay for that," Lord Montrose growled.

Anthony's gaze remained unyielding. "Leave, Montrose. Go slither back to whatever hole you crawled out of."

With a snarl, Lord Montrose swung his fist, landing a blow to Anthony's jaw. Anthony staggered back, bringing a hand to his reddening face.

"That was for the other night," Lord Montrose declared.

Before Anthony could respond, Elodie stepped forward, brandishing a rusty, bent nail from her reticule. "Leave now, or I will show you exactly what this nail can do."

Lord Montrose chuckled. "That is adorable, my dear."

"Come closer, and I will demonstrate how adorable it truly is," Elodie said, squaring her shoulders.

Putting his hands up in surrender, Lord Montrose responded, "Good evening, my lady. Belview." He turned and strode off into the shadows.

Elodie spun to face Anthony, her expression filled with concern. "Are you all right?"

"I will live," Anthony said, rubbing his red jaw.

"Lord Montrose is awful. Just awful."

"I will not disagree with you there," Anthony said. He gestured to the nail in her hand. "I appreciate what you did, but it truly was not necessary. I could have handled him."

"I know," Elodie said, "but we were already drawing attention. I thought it best to end it quickly."

Anthony smiled faintly. "Is that the infamous nail?"

Her expression grew thoughtful. "Yes, it is the nail I found when Melody and I were abducted. I kept it to remind me of that night."

"Is that a night you want to remember?"

"It is," Elodie said after a pause. "It was the night I learned to truly appreciate my sister."

Just then, Winston stepped out onto the veranda with Mattie on his arm. "There you are," he said with relief in his voice. "Montrose is weaving quite a tale about how he beat Anthony to a pulp."

"He did no such thing," Anthony declared.

"I believe you," Winston said, "but it would be wise to return inside so people can see Montrose is, once again, spewing lies."

Anthony offered Elodie his arm. "Shall we, my lady?"

She smiled, slipping her hand into the crook of his arm. "We shall."

19

Elodie lay in bed, staring up at the ceiling. She could hear the barking of the puppies drifting in from the window. But she did not dare move to the window. The thought of catching a glimpse of Anthony made her heart pound in her chest.

Her restless night had been plagued by memories of their conversation playing over and over in her mind. Anthony had said he cared for her. How had she been so blind? Had his teasing all along been an attempt to flirt? To express something deeper? She had missed it entirely.

And now he was done trying to win her over. He wanted to remain friends. But was that truly what she wanted? She cared for him, of course. There was no denying that. Yet perhaps it would be best to let things lie as they were, to remain friends and avoid the risk of making things more complicated.

The door opened, pulling her from her thoughts. Molly entered with a cheerful expression. "Good morning, my lady. Your mother has requested that you join everyone for breakfast."

Elodie groaned and grabbed a pillow, pressing it over her face. "Tell her that I died."

"You are not dead," Molly said. "Is something truly bothering you?"

Tossing the pillow aside, Elodie forced a weak cough. "I feel sick."

Molly raised an unimpressed eyebrow. "You are not sick, either. Do you want to tell me the real reason?"

Elodie sat up in bed. "I just feel discombobulated."

Walking over to the wardrobe, Molly removed a green gown. "Then let's dress you while you are trying to sort through your thoughts."

"I doubt that will help," Elodie replied, swinging her legs over the side of the bed.

Molly draped the gown over the back of the settee. "Did something happen at the soiree last night?"

"Yes... no... I don't know," Elodie admitted, removing her white wrapper and placing it on the bed.

"You are being very decisive today, I see," Molly teased.

Elodie moved to her dressing table and sat down in the chair. "What do you think of Lord Belview?"

Molly tilted her head thoughtfully. "I have never met him, but you speak rather highly of him."

"He can be very vexing."

"But he did buy you a miniature horse and a puppy," Molly said as she started brushing Elodie's hair.

Despite herself, she smiled. "He can also be very charming and kind. Do you see the problem?"

"I'm afraid I do not, my lady."

When Molly finished with her hair, Elodie turned in her chair to face her lady's maid. "He told me that he cared for me."

Molly's eyebrows lifted. "And what did you say?"

Elodie frowned, her hands twisting in her lap. "Nothing. We were rather rudely interrupted by Lord Montrose."

Molly sat on the edge of the bed. "If you hadn't been interrupted, what would you have said?"

"I don't know," Elodie admitted, standing abruptly and beginning to pace the room. "He said he was done trying to win me over. That he wanted us to remain friends."

"Is that what you want?"

Elodie stopped mid-step, turning back towards Molly. "Yes... no. Maybe? I do not dislike him."

Molly studied her carefully. "Do you care for him?"

"I think so."

"You do not sound so sure."

Elodie resumed pacing. "I have always considered Lord Belview to be the most vexing of men, but lately..." Her words trailed off. "It has been different."

Molly leaned forward slightly. "Different how?"

She stopped again, this time looking out the window. "I find myself hanging on his every word, as though I need to know everything that he is thinking. He is the first person who has made me feel like I am enough."

Molly gave her a knowing smile. "It sounds like you have developed real feelings for Lord Belview."

"Perhaps, but it is too late."

A knock came at the door, interrupting their conversation.

"Enter," Elodie ordered.

A young maid stepped inside, her dark hair pinned beneath her cap. "Lady Dallington requests your presence in the dining room, my lady."

Molly jumped up and retrieved the gown. "We should hurry. We can continue this conversation later."

Once Elodie was dressed, she made her way to the dining room. She approached and heard the sound of a familiar voice drifting through the open door.

Melody!

Elodie hurried into the dining room and saw her entire

family, including Melody and her husband, Lord Emberly, sitting at the table.

Melody spotted her and rose from her seat, rushing over to embrace her tightly. "Elodie! It is so good to see you."

Taking a step back, Elodie asked, "What are you doing here?"

"We decided to cut our wedding tour short so we can enjoy the Season with you," Melody explained, exchanging a loving glance with her husband.

"That is wonderful news."

Melody guided her to the table, her tone turning serious. "I understand that Lord Montrose has been bothering you."

"He has, but it is nothing that I cannot handle," Elodie replied, taking a seat next to her sister.

Her mother spoke up from the end of the table. "You certainly took your time in coming to breakfast this morning."

Elodie did not want to tell her mother that she had been lying in bed for hours, dwelling on Anthony. She decided to lie. "I overslept."

Bennett, sitting across from her, spoke up. "I do not know how you could have slept in with those puppies barking incessantly."

"Barking does not bother me," Elodie said, reaching for a piece of bread. She picked up her knife and began to butter it carefully. If there was ever a time she needed to eat something delicious, it was now.

Melody gave Elodie a curious look. "I understand that Anthony gifted you a miniature horse."

"He did," Elodie replied. "It is no unicorn, but it was a thoughtful gift."

Winston interjected, "Unicorns are not real, Sister."

Elodie set down her knife and fixed him with a serious look. "I want to live in a world where unicorns are real." She did not know why but she needed to believe that the impossible could happen.

Melody laughed and leaned closer. "What did you name your miniature horse?"

Grateful for the change in subject, Elodie replied, "Lord Henry."

"I like that name," Melody replied.

Bennett sighed. "It is a dreadful name for a horse. You should have named it Lord Bennie."

"Bennie is a nickname for Bennett," Elodie remarked. "Why on earth would I name my horse after you when I am so fond of him?"

"I hope your horse bites you," Bennett quipped.

Elodie laughed. "Lord Henry is rather ornery, but I like his spirit. It keeps things interesting."

Her father stepped into the room and took his place at the head of the table. "My apologies for being late. There were matters at work that required my attention."

"There always are, Dear," her mother said.

Turning towards Melody, their father smiled. "Welcome home, Melody."

"Thank you, Father," she replied.

Their mother rose from her chair. "Now that we are all here," she began, her tone suggesting she had been eagerly awaiting this moment, "I have the most wonderful news."

Melody leaned towards Elodie and whispered, "This cannot be good."

Elodie stifled a giggle behind her hand. "Definitely not," she whispered back.

"I have decided that we will host a ball," her mother announced. "It will be held here, in our ballroom, three weeks from now. Is that not wonderful?"

"I am still waiting for the 'wonderful' part," Bennett joked.

Their mother waved a dismissive hand. "You will adjust. It will be in three weeks' time. Plan accordingly."

Elodie raised her hand.

Her mother shook her head. "Yes, Elodie."

"Must I attend?"

Her mother furrowed her brows. "And why would you not?"

"I do not like dancing."

"Yes, Child, you have to come," her mother replied firmly.

Elodie took a bite of her buttered bread, savoring the taste. She hated dancing, but the thought of being in Anthony's arms for even one dance made her heart flutter. Perhaps she would not fight this ball too much.

"Is that all, Elodie?" Bennett asked, bemused. "No dramatic protests? No declarations that you would rather die?"

Elodie shrugged. "What is the point? It is inevitable that I must go."

Bennett pointed accusingly at her bread. "What kind of magical bread is that? Is it a bread that makes people compliant?"

"It is just bread, Brother."

Bennett sat back in his chair. "Elodie is acting odd, and I intend to get to the bottom of it."

"I am not acting odd," Elodie countered.

Winston chimed in. "I agree with Bennett. The old Elodie would have declared she would rather be eaten by wolves than attend a ball."

Elodie rolled her eyes. "You two are overthinking this."

"Leave poor Elodie alone," her mother chided lightly.

Bennett put his hand up. "Very well, but be warned, I am a master investigator. Nothing escapes my notice."

Delphine patted Bennett's arm. "Says the man who could not find his pocket watch this morning, even though it was in his waistcoat pocket."

"In my defense, I do not remember putting it there," Bennett said.

"That is not a good defense, my love," Delphine teased.

Elodie laughed. "Once I have had my fill of this magical bread, I will be back to my delightful self. No investigation necessary."

Melody reached for her cup of chocolate and took a sip. "I also heard that Anthony gifted you a puppy. May I see this dog of yours?"

Elodie did not want to see Anthony right now. Her emotions were too conflicted and she needed to sort through them. "You do not need to see Lulu," she said quickly. "It is just a dog. You have seen plenty of dogs before."

"But I want to meet Lulu," Melody pressed.

Elodie thought fast, trying to come up with a plausible explanation. "Lulu does not like meeting new people. He might bite you, and I could not live with myself if he did."

Melody's lips twitched. "I think I will take my chances."

"Are you sure? I once heard that if a dog bites you, there is a higher chance your child will be born a werewolf," Elodie said, trying another tactic.

Winston chuckled. "Where, pray tell, did you hear that nonsense?"

"It is common knowledge, is it not?" Elodie asked.

"Werewolves, much like unicorns, are not real," Winston replied. "Now, what is the real reason that you do not want Melody to meet Lulu?"

Elodie adopted an innocent look. "There is no reason. If Melody wants to risk raising a werewolf, I will gladly show her the dog."

"Then shall we go after breakfast?" Melody asked.

Elodie sighed in defeat. "Wonderful," she muttered, nibbling at her bread to avoid further protest.

Anthony sat at his desk, the ledgers spread out before him untouched, his attention instead drawn to the window. His gaze lingered on the gardens, where Elodie and Melody were laughing as they played with the puppies. Emma flitted around them, joining in their playful chaos. The scene brought a smile to Anthony's face. He wanted to join them, but he stopped himself. If his plan were to succeed, he needed to give Elodie time to realize she cared for him as much as he cared for her. He thought he had seen something in her eyes. But was it real, or was he merely being hopeful?

A knock at the door pulled him from his musings. Percy stepped in, his expression solemn. "My lord, Mr. Grady..."

Before Percy could finish, Grady strode into the room with purpose. "We need to talk."

Anthony offered Percy an apologetic glance and gestured towards a chair. "Take a seat."

Grady remained standing, gripping the back of the chair with white-knuckled intensity. "After you made the drop, I followed a man deep into the rookeries. I apprehended him and questioned him thoroughly. He is sitting in Newgate now."

"That is wonderful—" Anthony began.

The Bow Street Runner cut him off. "He was just the middle-man. It took hours, but he finally confessed to the mastermind behind the blackmail. And you are not going to like it."

Grady's voice put Anthony on edge, but his question needed to be asked. "Who is it?" he asked, bracing himself.

The Bow Street Runner's voice dropped, his tone grave. "Your brother."

Anthony blinked, stunned. "That is absurd. Why would Stephen blackmail me? His own brother?"

Grady leaned in. "I assumed you would feel that way, so I conducted further inquiries. Your brother promised his creditors he would pay them by the end of the day. He is desperate."

Anthony rose from his chair. He walked to the window and looked out again, but the cheerful scene in the gardens brought no solace. Could Stephen truly be capable of such betrayal? Deep down, Anthony suspected the answer was "yes." Stephen had always been selfish, and he would do anything to save himself.

"What would you like to do, my lord?" Grady's voice broke the silence. "I can arrest your brother."

Anthony closed his eyes briefly, then turned back to the room. "No. Let me speak to him first."

As if summoned by his words, the door opened, and Stephen entered. His hair was disheveled, his clothing wrinkled and carelessly thrown on. He sauntered into the room. "You rang, my lord?" he mocked.

Anthony turned his gaze to Grady, who explained, "I anticipated you would want to address this immediately, so I had your butler summon him."

Stephen's eyes flickered to Grady, his expression critical. "Who is this man?"

"This is Grady," Anthony replied. "He is a Bow Street Runner who is looking into an important matter for me."

Unperturbed, Stephen flopped into the chair across from the desk. "So, what is this pressing issue that required waking me at such an ungodly hour?"

Anthony moved to lean against the desk, folding his arms. "Grady has brought me some distressing news."

Stephen, studying his fingernails, barely glanced up. "Oh? And what is it?"

Taking a deep breath, Anthony decided it was time to just say what needed to be said and be done with it. "Are you blackmailing me and Lord Westcott?"

Stephen's hand froze mid-motion, but his expression remained disinterested. "What? No. Why would you even suggest such a ridiculous thing?"

Grady stepped forward, his voice sharp. "A man in Newgate says otherwise. He confessed to working for you, retrieving money left in an alleyway."

"That man is clearly lying," Stephen said, standing abruptly. "I do not have time for such baseless accusations—"

"Sit down, Stephen," Anthony interrupted.

Stephen's eyes flashed with anger. "I do not answer to you."

"No, but I could have you arrested for your part in blackmailing me," Anthony said.

His brother glared at him, his face contorted with fury. "You would not dare!"

"Do you want to take that chance?" Anthony asked, stepping closer.

Reluctantly, Stephen sank back into the chair, though his body remained tense. "Why does it matter, anyway? You don't need the money. I do."

"So you admit it?" Anthony pressed, his voice hard.

His brother shrugged. "I needed money, and you were being stubborn about not paying off my debts. I had no intention of ruining anyone's reputation."

Anthony stared at his brother. "Do you feel any remorse for what you have done?"

"Why should I?" Stephen demanded. "If I do not pay my creditors, I will be sent to debtor's prison. What choice did I have?"

"Do you care about anyone but yourself?" Anthony asked.

Stephen scoffed. "Why should I?" he asked, repeating himself.

Anthony frowned, knowing what he needed to do. "I want you to leave and never come back."

His brother shot up to his feet, his face twisting with outrage. "You are disowning me?"

"I am."

"You have been looking for a reason to get rid of me since Father got sick," Stephen spat out. "What would our parents think of this?"

Anthony stood firm, his expression unyielding. "I do not care. It is time that you find your own way in the world."

"With what money?" Stephen demanded. "If I leave here, I will end up in debtor's prison. Is that what you want?"

"It is what you deserve."

Stephen narrowed his eyes. "Why should I be punished for being the second son? You are the precious heir, and I have been left with scraps my entire life."

"You were given the finest education," Anthony shot back, his voice rising. "And you squandered it when you were expelled from Oxford for cheating."

Stephen moved to stand in front of Anthony, his nostrils flaring. "I will leave, but you will give me the money that is owed to me."

"Nothing is owed to you. Not anymore," Anthony replied.

Stephen's lips curled into a sneer. "Fine. Then I will take Emma with me."

Anthony's jaw tightened. "You will do no such thing."

A smug smile spread across Stephen's lips. "Our parents adore that little girl. Imagine their devastation if I take her away. What do you think will happen, Brother?"

"You do not even want to raise a daughter."

"Does it matter?" Stephen asked, his sneer morphing into something colder. "She is my golden ticket. As her father, there is nothing you can do to stop me."

Anthony grew tense. He could not let Stephen take Emma, but the law was clear. Stephen, as her father, held the power. Helplessness gripped him as he struggled to find a solution.

Grady's voice broke the tense silence. "If I may interrupt, I believe I have something of interest to say."

Stephen shot the Bow Street Runner a withering look. "Nothing you have to say interests me, Runner."

Grady smiled at Stephen, appearing unbothered by the insult. "After I got your middleman to confess, I took the liberty of visiting the gambling establishments you owe money to. Let's say they were very unhappy to hear you would not be paying your debts."

Stephen's face paled slightly, though his sneer remained intact. "Why would you do something so foolish?"

"Because I suspected that this was your plan all along," Grady replied. "You are a rich, entitled lord who thinks nothing of trampling others to get your way. That kind of arrogance deserves a comeuppance."

Stephen's mask slipped, and for the first time, real fear flickered in his eyes. "What did you do?"

Grady turned towards the door. "Constable Chandler, if you would join us?"

A tall, dark-haired man stepped into the room. He tipped his head at Grady before turning to Stephen. "Is this Mr. Sackville?"

"It is," Grady confirmed. He turned back to Stephen. "Your creditors have called in your debts. Since you are unable to pay, Constable Chandler will escort you to King's Bench Prison."

Stephen's eyes widened with panic. "No! This is just a ruse. I am the son of an earl. You cannot send me to prison!"

Constable Chandler stepped forward, his voice calm but firm. "You will remain in prison until you settle your debts."

"But I have no funds!" Stephen shouted, his desperation mounting.

"Then you could remain in prison indefinitely." Constable Chandler extended his hand. "Shall we?"

Stephen spun towards Anthony, his expression frantic.

"Would you truly do this to your own brother? Have you no mercy? No soul?"

Anthony kept his face expressionless. "You blackmailed me and threatened to ruin Elodie's and Lady Eugenie's reputation. And now you would use Emma as a pawn. Yes, Stephen, I think it is time you learned there are consequences for your actions."

His brother jabbed a finger at him, his face red with fury. "You are no better than me. The only reason why you are not in my position is because you were born first."

"I never claimed to be better than you."

Stephen puffed out his chest, his voice shaking with rage. "This will not end well for you, Brother. I will get out of that prison, and when I do, I will take what is owed to me."

Constable Chandler stepped forward and took Stephen by the arm. "It is time to go."

Stephen tried to yank free, but the constable held firm. "Let me go! I am the son of an earl."

"A broke son of an earl," Constable Chandler responded with a smirk.

As Chandler dragged Stephen towards the door, he twisted around to glare at Anthony. "You will pay for this!" he bellowed before being hauled out of the room.

Once they were gone, Grady met his gaze and said, "You did the right thing, my lord. Your brother left you no other choice."

Anthony exhaled deeply and dropped into a chair. "I know, but I wish it had not come to this. What am I going to tell my parents?"

"The truth, my lord."

He winced. "I worry how this will affect my father's health."

Grady placed a hand on Anthony's shoulder, a rare showing of compassion. "You are protecting your family by sending him to prison. Do not lose sight of that."

"Thank you."

Grady released Anthony's shoulder and took a step back. "If you need anything further, you know where to find me."

With that, Grady left the study, leaving Anthony with his thoughts. He stared at the ceiling, knowing he needed to face his parents. They deserved to hear the truth from him before news of Stephen's imprisonment reached the newssheets.

Rising, Anthony made his way to his father's room, hesitating before knocking. The door opened promptly, and he stepped inside to see his mother sitting beside his father in bed, both leaning back against the pillows.

"Anthony," his mother greeted warmly. "You were just here. Is everything all right? You look troubled."

He came to a stop beside the bed, his hands clasped tightly. "I have come bearing bad news."

His father furrowed his brow. "What has happened?"

"Stephen has been sent to debtor's prison," Anthony revealed.

His mother gasped, her hand flying to her chest. "Dear heavens, we must get him out of there immediately!"

Anthony moved to sit in a chair positioned next to the bed. "His debts amount to nineteen thousand pounds. A sum that would drain the family coffers. When I refused to pay, Stephen turned to blackmail."

"Who did he try to blackmail?" his father asked.

"Lord Westcott and me," Anthony admitted. "He threatened to ruin Lady Elodie's and Lady Eugenie's reputation over an incident that happened many days ago."

His mother sat up in bed. "We cannot let Stephen stay in prison—"

"It is where he belongs," his father interrupted firmly. "Anthony, you made the right decision."

"Surely there is another way?" his mother pleaded, glancing between them both.

Anthony paused before sharing, "Before the constable

came, Stephen threatened to take Emma. He planned to use her to manipulate us into giving him money."

His mother's face crumpled. "Stephen would not do something so cruel."

"He would, Mother," Anthony said.

His father reached for her hand. "I love Stephen, but it is time that he is held accountable for his actions. We must protect Emma, at all costs."

Anthony nodded, though the heaviness in his chest remained. The truth had been spoken, but the pain of it would linger far longer.

20

E lodie stood on the pavement, gazing at the storefront display of elegant hats. The array of ribbons, feathers, and fine lace was mesmerizing. Did she really need another hat? No, but they were so pretty. Yet, after hours of shopping, her feet ached, and her enthusiasm waned.

Melody appeared beside her. "Shall we go to Gunter's for some lemon ice?"

Elodie perked up. "That is a lovely idea," she said with a smile.

Looping her arm through Elodie's, Melody led the way down the bustling street. The scent of freshly baked bread wafted from a nearby bakery, mingling with the crisp afternoon air. "How are you faring, Sister? And I would prefer the truth."

"I am fine. Just fine. Perfectly fine, in fact," Elodie replied, her words spilling out in quick succession.

Melody gave her a knowing look. "Perhaps if you said 'fine' one more time, I might believe you."

Elodie laughed. "I am far more interested in you. How is married life?"

That was the right thing to say because a bright smile came

to Melody's lips, spilling into her eyes. "Marrying Wesley was the best decision I ever made. I am happier than I ever dreamed possible."

"Well, I am happy that you are happy."

"Thank you, Sister," Melody said, glancing over at her. "Dare I ask how being the diamond of the Season is going?"

Elodie groaned. "It is awful. It should have been you."

"I would have been miserable as the diamond," Melody said. "I much prefer anonymity."

"As do I," Elodie admitted, "but the queen decided to ruin my life."

With a shake of her head, Melody replied, "The queen did not ruin your life."

"No, but I am tired of all the stares and whispers," Elodie said, her voice tinged with frustration. "I am expected to dance at balls and perform at social events. It is exhausting."

"What a dreadful burden," Melody teased. Then her tone shifted. "Now, tell me the truth. What is going on with you and Anthony?"

"Nothing," Elodie rushed out.

Melody's gaze sharpened. "That is not what Bennett and Winston told me. They said you two have been spending a considerable amount of time with one another."

"We are merely friends," Elodie insisted.

"Very well, do not tell me," Melody said.

Elodie hesitated, then bit her lower lip. "How did you know that you were in love with Wesley?"

"My heart told me that the search was over," Melody said. "I am not saying that it was easy, but it was worth it."

In a low voice, Elodie said, "Anthony admitted that he cared for me."

"I see, and what did you say?"

"Nothing," Elodie confessed. "We were interrupted, and the moment passed."

Stopping on the pavement, Melody turned to face her sister. "Do you care for Anthony?"

"I do," Elodie said, seeing no reason to deny it. "But he wishes to just remain friends."

"Is that what you want?"

Elodie shrugged, a gesture that failed to mask her turmoil. "Does it matter?"

Melody huffed. "Of course it matters," she replied. "Sometimes you must fight for what you want. Do you want Anthony in your life?"

"You make it sound so simple."

"It is simple," Melody argued. "Life is too short for regrets. If you care for him, tell him. Do not let fear hold you back."

Elodie sighed, resuming her walk. "If I do not get lemon ice soon, I might wither away and die."

Melody matched her stride. "You can run from the truth, but you cannot hide from it."

"Then I shall never stop running," Elodie retorted with a grin.

But Melody was not deterred. "Do you love him?"

Elodie stopped abruptly, turning to face her sister. "Love? I said nothing about love."

"You did not have to," Melody said. "I can see it in your eyes when you speak of Anthony. You love him."

"Love is a strong word," Elodie declared.

Melody placed a hand on Elodie's shoulder. "Sometimes, the mind takes longer to accept what the heart already knows."

"And what does my heart know?"

Leaning closer, Melody said, "You love Anthony."

Elodie's lips pressed into a thin line. "I care for Anthony, but love... that is impossible." Her words stopped. "He is vexing and troublesome... and kind. Considerate."

"Handsome?" Melody pressed.

Elodie's cheeks flushed. "Yes, he is very handsome. But none of that matters. I could never marry him."

"Whyever not?"

Elodie reached up and adjusted the brim of her straw hat. "It is safer to remain friends."

Melody nodded, though her expression remained thoughtful. "You are right. It is safer."

"Thank you," Elodie said.

"And I have no idea what is going to happen next or how things are going to work out. All I know for sure is that Anthony makes you happy. Is that not enough?"

Elodie stared back at her sister with exasperation. "Why are you encouraging this?"

"Because I know you, and I know you need Anthony."

"I don't need anyone."

Melody smiled. "That is the lie you tell yourself. Trusting someone, relying on them—it is not a weakness. It is a strength."

Elodie's gaze drifted over her sister's shoulder as she asked the one question that she feared the answer to. "What if I make a mistake?" she asked softly.

"What does your heart tell you?"

Closing her eyes, Elodie saw Anthony's face, clear as day. Realization washed over her, sudden and undeniable. Somewhere along the way, she had fallen for him. And not just fallen. She loved him deeply, with all her heart.

Melody gently placed a hand on her sleeve. "You should tell him how you feel before it is too late."

"But it is too late," Elodie said. "He said he wants to remain friends."

"I promise you that his actions suggest otherwise," Melody responded.

Before Elodie could respond, a black coach came to a jerking stop beside them. The door swung open, and Lord

Montrose stepped out, his expression dark and determined. Without warning, he grabbed Melody's arm.

"Unhand me," Melody shouted, struggling against his grip.

Lord Montrose's gaze flickered between the two sisters. "Good gads, there are two of you. Which one of you is Elodie?"

Melody narrowed her eyes. "Why should we tell you?"

With a smirk, Lord Montrose replied, "Because Lady Elodie and I have a date with an anvil priest."

Elodie scoffed, her voice laced with defiance. "I will never marry you."

"Ah, so you are Elodie," Lord Montrose sneered, reaching for her.

Melody stepped between them, swatting his hand away with unexpected ferocity. "Do not touch my sister."

Lord Montrose's laugh was harsh and mocking. "Or what? What are you going to do? You are just a woman."

Melody's expression grew determined as she reached into her reticule, withdrawing a small pistol and pointing it squarely at Lord Montrose's chest. Her voice was steady. "Leave us alone," she ordered.

For a moment, Lord Montrose's smug expression faltered, but then he grabbed Elodie's arm, yanking her in front of him like a shield. "You would not dare try to shoot me and put your sister in harm's way."

A calculated gleam came into Melody's eyes. "I assure you, I do not miss."

"No one is that good of a shot."

Melody cocked her pistol. "Do you want to take that chance?"

With a swift motion, Lord Montrose shoved Elodie towards Melody, forcing the sisters to stumble into one another. He took a step back towards his waiting coach. His voice was loud and cantankerous. "You may have won this time, but it is too late. Lady Elodie's reputation is already ruined." He gestured to the growing crowd "I will marry Lady Elodie one way or another. She will be mine."

Without another word, Lord Montrose climbed into the coach and slammed the door shut. The carriage rolled away, leaving a trail of dust in its wake.

Melody wrapped her arms protectively around Elodie. "Are you hurt?"

"No, thanks to you."

"Who was that man?"

Taking a step back, Elodie steadied herself. "That is Lord Montrose. He is an awful man who made a bet in the betting book at White's that he would marry me."

Melody grew tense. "Well, he is going to be sorely disappointed."

Elodie glanced around at the crowd, their gazes piercing and judgmental, their whispers hidden behind fluttering fans. "We need to leave. Now."

"Yes, we should," Melody agreed.

They did not speak as they walked towards their coach. A footman opened the door and they stepped inside. Once the door was shut, Elodie leaned back and exhaled, her voice tinged with anger. "You should have shot him in the foot when you had the chance. It would have served him right."

"Perhaps I should have."

Elodie glanced out the window. "Lord Montrose is right about one thing. When the *ton* gets wind of this, I am ruined."

"You did nothing wrong."

"Does it matter?" Elodie asked. "Reputations have been ruined for far less."

Melody leaned forward, her voice filled with conviction. "Do not worry. I will fix this."

"Some things cannot be fixed, and I do not want them to be," Elodie said. "I am not afraid of being a spinster."

Even as she said her words, a pang of regret stabbed at her

heart. What would Anthony think? Would he distance himself from her—a walking scandal? That thought terrified her more than she wanted to admit.

Melody reached for her hand. "I know that look. You want to give up. But now is not the time. It is the time to fight."

"Fight for what?" Elodie asked, her voice rising. "Lord Montrose will ensure that I am ruined to force my hand in marriage."

Rearing back, Melody asked, "You would not consider marrying that audacious man, would you?"

"Heavens, no," Elodie responded. "I would rather wrestle a crocodile with my bare hands than walk down the aisle with Lord Montrose."

Melody relaxed slightly, a smile on her lips. "That is good."

Elodie clenched her fists, her frustration palpable. "I should have punched him again."

"You have hit him before?"

"Yes, and it was quite satisfying," Elodie replied, her tone brightening for a moment.

Melody released her hand and leaned back. "I would not leave the townhouse for the foreseeable future. I fear that Lord Montrose will be stupid enough to try abducting you again."

Elodie smirked, her defiance returning. "Next time, I will strike him down with my nail."

Her sister arched an eyebrow. "You still have that nail?"

"I do, and it has come in handy a time or two," Elodie replied.

Their conversation came to a halt when the coach stopped in front of their townhouse. Elodie was furious that Lord Montrose had done something so dishonorable and in front of so many witnesses.

But one thing was certain. She refused to let Montrose win —not with her reputation and certainly not with her future.

Anthony sat in the dim corner of White's, his glass of brandy swirling slowly in his hand. The lively hum of conversation and clinking glasses around him felt distant, muffled by his troubled thoughts. He had chosen the solitude of this corner intentionally. He was not in the mood for company. The looming scandal of Stephen being sent to debtor's prison hung over him like a dark cloud. The *ton* would soon learn of it, and the ensuing gossip would be merciless. Yet that was not what truly troubled him.

It was Elodie.

What would she think of him? Would she see his actions as justified, or would she view him as cold-hearted for sending his own brother to prison? He had made the only choice he could, but the thought of losing Elodie's good opinion twisted his gut. Worse still, the idea of losing her altogether was unbearable.

He took another sip, the brandy doing little to help with his unease. His thoughts were abruptly interrupted by the smug, drawling voice of Lord Montrose.

"Well, well, look who it is," Lord Montrose sneered, swaggering up to Anthony's table. "I assumed that I would find you here."

Not bothering to look up, Anthony asked, "What do you want, Montrose?" His tone was clipped, his patience thin.

Lord Montrose sank into the chair across from him, a triumphant glint in his eyes. "Elodie is mine now."

Anthony's grip on his glass tightened, his knuckles white. He set the drink down deliberately before responding, "She will never be yours."

"Ah, so you have not heard?" Lord Montrose asked. "We were to elope to Gretna Green, but her meddling sister got in the way."

"Elodie would never agree to marry you."

Lord Montrose's grin widened as he leaned forward. "She has little choice in the matter. No one will want her now."

Anthony's jaw clenched, his voice a growl. "What did you do?"

Lord Montrose shrugged. "Nothing. I merely suggested we marry, and she all but leaped at the chance."

"Montrose!" a familiar voice shouted.

Anthony turned his head to see Bennett and Winston striding towards them, their faces flushed with barely contained fury.

Bennett reached the table first, leaning over Lord Montrose with a penetrating glare. "How dare you try to abduct my sister!"

Anthony shot to his feet, his chair scraping loudly against the floor. "He did what?" The words came out in a shout.

Lord Montrose's smirk was unwavering. "It was all but a misunderstanding, I assure you. But now that you are here, what shall we do about this little scandal?"

Leaning closer, Bennett's face hardened. "You will stay away from my sister. Or else."

"Or else what?" Lord Montrose asked with a chuckle. "Face it, gentlemen, Lady Elodie will marry me. I have made sure of it."

Winston stepped forward, his fists clenched. "I should challenge you to a duel."

"Name the time and place," Lord Montrose said.

Anthony's voice cut through the rising tension. "No one is challenging anyone to a duel." He pointed a finger at Montrose, his voice firm. "You have gone too far this time."

"Not from where I am standing," he responded, rising to his feet. "Now, if you will excuse me, I am going to call on your sister and offer for her. Perhaps she has come to her senses."

Taking a step closer to Montrose, Anthony said, "You are a blackguard."

Lord Montrose tsked. "Name-calling, Belview? You must be desperate. Jealous, even. I bet you are upset that you did not think of this plan first."

Anthony's voice was calm, though every word was measured. "I would never force Elodie into a marriage she did not want."

"That is why you are going to lose," Lord Montrose said with a cocky smile. "And if this approach does not work, there are other ways to force her hand."

Unable to stop himself, Anthony reared his fist back and punched Lord Montrose squarely in the nose. Lord Montrose stumbled back, collapsing into his chair, blood trickling from his nose. He stared up at Anthony with wide eyes, his voice shaking. "You broke my nose!"

"If you ever go near Elodie again, I will do more than that," Anthony warned. "This is your last warning."

Without waiting for a response, Anthony turned on his heel, striding purposefully towards the door. He knew what he had to do. There was only one thing that could be done to save Elodie's reputation. He had to convince her to marry him, and quickly. The question was whether she would agree.

Bennett and Winston followed closely behind as they exited White's. On the pavement, Anthony turned towards his coach, only for Bennett to grab his arm and stop him. "Where are you going?"

"To Elodie," Anthony replied.

"Why?" Bennett asked.

Anthony faced him, his jaw set with determination. "To convince her to marry me."

Bennett crossed his arms. "Again, why?"

He hesitated for a moment before admitting, "It is the only way to save her reputation."

Winston's lips curled into a knowing smile. "Try again."

Anthony knew it was time for him to confess his feelings and hope that his friends would not object. "Because I love her. I always have, and I always will."

Winston's smile grew. "We know."

Anthony blinked in surprise. "You do?"

Bennett nodded, his expression both amused and serious. "It was painfully obvious when you bought her that miniature horse. But somehow, Elodie did not see what was right in front of her."

"You have no objections?" Anthony asked.

Bennett smirked. "I have many, but none that truly matter. You are exactly what Elodie needs."

"I agree," Winston added.

Anthony could not help but be buoyed by his friends' responses, but doubt still lingered. "Do you think she will agree to marry me?"

The smirk faded from Bennett's lips. "Not if you tell her that it is the only option. My advice is to confess your love and hope that is enough."

"And if it is not enough?" Anthony asked.

Winston chuckled. "You could always keep buying her animals until she agrees. I hear that pet pigs are all the rage right now."

Anthony took a deep breath, his resolve hardening. "Wish me luck."

Alone in the coach, Anthony tried to compose his thoughts. He had planned out a speech in his mind, but the words felt wholly inadequate. How could he convince Elodie of the depth of his feelings? As the coach rolled to a stop in front of her townhouse, he knew one thing for certain: he needed to be completely honest with her.

He pushed the door open before the footman could assist

him. The butler greeted him with a knowing look as Anthony stepped into the entryway.

"Where is Lady Elodie?" Anthony asked.

Gesturing towards the rear of the townhouse, the butler replied, "She is in the gardens."

Anthony did not need to be told twice. He strode purposefully towards the gardens, stepping out into the soft glow of the afternoon sun. There she was, crouched next to Emma, laughing softly as the puppies tumbled around them. The sight sent a warmth spreading through his chest. How had this woman come to mean so much to him?

"Elodie," he said, his voice surprisingly steady.

She turned, her face lighting up with a smile that lifted his spirits immensely. How did she hold so much power over him? "Anthony."

Anthony kept his face expressionless. "We need to talk."

Her expression quickly shifted to one of caution. "I assume you heard the news."

"I did."

She turned back towards Emma and placed a hand on the little girl's shoulder. "Why don't you take the puppies inside for a treat? I promise I will be along shortly."

"*We* will be along shortly," Anthony corrected.

Elodie's eyes softened with approval. "Yes, *we* will."

Anthony watched as Emma headed towards the door of his townhouse with the puppies following closely behind her.

Once they were alone, Anthony said, "I broke Lord Montrose's nose."

Elodie did not look the least bit bothered by the news. "Good, he deserved it."

"I will not disagree with you there," Anthony said. "What he did to you was horrific and I am sorry."

Her brow furrowed. "Why are you sorry?"

He took a step closer to her. "I should have been there to protect you. I *want* to be there to protect you."

"You cannot protect me from everything, Anthony," Elodie sighed. "Because of one mishap, I brought scandal to my name and my family's."

Anthony closed the distance between them. "You did nothing wrong."

Elodie's eyes grew downcast. "At least I do not have to worry about being the diamond of the Season anymore."

"Do you want to know what I believe?" he asked.

"What is that?"

He tipped her chin up gently, forcing her to meet his eyes. "I believe that everything happens for a reason. Every single thing, the good and the bad, leads you to right where you are meant to be."

Elodie's eyes held vulnerability as she stared up at him. "And where is that?"

Anthony hesitated, his carefully rehearsed speech forgotten. Now that he was standing in front of Elodie, his mind went blank.

He cleared his throat and hoped for the first time that his words were enough. That *he* was enough. "I do not know the precise moment when I fell in love with you, but I did. I love you wildly, madly, infinitely. And I do not apologize for it. I never will."

Elodie's eyes widened slightly. "You... love me?"

"I do," he said, placing his hand over his heart. "I have waited for you my entire life, and I do not regret a single moment."

"Anthony—" she began.

He interrupted her. "You do not have to say anything. But you do have to accept it. I love you. I want you always in my life as my wife. I want to love you the way you deserve."

Elodie lifted her brow, her expression unreadable. "Since

you are apparently planning out our future, may I say something?"

"Of course," he said with a slight wince.

"I have always found you vexing. Maddening. The bane of my existence," she started. "But something has changed between us. I was afraid to admit it, afraid of what it meant."

"Elodie..." Anthony started.

She placed a hand on his chest. "Somewhere along the way, I fell in love with you, too. I fell in love with what I found in you. And I saw home in your eyes. I am sorry that it took me so long to realize that."

Relief flooded Anthony's chest as he took her hand in his. "Before I convince you to marry me, I need to tell you something. Stephen is in debtor's prison. He was behind the blackmail, and he planned to use Emma as a pawn. I had to protect you and her. I hope you understand."

Elodie's gaze was filled with compassion. "You did the right thing."

"There will be a scandal," he warned.

Elodie's eyes twinkled with merriment. "I have a scandal of my own. We will be scandalous together."

Anthony's lips quirked into a smile. "Do you truly mean that?"

She grew serious. "My heart has waited so long to be loved by you. I do not want to wait another day to start living with you."

Anthony leaned closer, making their faces inches apart. "I suppose now that we are in agreement, we should kiss on it."

"You'd better be a good kisser," she teased.

Not wanting to wait another moment, he pressed his lips against hers. Her lips were soft and warm beneath his, responding with a sweetness that stole his breath. He poured everything he felt into that single moment—his love, his devotion, his hopes for the future.

How he loved this woman! She completed him in a way that defied explanation, as though she had always been a part of him, waiting to be found.

A cheer went up around them, causing them to break the kiss.

Anthony turned his head and saw Elodie's entire family gathered by the door. Bennett approached them with a paper in his hand. "I thought you might need this."

He accepted it and realized it was a special license for them to wed. He looked up in astonishment. "When did you—"

Bennett smirked. "Winston and I appealed to the Archbishop of Canterbury about your peculiar circumstances, and he agreed that you two should be wed at once."

"What do you think?" Anthony asked, turning to face Elodie. "Shall we wed tomorrow?"

Elodie grew thoughtful. "How long do you think it would take for me to make a waistcoat for Lord Henry?"

"Why does your horse need a waistcoat?"

"I would assume you would want Lord Henry to look his finest at our wedding."

Anthony chuckled, shaking his head. "It might be best if we leave the animals at home during our ceremony."

Elodie feigned a dramatic sigh. "Very well, but Lord Henry will be quite disappointed." Unable to resist, Anthony leaned in, capturing her lips in a soft, lingering kiss. His hand rested gently on her waist as he pulled her closer. "I promise I will make it up to you," he murmured.

"You'd better," she retorted, her playful smile tugging at his heart.

"So, tomorrow?"

Elodie tilted her head as if considering. "Yes, but I will need to work it around my nap."

With a chuckle, Anthony turned them to face her family. "We are getting married tomorrow!"

"It is about time," Bennett quipped, casting a glance over his shoulder at Lady Dallington. "Mother has been planning the wedding luncheon for weeks."

The back door of his townhouse opened, and Anthony's gaze shifted as his mother stepped out, guiding his father with tender care. Despite his father's frailty, both parents beamed with happiness.

"We have been watching shamelessly from your father's room," his mother admitted, her eyes glistening with emotion. "And we could not be happier for you two."

Elodie glanced up at him, her gaze warm. "I do not think tomorrow will come soon enough."

For the first time in a long time, Anthony felt utterly content. He held the woman he loved in his arms, surrounded by family, and a lifetime of happiness stretched out before them. Forever could not come soon enough.

EPILOGUE

Five years later

The morning sun streamed through the dining room windows as Elodie sat between Emma and her four-year-old daughter, Charlotte. Elodie picked up a slice of bread and held it up with a playful smile. "Shall we begin?"

Emma and Charlotte followed her lead, picking up their own slices of bread. Elodie reached for the knife and dipped it into the butter tray. "Now, you must ensure the butter reaches all the corners of the bread. That is the key to achieving the perfect bread-to-butter ratio."

As she meticulously spread the butter, Charlotte plopped a thick pile onto her bread. "I like my bread this way," she announced proudly.

Emma wrinkled her nose. "Your way is wrong."

Elodie laughed softly, shaking her head. "Everyone can butter their bread their own way. There is no right or wrong way to do so."

Emma held up her neatly buttered slice. "But I like your way best."

"And that is why you are my favorite," Elodie teased.

Charlotte huffed in protest. "Why is Emma your favorite?"

Elodie smiled. "You are my favorite, too."

"How can we both be your favorite?" Charlotte asked.

Placing her bread down, Elodie explained, "It is a mother's prerogative to have as many favorites as she likes. And I have three."

Charlotte seemed satisfied by the answer, but Emma leaned closer, her voice low. "I thought I was your favorite on Wednesday."

"You were, my dear. And today, you both are," Elodie replied as she affectionally patted her on the head.

The door creaked open, and Anthony stepped into the room. He smiled through tired eyes. "William is finally asleep," he announced.

"I do not know why you didn't let your mother put him to sleep," Elodie said with a knowing look. "She seems to have the magic touch."

"Because William is my son," Anthony replied with a sheepish smile. "And, honestly, I thought it would be easier."

Elodie raised an eyebrow. "William is a terrible sleeper."

"That he is, but he should outgrow it soon enough," Anthony said.

"Come, join us for breakfast," Elodie said, gesturing to the table.

Anthony kissed the tops of both girls' heads before taking a seat. A footman promptly set a plate of food in front of him. "What were you discussing before I arrived?" he asked, picking up his fork.

"Who Mother's favorite is," Charlotte replied.

"And what was decided?" Anthony asked.

Emma answered confidently, "It depends on the day."

"That sounds about right," he said with a nod. "But you'd better hurry and eat if you want to make your riding lesson."

Emma picked up her fork and took a bite of her eggs. Once she had taken a bite, she asked, "When can I ride a horse like you and Aunt Elodie?"

"Is there something wrong with your pony?" Elodie asked.

"No, but I want to ride like you," Emma replied.

Anthony gave her a thoughtful look. "How old are you?"

Emma straightened in her seat. "I am nine years old."

"Ah, yes, you look about old enough," Anthony said. "I will speak to the groom about finding you a proper horse."

Charlotte held her bread up for inspection. "Look, Father. I buttered it all by myself."

"Well done!" Anthony praised before turning his attention towards Elodie. "How are you doing this fine morning, Wife?"

"I have no complaints."

Anthony gave his wife a curious look. "Have you given more thought to Emma's education?"

Elodie sighed, setting her cup down. "I have. I can't bear the thought of sending Emma away to boarding school. However, I enjoyed my time immensely there."

Emma perked up. "I want to go to boarding school like you, Aunt Elodie! If I go, do you think I can become the diamond of the Season someday?"

Elodie reached out to smooth Emma's curls. "Of course, I do, my dear. You have all the charm and grace to be the brightest diamond the *ton* has ever seen."

Anthony's gaze shifted towards Elodie's portrait, where she stood proudly next to Lulu and Lord Henry. "I still find it remarkable that Queen Charlotte herself commissioned this portrait as a wedding gift," he said, his tone contemplative. "It was more than a gesture of approval. It silenced the scandal with Montrose entirely."

"He was utterly unprepared for the cut direct he received from the *ton*. No one dared to align themselves with him after that," Elodie said.

Anthony smirked. "It was a swift fall for a man who fancied himself untouchable."

Percy stepped into the room and announced, "A Mr. Skye wishes to speak with Your Lordship."

"I do not know a Mr. Skye," Anthony said. "Send him away."

Percy hesitated. "He was rather insistent that he should speak to you. He said it was about your brother."

Anthony frowned. "Very well." He shoved back his seat and stood. "I will see what this is about."

"Would you like me to join you?" Elodie offered, rising from her seat.

Holding out his arm, Anthony replied, "Always."

As they walked towards the study, Elodie said, "Do not forget that my family will be here for supper."

"That is wonderful news," Anthony said, though his jaw remained tight. "It has been far too long since we were all together under one roof."

Elodie saw the tension in his posture and offered him a reassuring look. "It will be all right. I am sure Stephen hasn't done anything too foolish. This time."

Anthony did not quite look convinced. "Stephen never fails to surprise me. Considering he has tried multiple times to sue me for his inheritance, claiming I stole it from him. I would not put anything past him."

She patted his arm, but she knew her husband was not wrong. Stephen had made a nuisance of himself these past few years, despite being in debtor's prison.

They entered the study to find a short man with dark, thinning hair waiting. He bowed stiffly. "My lord. My lady. I am Mr. Skye, a coroner here in London."

Anthony's frown deepened. "What has my brother done this time?"

Mr. Skye grimaced. "I'm afraid it is worse than that, my lord. Your brother is dead."

"Dead?" Anthony repeated, his tone sharp. "How?"

"He was involved in a duel," Mr. Skye explained. "Mr. Sackville was granted permission to leave prison during the day, assuming he would return at night, and he challenged Mr. Ramsey to a duel over his sister. Your brother was fatally shot."

"Mr. Ramsey?" Elodie asked. "As in the heir to the Ramsey merchant fortune?"

"The very same, my lady," Mr. Skye confirmed. "Apparently, your brother intended to elope with Miss Ramsey and her brother caught wind of it."

Anthony sank into a chair, running a hand over his face. "Did my brother suffer?"

"No, it was a single shot to his heart," Mr. Skye shared.

Elodie knelt beside Anthony, taking his hand in hers. "I'm sorry, my love."

Mr. Skye shifted uncomfortably in his stance. "I do apologize for being the bearer of bad news. I shall see my way out."

Once the coroner departed, Elodie squeezed her husband's hand. "How are you faring?"

Anthony met her gaze. "A part of me is relieved. Emma is safe now."

"And the other part?"

His eyes glistened with unshed tears. "I worry about how my mother is going to handle the news. First my father, and now Stephen..."

Emma's soft voice came from the doorway. "Is it true? Is my father dead?"

Anthony stood, opening his arms. "It is true," he replied.

Emma ran into his embrace. "I am so relieved," she whispered. "I was always so afraid he would take me away."

Anthony crouched down, holding her tightly. "You are safe now. You are part of this family, Emma. Always."

Emma let out a sigh of relief. "Thank you, Uncle Anthony."

"Now run along," Anthony said. "You have your riding lesson right now."

"Will you come watch me?" Emma asked with a hopeful expression.

Anthony bobbed his head. "I would love that. Will you give me a moment with Elodie?"

As Emma skipped off to her riding lesson, Anthony turned to Elodie. She wrapped her arms around his neck. "You are a good father."

Resting his forehead against hers, Anthony murmured, "We have built a beautiful life together, haven't we?"

"We have. But I do believe our family is not quite complete yet."

Anthony raised an eyebrow. "Are you suggesting..."

"I'm pregnant," she shared.

His eyes went wide. "You are?"

"I am," Elodie replied, her voice trembling slightly. "I know this might not be the best time, but—"

Anthony kissed her deeply. "There is no wrong time to tell me such joyous news."

"You are happy?"

"How can you even ask me that?" he questioned, moving to place a hand on her stomach. "I have never been happier."

Elodie bit her lower lip. "I was hoping to tell my family tonight over dinner."

"That is a grand idea!" Anthony exclaimed.

"Do you want a boy or girl?"

Anthony shrugged. "Does it matter?" he asked. "All I want is a healthy child."

Elodie felt joy bubbling up inside of her. Never had she imagined she could be so happy. Since the day she had married Anthony, there had not been a night when she didn't fall asleep thinking of him.

She knew, in her heart, that even as she grew old, it would always be Anthony. Her soul had found a home.

The End

NEW SERIES:

COURTING THE UNCONVENTIONAL

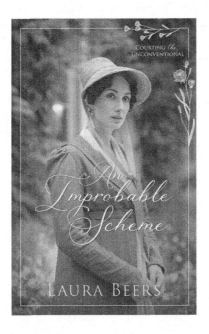

Some secrets are worth stealing. Some hearts are harder to escape.

Lady Elsbeth Caldwell has long suspected that her stepfather is hiding something far more sinister behind his polished façade. Determined to uncover the truth, she embarks on an investigation that leads her to take desperate measures, including robbing a passing coach under the cover of night. Unfortunately, the coach belongs to Niles Drayton, Earl of Westcott—a man with a sharp tongue, a sharper wit, and a maddening ability to remain amused in even the most scandalous circumstances.

Niles has no patience for matchmaking schemes, particularly those orchestrated by his well-meaning aunt. But when he's introduced to the opinionated and undeniably intriguing Lady Elsbeth, he is determined to keep her as far away from his sister—and himself—as possible.

As threats begin to close in around Elsbeth, Niles is pulled deeper into her world. What begins as a reluctant association soon becomes an uneasy alliance, and then something far more dangerous: a fragile, undeniable connection. When long-buried secrets come to light and the true extent of the deception surrounding Elsbeth is revealed, the two must trust each other if they hope to survive.

Because this time, it isn't just Elsbeth's heart at risk—it's her life.

ABOUT THE AUTHOR

Laura Beers is an award-winning author. She attended Brigham Young University, earning a Bachelor of Science degree in Construction Management. She can't sing, doesn't dance and loves naps.

Laura lives in Utah with her husband, three kids and her dysfunctional dog. When not writing regency romance, she loves skiing, hiking and drinking Dr Pepper.

You can connect with Laura on Facebook, Instagram or on her site at www.authorlaurabeers.com.

Made in United States
North Haven, CT
28 July 2025

71074336R00173